Stella Duffy ... ... *ng Cake* and *Immaculate* ... ... Martin crime ... ...ies *Calendar Girl*, *Wavewalk...* ... *the Blonde*, *Fresh Flesh* and *Mouths of Babes*. She has published ...e than thirty short stories, many feature articles, and also writes for radio and theatre. With Lauren Henderson, she edited the anthology *Tart Noir*, from which her story 'Martha Grace' won the 2002 CWA Short Story Dagger Award. Her novel *State of Happiness* was long-listed for the Orange Prize 2004.

Stella Duffy was born in the UK, grew up in New Zealand and now lives in London. In addition to her writing work she is an actor, comedian and improviser.

Praise for *Par...*

'A tart look at glitzy ... ... and general naughtiness . . . Duffy ... ...d completely convincing' *Even...*

'Welcome to a world in ... ...e to make believe is even stronger off set than on, and no one is quite what they claim to be. Poison-pen letters, betrayal, even murder, all play a part in [this] movie-biz comedy' *You* magazine

'Smart, sexy and suspenseful' *Bella*

'Stella Duffy has made a name for herself with smart, tart thrillers, and *Parallel Lies* is no exception' *Image*

'*Parallel Lies* has it all – sex, movie stars, threatened blackmail, scandal and murder. Duffy's story rattles along at breakneck speed . . . [it] easily confirms her place in the pantheon of contemporary British authors' *Gay Times*

'Tense and engaging' *Diva*

'Witty, fast-paced and entertaining . . . *Parallel Lies* is disturbingly exciting' *Herald*

PARALLEL LIES

STELLA DUFFY

virago

VIRAGO

First published in Great Britain in February 2005
This paperback edition published in April 2006

Copyright © Stella Duffy 2005

A CIP catalogue record for this book
is available from the British Library

ISBN: 978-1-84408-025-0

Typeset in Bembo by M Rules

Virago Press
An imprint of
Little, Brown Book Group
100 Victoria Embankment
London EC4Y 0DY

An Hachette UK Company
www.hachette.co.uk

www.virago.co.uk

Acknowledgements

My thanks to the Russian dolls Alla Shteinman, Elena Poletskaya, Igor Alyukov, Andrei Konstantinov, Francesca Canty, Masha Koslovskaya, and the American dreamers Chris Manby, Brian Lohmann, Doug Nunn, Dan O'Connor. To Lauren Henderson for saying her spine shivered, Antonia Hodgson for the best editorial notes ever, Stephanie Cabot and Shelley Silas for their constant support and enthusiasm. I am grateful to the British Council for sending me to Novosibirsk. Twice. Thanks also to Ludmilla Turisheva, Nelli Kim, Olga Korbut, Norah Givens, and the Board.

One

When we visited Yana Ivanova in her own home, she
gave us her story in her own words. On a sunny afternoon in the hills, sitting by the very cool pool, set in a
secluded herb garden, Yana spoke to us at length about
her journey to fame and fortune, the heartache and the
joy . . . and, to those of us used to the fickle nature of
'star' behaviour, Yana came across as one of the best.
Not only was she charm itself in the way she welcomed
us, but she also greeted the occasional interruptions from
her pretty British assistant with calm and polite attention.
In this town, the true nature of a celebrity is better
judged, not in how they welcome the press to their door,
but in how they treat their 'people'. Yana Ivanova does
both extremely well. (And her delightful housekeeper
makes a dangerously tempting apricot bread . . . gluten-
free, of course!)

(inside: pages 10, 11, 13, 14)

Yana Irina Ivanova was born in a small town halfway
between Moscow and Novosibirsk. Just over a hundred
years earlier the ruling fathers of Yana's small town had
underestimated the bragging potential of the locomotive
and chosen not to be a stop on the thundering new Trans-
Siberian Railway. Which meant her small town remained
a small town. Certainly it did not feature on any traditional
Western maps, those that place the United States at the
centre of the known universe and limit what was the

Soviet Union to a squashed chunk of the upper quadrant, the magic of flat-plane projection shrinking Russia to half its true size. Though it must be said, even on Soviet maps, the town was not guaranteed a place. While in Lenin's time it had boasted a gracious town hall, and a respected school, by the end of Stalin's reign the air of bright possibility had faded to a cool grey. The market stands were dismissed by local farmers in favour of a village twenty miles closer to the railway, the centre suffered accordingly, and the sweeping arcs of Russian art nouveau on the town hall façade were plastered over to provide a focal point for bulletin boards.

> Dedicated and encouraging teachers at the local school, Yana's parents knew right from the start that their little girl was destined for greatness. Whether starring in the school play or beating her older brothers at chess, Yana was already beginning to shine – even in the dark of Soviet Russia!
>
> *(see photo: left to right: brothers Serge, Pavel, with three-year-old Yana on his knee, Masha and Andrei proudly standing behind their three children)*

Masha and Andrei fell in love at university in Moscow, married young and accepted jobs in this little town that could at least offer them a home of their own. They moved into an old-new apartment and began teaching immediately after graduation. The place was tiny but they had their own kitchen and bathroom, and a half-balcony from which to admire their newly attained marital bliss. They were in love and youthful and eager to start a family. And they had three children, which was unusual in their circle, unusual in general at that time. Not for the Chinese-style imprecations the West assumed most Soviets were subject to, but more for reasons of practicality. Masha and Andrei each had their own careers, she an English-language specialist, he a biochemist, and the norm among their friends and peers was one, maybe two children. This generation, marrying young and breeding early while Western women were only just discovering the possibility of doing neither, still had their own parents' tales of war-bred poverty ringing in their ears.

Naturally, it was far easier to give your all to one instead of two, two rather than three. Children desired and cherished. Five-Year Plan children. Yana was not planned. She came unexpected, positively unwanted, into her parents' life just at the stage when a divorce might have been preferable. Her brothers were already into their teens, able to take care of themselves. Andrei had recently begun a new course of study, alongside his regular work hours, and Masha was thinking of expanding her own horizons. Ideally in the direction of another man, any other man, this one who had seemed so bright and shining when she was twenty, now tarnished with age and indifference at thirty-six. Unfortunately she allowed her hunger to linger with Andrei that one last time and Yana was the product not of love or of passion, but a bored late-night fuck.

> We asked Yana what childhood was like, so far from the dream life she lives today: 'You know? I didn't know any different. Everyone had tiny apartments, parents who worked really hard, enough to get by and no more. When everyone else around you has the same standard of living it doesn't seem that big a deal. My parents loved us, I guess that's all that really matters.'
>
> *(photo, top right: Yana receiving school prize for languages, Masha in background)*

Masha could have had an abortion easily enough, was certainly advised to do so by all her friends, her own mother, and her husband. She very nearly did, except that on the morning she had taken off from work to go to her doctor, she went into the small extra room they'd bargained for in an apartment swap with an older couple, the room where her too-rapidly expanding sons now explored their vigorous lives in long late-night conversations. She went into her sons' room to pick up clothes and straighten dirty shoes and cover the uncovered youth-stained sheets. She went to collect teacups from beneath the lower bunk bed where they gathered first dust, and then a mould her scientist husband would have been proud of. She went to tidy up her boys-becoming-men. And standing among the detritus of teenage male hormones, it occurred to Masha that maybe a daughter would make all the difference. A daughter might be a new possibility, one which, unlike a new husband, wouldn't involve the turmoil of divorce and re-housing and starting all over again. She gathered an armload of washing, retrieved several verdant teacups, and cancelled the doctor's appointment.

Seven months later, on the day that Olga Korbut became the world's darling at the Munich Olympics, Masha was handed her very own tiny Russian doll. Three years on, Andrei left home to move in with a young woman from his post-graduate course. The precious baby daughter was not enough to keep him home when he had a barely post-pubescent girl throwing herself in his direction at work. When Yana was five, Serge went away to university; when she was eight, Pavel too left home. But none of it mattered to Masha by then, because Masha had her little Yanotchka.

As Yana herself says: 'My parents were very supportive from the start. I guess being so much younger than my older brothers made a difference. Of course their divorce was difficult, it always is for children. But we carried on, as best we could, and my mother made sure I was well taken care of. She had always wanted a little girl, we were very close and she was so proud of everything I achieved before she died. I still miss her terribly.'

And Yana Irina truly was everything that any mother who secretly and fervently gave seven months of her life to hoping for a little girl instead of a little boy could have wished. Fine and delicate and huge-eyed, yet also bright and questioning and brave. Yana was not an easy child, she was inquisitive and invigorating and her rushing, tumbling, urgent body brought an exhausted excitement into the emptying apartment. From the first, Masha read stories to Yana in English – American and English stories – teaching her both the Cyrillic and the Latin alphabets long before the other nursery children had mastered the calligraphy of their own names. When she was at school, the same school where her estranged parents still shared a staff-room locker, Masha listened out for Yana's voice from her patrol in the senior playground, heard first-hand reports from the junior teachers, peered in through alphabet-shrouded windows at Yana's progress in class. She spun a protective dream over her baby. From the age of nine Yana kept a diary, each page the carefully phrased yearning of a youthful soul who didn't yet know what she wanted to be or how to get there, but knew it would be somewhere important. Each page in grammatically perfect English. Masha was a prescient mother, she knew change was coming and she wanted her daughter to be ready for it. By the Moscow Olympics of 1980, Yana could have slowly conversed with any member of the no-show United States team; by 1984, when Mary Lou Retton swept the gymnastics board – no tiny Russian girls to bounce her off the podium – Yana's English accent was just-foreign-enough; and in September 1990 Yana Ivanova was living in an overcrowded flat off Kensington High Street, slowly but successfully touting her portfolio to the fashion editors of all the London-based magazines.

> Yana again: 'My mother made it possible for me to live the life I do today. If she hadn't encouraged me to learn English so early, and taught it so well herself, if she hadn't pushed me into speaking only English whenever I could – which is why I hardly know any Russian any more, really – I don't think I could ever have been as successful as I have. It can be hard to be different, my family's faith in me made it possible for me to be accepted anywhere.'

Masha had not brought up her beautiful daughter to be a fashion model, but then she hadn't brought her up to be anything else either. She had wanted to create the perfect girl – beautiful, but also bright and strong. What Yana actually did with her perfection was not within Masha's sphere of influence. Bright, personable and completely certain of her own glorious charm, at seventeen and in her last year of school, Yana joined a state-sanctioned fortnight exchange visit to a Manchester family. On her third day in the sadly not-so-decadent West, Yana's high cheekbones, long hair, longest legs and huge-eyed enjoyment were singled out from among a group of late-teenage girls in the Arndale Shopping Centre. She and a girl called Kathy also loitering in the Centre were encouraged to call the agent's office and make an appointment. The next morning she called the number the scout had given her. There followed several shall-we/shan't-we coffees, a shoplifting foray with Kathy to get appropriate clothes and a midnight packing

6

session with her two host schoolgirls, silent as possible so the responsible parents wouldn't find out and ban Yana from the London adventure. Neither girl had the money to get to London and Kathy took Yana on a hitchhiking and stolen-train-ticket journey as far as Coventry, where she disappeared into a drunken night and failed to return. Yana, on the other hand, made it just in time for her first interview, gave great face in a Polaroid proposal, and never went home again. The scout who'd asked them to call was disappointed with Kathy's no-show, the two tall fair teenagers would have looked good together, similarly striking, might have been a nice catwalk pairing. But it didn't matter to the booker who took her on, Yana was a fine piece of raw material.

> 'I didn't know what I was doing when I walked into that agency. I knew they'd been looking for matching girls really, for one job in particular, I was scared they might not want me when I turned up by myself. But I figured I had to give it a go. And anyway, I was in London, seventeen and all alone. I had hardly any money. What else was I going to do? I thought if I could at least prove I'd tried to get work, my mother and the people who'd organised our trip might forgive me for running off. After that, one job just led to another . . . not that I didn't work hard, or that it wasn't long hours and sometimes very difficult, but at the beginning, when you're that young, everything's an adventure, isn't it?'

Yana was filming her first New York shoot on the day Masha called to announce Andrei's death. The phone call was brief and conducted entirely in English because Yana now refused to speak anything else. Masha did not want to attend her ex-husband's funeral, she had no intention of persuading her daughter to go in her stead. And Yana was way too involved in her new life to pay a mock-grief homage to the man who had left when she was so young. As the months passed, Yana limited her Russian connections to a very few financially prudent telephone calls and, eventually, to sporadic, neatly written letters which, even after the advent of email, remained infrequent and brief. Masha had wanted a walking-talking doll, Yana was a forced-growth baby who was more than tired of the close confines of her showcase. She was ready to take care of herself. The fashion editors couldn't have been more grateful.

(see photo, left: Yana Ivanova (in black wig) in Jean-Paul Gaultier's shocking summer swimsuit/dinner jacket combination)

After two years of modelling, Yana finally accepted the catwalk's limitations and realised her boredom there wasn't going to go away. She started acting classes. There was little encouragement in London where regional accents had replaced the standard RP as the voice of choice – regional, never foreign – but in New York and LA the startlingly beautiful model-turned-actress was not such an unusual sight. Not so unusual anyway that Yana couldn't get six months' work in a daytime soap, followed by a regular role in an early-evening sitcom, and then, making the transition that so many actors dream of but so very few achieve, a big-budget major motion picture. Her looks definitely helped, her undoubted acting ability was useful, her perfect if not-quite-definable accents gave her the edge of sexy outsider status, but most of all, Yana helped herself. Masha had brought her up to believe she was wonderful and beautiful and worthy. And she behaved it and she believed it and so did everyone else.

Not many young hopefuls make that difficult transition from model to actress. Certainly the trail is littered with the broken hopes of many other youthful soap stars who slip on the road to their dream. Fewer still, no matter what their transition, attain the dizzy heights of Yana Ivanova's current success. Beauty, fame, critical approval, and a happy relationship – not to mention her lovely home, she certainly seems to have it all. But we'll leave the last word to Yana: 'I know I'm lucky. It hasn't all been easy, it was hard to leave home, to make that break, to live in a new country. But I'm so glad I did. To be born an American is one thing – but to be accepted here, welcome to live and work and be part of this life – I know just how lucky I am. And having Jimmy as my partner, to enjoy it all with me, is the icing on my cake. I couldn't ask for more. I just want to keep working and doing my best.'

And now, many years since the day she illicitly boarded a train at Manchester Piccadilly, her travel documents and precious diaries in a box under her arm, she is a Queen. Goddess. Angel. Yana Ivanova is a bona fide star. London, Paris, Rome, Milan prostrate themselves before her perfect twinkling toes. The Berlin Wall would rebuild itself if she merely asked; Buda and Pest settle themselves willingly on the same shore if she deemed it necessary. Yana has all the attributes of perfection, in a just-like-us personality. Her past is an East-to-West, Iron Curtain glory story. Her present an endless round of right people, right places, right choices. She lives on a knife-edge of perfection, tightrope walking her way to greater success, never dull, always daring, pushing the boundaries and yet winning through in the end. And even those who might envy her gloss and sheen don't really want to see her fall. Not this one. Yana is as close as we get to an angel, we need her to maintain the heavenly trajectory, blessing us with her magical bounty. Yana Ivanova is the Russian-born American-living schoolgirl dream; olive skin, dark eyes, long straight fair hair, smooth rounded arse, and high creamy tits – the finest example of cross-cultural fertilisation since the Spanish paid an Italian to discover the New World – and he named it America thinking it was India. Yana Ivanova is all that.

Two

OK. So that's the public version. But to tell the truth – speak it secretly, whisper into your pillow, mumble into a clenched fist – actually, Yana Ivanova isn't that fuck-all hot. Perhaps her hair isn't totally shiny and manageable every single day of the year. Maybe Mother Nature didn't hand down those perfect white teeth without any struggle between dentist and purse-strings, she's definitely come a long way since the burgeoning Soviet swan in the teenage photos her mother sent over years ago. Certainly there is at least one camera angle that, given a short skirt and a long lens, would suggest a hint – if not more – of really truly cellulite. I've seen it on one or two occasions and the *National Enquirer* has proved it so. All right, her body wasn't born perfect. Maybe she works at it, has turned herself into this paragon of beauty we now know so well, but that just makes her more reachable, more real. Why else was Princess Diana so eager for the world to see her rushing off to the gym every morning? Why would Madonna spend her thirties sweating her way round a running track, bodyguards and paparazzi in her wake? Why would anyone, who supposedly loathes press intrusion and who has the guaranteed privacy of their own home or hotel gym in which to work out, make a public show of their exercise regime? Except that everyone hates a born skinny. Whereas a woman who has to work for her fine physique,

11

and what's more, shows us how hard she is trying? Hell, we can all aspire to that, admire that. Yana's current gloss may make her far removed from the real world, but it's the flaws that pull her back down to earth, closer to us. We love her, she is distant; we see the imperfections, she is close. And because she is close – we love her again. So it continues.

On the family side, Yana can be grateful she has not had an alcoholic father or estranged mother to deal with, spilling their guts and the photo album to the press at ten grand a shot. But it must be noted, Yana hasn't found the geographical distance too hard to bear. Sad as it is that both her parents are now well and truly dead, even when Masha was alive, her perfect little Yanotchka wasn't exactly ringing home every week. Month. Year. From that first week in London, once she'd started with the agency, Yana spoke only in English – she leaped at every opportunity to perfect her new language, adopted accents, explaining it had been her mother's dream that Yana would work in the West. Which was only stretching the truth a little distance, over the border. And while Masha's English had always been impeccable, age and infirmity slowly stole the words from the older woman, just as time and inclination removed most of Yana's Russian, until their mother–daughter conversations became as stilted as the crackling line along which they travelled. Instead Yana sent out-of-season flowers and overflowing hampers and first-print magazines and her ageing mother seemed happy enough with a Post-it postscript. Newspaper clippings – even unflattering ones – were always faithfully forwarded on. Masha pored over the dot matrix photographs and marvelled at the uses of fame and fortune, which had apparently smoothed down her daughter's sharper features, rounded off what she knew to be a slightly pointed chin, an almost too-thin nose, blanched out what should have been her work-shadowed eyes. The big brothers were more interested in the words. And the money.

And even now, years later, Serge and Pavel have no complaints on the money front. Yana faithfully collates the photos her big brothers send of their young and not-so-young families, but she has yet to follow up on the hint of a whole-family trip to Disneyland. She carefully reads the stilted-English, awe-filled letters from her teenage and smaller nieces and nephews, committing their stories of her home town to memory and putting the crayoned pictures away in a drawer for safekeeping. What she sends in return is another international cheque. Yana may not be the most touchy-feely of baby sisters, but she is very happy to provide. (The dollar–rouble exchange rate makes them all smile. A family heritage lopsided grin that slopes to the left. Though not Yana's, not any more. Yana has trained her smile into balanced perfection.) And if the public read the occasional article suggesting Yana Ivanova's behaviour towards her family is slightly distant, who is to say what it must be like for her? The Evil Empire so far behind, the American Dream held tight in her hand, maybe any one of us would be the same, living the fantasy-come-true, not necessarily wanting to be reminded of what we've had to leave behind. And as long as her manager makes sure Yana plays a life-saving surgeon or grieving young mother in every third movie, the public are just as likely to believe the latest character shows her true heart as the occasionally less flattering stories they read in the tabloids.

Yana Ivanova has been known to snarl at paparazzi more than once. She has been seen to pout when not offered the finest table in a restaurant. It is not unheard-of for her to complain to her publicist about the endless round of interviews she is obliged to undergo – and then complain a month later when interest is lacking and she fears her star is waning. (Her star is not waning, but it's hard for Yana to know that for definite, all the time, throughout the long soul-searching night.) So she is a normal star. Albeit one with a wide shelf of English-translation Russian classics in the sitting room, and a Russian copy of *The Master and Margarita* by her bed. She demands notice and hides from it, courts publicity and spurns it, wants adoration and tires of attention. Yana works hard at her job and she works hard at pleasing her public and, no matter who else she infuriates, she always remembers the fans. She is nice when it suits her – often she is nice even when it doesn't – and every now and then she lets rip with an ear-splitting mouthful of oddly-accented nasty invective directed at some unsuspecting probably-innocent who gets in her way. Which, in most people's eyes, just goes to show she is human. The occasional Bloody Mary being so much more trustworthy than the constant Shirley Temple.

So maybe Yana Ivanova isn't that fuck-all hot. Not in reality. But mostly she thinks she is. And I certainly think she is. And you think she is too. (Don't you? Of course you do, you know you do, you want to have her, be her, she is the firm-fleshed blow-up doll of your teenage dreams.) The power of conjoined thought is so immense, so strong, that between us we could think the Third World sated if we chose. But we don't. We'd rather think her a star. Talk her a star, buy her a star, name her a star. And so she is. The movie magazines publish column after column explaining in elaborate detail why Yana Ivanova is the finest thing since Marilyn fucked some dead Kennedy on a White House floor and the CIA realised they'd forgotten to put film in the camera. And the panels who vote on the Oscars and the Golden Globes and the Emmys (when she occasionally appears on the smaller screen, lowers her sights to raise our expectations) all know – admittedly often before the screening – that she is worthy of their highest accolades. Of three nominations, she's had to smile 'Oh well done, how right!' twice. And both times the prize went to some old bitch who was planning to die in the next twelve months anyway. When competing against her peers however, Yana is, more often than not, the peerless winner. And she makes people laugh in her acceptance speeches. That helps. A well-paid comedian writes her off-the-cuff quips, Yana remembers not to cry. Maximum humanity, minimum tears, nothing to embarrass the folks back home. Between us, we've got it covered.

Meanwhile Jimmy (named for Garner not Dean, though he'd rather not talk about that, thank you) is her perfect consort. He is the brother-boyfriend, pretty enough and witty enough to shine beside her, yet never eclipse Yana's silvery light. Jimmy's career is really good but not totally great, his wealth sufficient but not vast, his image not above a touch of wild living if Yana's box-office booty needs spicing up. For five years now they have been together at every premiere, every party, every charity gala. In interviews she makes jokes about him, he talks about her with a real fondness and respect – not only for her talent, but also for her normality. The way Yana is when they're at home together. Just the two of them. Ordinary. Quiet. Regular. The public love to hear that she can't cook. Won't cook, but that's another story. They smile to read that he has a Russians-in-translation reading pile on his bedside table, but that so far even *The Idiot* is a name he applies to himself rather than his must-read-again list. (Jimmy is not stupid, he is something of a Shakespearean scholar on the quiet – but they keep it very quiet. Too-clever boys are not the order of the day.) The public lap up these interviews. Just like us but not. Everyday but different. Same but special. And they look so good together.

Yana and Jimmy are both light-olive-skinned and glowing. She is model-tall and, unusually in Hollywood, even more so for a made-for-TV actor, he is taller than she. Not for Yana the prison of flat heels. They laugh in public and hold hands on holiday and cater for the hungry needs of our fairy-tale dreams. They take the empty places that were Bogey-and-Bacall, Hepburn-and-Tracy and, with a little adjustment for height and breadth and age (and the removal of the cigarette silhouette), they fill the space quite nicely. Yana Ivanova and Jimmy McNeish get to be the golden couple, she gets to be the shinier of the two, and Jimmy gets around two million a year for his pains.

I, on the other hand, have sex with a new man every six months. I do this because the men I sleep with are bound to tell someone that they nailed the woman who works for Yana Ivanova, the woman who manages her diary, answers her telephone, reads her mail, eats at her table, sleeps in a room just down the hall; the woman who is Yana Ivanova's right hand. Having me is one degree of separation from the most desirable woman in town. I also screw these men because I quite enjoy the partying and a little wildness on occasion. Working and living so closely with such hot property means we all have to be careful about where we go and who we see and where we can play. When I am away from Yana and Jimmy I can let down my guard a little. The papers would have a field day at the very thought of Yana Ivanova tasting a line of coke in a late-night club. And it's possible they might even notice me doing it – if I was right beside her. Away from her orbit though, I'm just another cute-enough Brit chick making it in LA. I happen to have a fantastic job and a brilliant name attached to my resumé, but when the name isn't around, I'm as anonymous as the next girl. And, this being LA, a little shorter than most. With real tits that lie down when

I do. No matter how hard I want to play though, I only ever sleep with the finest specimen of the gender I can find on any given evening – and ideally one I won't mind seeing for another week or two, a month at the most. It's not much of a hardship. I screw the men because I can, because I know it will give them a thrill, and because it is appropriate to maintain my image as something of a good-time slut – an image more easily achieved by the British over here than your average soft-drinking Yank.

There is one other reason for my carefully timed launch into the world of the single sex kitten. I fuck some good-looking, loud-mouthed guy for a few weeks maybe twice a year. Because the rest of the time, I fuck her.

Three

When Yana and I first met I knew straight off there was something different about her. We were at a friend's house for dinner – contrary to popular belief the very famous do not spend all their time hanging out with the other very famous. At the least it would be boring, at worst they'd find out too much about each other and run the risk of losing that slight edge – the one that usually means Yana gets the part another woman doesn't. It is an edge that comes, conversely, from not being in perfect focus for too many people. Not being known inside out reinforces the illusion of a casting hierarchy – just now, Yana is close to the very top, and there is nothing more levelling than the whole. So while Yana is happy for the public to think they know about her private life – little titbits dropped by her manager into an interview here, Jimmy's passing comment there – her real strategy is to remain at a slight distance. It's worked well enough until now.

And nor was the difference her sexuality. Yana is way too clever for that. Anyway, I have never believed that bollocks about one gay person knowing another a mile off. God knows why so many gay men have affairs with married men if that's really the case. Unless of course it's the married men who just can't tell. Whatever, I've simply never thought who you sleep with is that big a deal. It isn't for me. Of course they have to be clean, able to hold a conversation, ideally good-looking verging on beautiful. But I just don't see that much difference between men and women. I can make myself fancy anyone, decide the turn of their head does it, or the way they laugh at my Brit-girl humour, or their inability to sip a third drink at those LA-AA parties, but it doesn't have much to do with boy or girl. The labels don't work for me, and nor do I want them to. I'm happy not fitting in. Perhaps that's why I came to the States in the first place. As soon as I could I moved from Southend to London, but after a while even that wasn't big enough. I needed somewhere truly anonymous. LA is truly anonymous.

Yana, though, always wanted to fit in, to be part of it, known as a linchpin, a central figure. Which brings its own difficulties. Yana does not fancy just anyone, she loves me. Despite the warnings of her manager, despite her trying very hard not to go where her heart – and her body – were taking her, we are together. Not easily and not without problems, but Yana has chosen to be with me. Unfortunately her work-place is this incestuous, insane business that knows no other society. Yana has seen the career nosedives taken by those ear-lier brave/stupid women. Either of us could name you a dozen or more men and women at the top of their profes-sion, each clutching a breastful of awards, and every one of them living glorious lies. It's hard enough for the girls to make the public believe they really do fancy the star guy twenty-five years older than them, but if the public thought a star was acting out of her sphere of sexual proclivity as well? Oscar will be a centenarian at least before the Academy gives its golden kiss to the next rank of forgotten woman, the gen-ital-free golden boy way more likely to go to the straight chick bravely portraying yet another hysterical historical dyke. The odd thing is, I never used to care. I am so not a freedom fighter in any of this, I'm way too easily bored to hide in any one ghetto. But it is Yana's problem. And because it's her problem, it has become mine. Love's complications spread like blood in bathwater.

Yana is not who she seems. And the only people who know the truth are Yana, me, her manager Felix – who found Jimmy for her – and Jimmy himself. And that's it. I think actually that's why she doesn't want to be properly in touch with her family, why she didn't speak to her mother for so long. Yana doesn't want to change the world, she wants to light it up. She believes in old-fashioned Hollywood glamour and, just like the past stars, she believes in her right to lie. So do I. And that's what I noticed that night I first met her. Not the rattle of a hidden secret, but the held certainty of a control freak. There is little I find more attractive than someone who looks like they have secrets. Yana holds it all in. Answers questions with one or two words, asks more than she answers, listens and looks as if she's taking even the most flippant remarks seriously. It makes you think about what you're saying, makes you step back and take a look at yourself. And if, as I was, you're a bit pissed and a little stoned, it makes you very hungry for still more of her carefully parcelled-out attention.

We met at a dinner, mutual friend – ex-shag in my case, ex-screen lover in hers. Though I didn't know it at the time, Yana and I had the same system: once you've exchanged bodily fluids, glycerine-enhanced or real, keep the other close. There's nothing more unsettling than an unfriendly ex-lover. I ate my meal, she pushed hers around the plate in the actress tradition of dining-approximation, and we talked about London. I knew she'd lived there when she was a model, I'm a few years older than her, but she was a very young model and I was a bit of a late starter.

Our London stories were of the same time and place. Not that a fashion shoot for *Vogue* and temping on the switchboard of the *Evening Standard* had all that much in common, but we did both know Kensington High Street a little too well. We liked the look of each other, so I made sure Yana knew I was looking for a job. Of course I already had a job, PA to a younger woman I was just starting to realise wasn't ever going to be as big as either of us had hoped she would. I'm a good PA. A really present assistant. I don't just deal with needs, I pre-empt them. Even back then, I had a pretty good reputation. While I may tell my own secrets readily – those I feel need telling – I have always been superbly discreet with other people's. Being British – and over here they honestly can't tell the difference between Sloane and Estuary – set me still further apart. I am immune to the twin American illnesses of alcoholism and drug addiction – I may happily do them both, but they aren't dangerous for me; cancer is a disease, alcohol is my choice. And I work through my hangovers.

More importantly, I am unaffected by that other Hollywood illness of success-by-association. I truly have no desire to become a star, there's no hidden agenda. I have never believed in the American myth that anyone will make it if they're good enough and anyway, I do not want to. I'm happy to work hard, I want to earn bloody good money for my work, and moreover I need to have fun in the process. But that's it. No other ambition. Unfortunately my employer at the time was on her way down. Having only made it halfway up in the first place. At twenty-four (though claiming twenty-one) she was never going to make it from teen-dream to adult fulfilment. This meant I was not earning anywhere near the figure I had been counting on, nor was I likely to as long as I stayed with her. It also meant she was absolutely no fun at all. Not her fault, Corinna wasn't the

21

brightest girl I'd ever met, but even she could see that second lead in a fourth-sequel horror movie, replacing the starlet who'd left the team for a better job, wasn't what she'd been hoping for from her sixth year in LA. It was time for both of us to move on. There was nothing I could do for her now and still less that she could do for me. Yana needed an assistant, someone enthusiastic and hard-working and vibrant and discreet. And, I had an idea, she needed something else as well. Which is why I agreed to take the job. I didn't know what the something else was. I was used to long days, no fixed hours, constant on-call for any task from message taking to paranoia sating. Finding out what Yana was hiding, that was the challenge that really attracted me. I like to know what else is going on. I'm good at other people's secrets.

I started the new job a week after that dinner. Corinna was simultaneously pissed off and relieved to see me go. I'd been something of a status symbol for her, but one she could no longer afford. I told her that it's always better to leave on your own steam rather than hanging around until you're asked to go. I spoke as if I were talking about myself, but left the implications to her. She didn't need much convincing. I pointed out she'd get more press attention for way less cost just carrying a very expensive dog. Or a slightly cheaper baby. I believe she appreciated my adopted-American candour. She's happily married and mothering back in Chicago now, my leaving was all the push she needed. She does a little theatre every now and then, it's amazing how well known she is from those late-night re-runs of her first and most successful movie. And the hard-hitting journalists of the Midwest press never question her smooth-faced assertion that theatre always was her one true love.

At first I worked for Yana from her home but stayed at

my own. I'd get up at seven, be at hers by eight, often not leave for twelve hours or more. Very quickly I took the necessary steps to prove how careful I was, how trustworthy. I mentioned several people we both knew to have various hidden stories, waited to see if she would tell on them. She kept quiet and so did I. I noted our mutual reserve on certain subjects. Truthfully, I have no natural reserve, but I know how to spot it in other people, I know how to copy it in other people. I kept working, getting used to Yana, following her, flowing with her, looking to see where I could jump forward and anticipate her desires before she asked. With time, I knew I would get to the point that I could provide her wants before she noticed she was hungry. But I would have to understand her control before I knew her that well. I would have to understand what she was trying to control. PA is the modern term, in the old days it was servant. And good service is the easiest thing in the world. Once you give in to it. Most people, though, don't want to give in, it hurts them to bend. Personally, I'd always rather bend than break, serve than be served. Those who dislike giving service don't understand how much power there is in being the one who knows what happens next.

I learned her schedule. If Yana was filming, she did absolutely nothing else other than work on the part. And her body, of course. Always her body. She accepted no invitations, went nowhere, even if her location was in LA, even if she had several days off or a week's break. But when she wasn't working, she went out as often as possible. When filming I was her first-call bodyguard, deflecting any requests that might divert her attention from the job in hand, when she wasn't working I was the conduit through which all her invitations flowed. And for someone of her stature, even then, there were a hell of a lot of invitations.

Pretty quickly I learned her likes and dislikes. There were only two charities she was prepared to give any actual time to (though a handful of others to which she regularly, privately, gave money), and just five people she had decided to know well enough that she was prepared to dine at their homes, and only three of those she would welcome back to her own. Unless Felix insisted she hold a party – so far there'd been just three, in which case it was open house to all but the closed (and locked) rooms. Other than these manufactured social occasions there was the occasional premiere and less frequent restaurants. My task was to negotiate the delicate balance between working for Yana, my boss – and what was necessary to please Felix, in reality, her boss. I'm not much of a believer in the chain of command. I did what I wanted. I wanted to please Yana. It worked.

There is little more desirable than someone who truly wants to make you happy. Within four months I had moved into my own rooms in Yana's house: en suite, kitchenette, private sitting room, walled patio. With fountain. No boyfriend yet, Jimmy arrived a year later. Six weeks after I'd moved in, an hour after her housekeeper Marina had left for the evening, while we sat in front of the huge DVD screen in her vast sitting room, Yana asked me, in passing, disinterestedly, if I had ever kissed another woman. I kept my eyes on the movie and replied that I had, more than kissed, more than once. That I would no doubt do so again. That night I made her dinner. The next morning I made our bed.

Four

What Yana was hiding was not her sexuality, or her fear of it being found out, or the truth of her relationship with Jimmy. The truth is that Yana and Jimmy get on very well. In their own way. They love each other. They have a working friendship of the kind that will never fall over into a fuck. Not that Jimmy wouldn't. But that it would mess things up, shuffle the clean lines of their arrangement. And it would piss me off no end. Though I don't imagine that figures in Yana's equation. Or Jimmy's. She doesn't fancy him though. Doesn't fancy boys. Never has. Nor men. Just not interested. Not that she can't appreciate Jimmy's beauty, the smooth lines of his well-worked torso, the slim hips, the wide mouth, bright teeth, that perfectly placed upper-lip scar. Not that she hasn't fucked men in the past. When it was relevant. But she doesn't have to fuck Jimmy. She merely has to love him. So she does.

Jimmy's needs are carefully catered for. He gets his whenever he needs it. Yana's manager who is Jimmy's manager has all the right phone numbers for all the right girls. Women. Boys. Men. Whatever his clients need, Felix Berger, the man born into a family of Hollywood greats and now greater than any of his antecedents, can find it. The ladies who come to the house for Jimmy, the girls who meet him on set, the women-acting-as-journalists who take him out to lunch, are simply performing the same function they offer for plenty of other men in the business. They do not need to know they are required because Jimmy is not getting it from Yana. These working women understand it is perfectly normal for a Hollywood handsome to need more sex than he can get from his equally beautiful, equally famous, possibly even more hard-working wife. It's where most of their employment comes from. Happily married men. The clients of these secluded hills are not so different from the happily married men who crawl the suburb curb in darkened cars. These men just pay a whole lot better. Via their managers. Direct to the account. And the women who service them under-stand the vital importance of maintaining the highest standards. Of discretion as well as fucking. Jimmy has three different women he gets on really well with. And they like him too. And hell, even if he did get found out in an extra-relationship liaison, he wouldn't be doing anything any other bloke in a long line of Hollywood stars hadn't done, from Chaplin, on the road to Bing and Bob, all the way down to our very modern, easily-tempted heroes. Certainly no one would ever think his behaviour cast any aspersions on Yana's manifest heterosexuality. All nice and sorted then.

It took me a while to work out what exactly Yana was hiding. It took me living with her, seeing her get ready for a new job, planning her day around a meeting with a pro-ducer. The physical workouts, the voice coaches, the acting classes. The pain before those endless rounds of meetings. She who is too successful to be asked to audition, must still be tested. At Yana's level, though, they are not called screen tests. There are meetings. Lunches. Dinners. Parties. Walking the dog, going to yoga class, ballet class, picnic on the beach. Everything is an audition. And every time it means Yana is on show, watched, analysed. No one these days wonders if she can do the accent, look the part. Not now she is so well established. That's what the dialect coach is for, the make-up women, her hairdresser. Yana no longer has to look or sound like the role she is up for. She just has to be likeable, glowing with the indefinable spark that will appeal to this new employer or that. And every time, of course, it is a different spark that is needed. Will she and the producers get on? The director may love her, but it's not his dollars making the film. The distributors may adore her, but they are only looking at what she'll bring them once the product is made. And the writer may want Yana and only Yana for the part. But the truth is he's written sixteen drafts of this film already and in his original dream he meant the role for Debra Winger – until the producer decided a younger woman was better box office. Besides, the director expects to write the final draft anyway, the writer will be long gone by then. No, Yana must make herself attractive to the producer. And he – ninety per cent of the time it is a he – may be anywhere. At dinner, lunch, an arranged meeting. He may not be making the next movie she has lined up, or the one after that. But some time he will think about her, and Yana must be ready for it. And so she is constantly on show, always ready to impress with her blend of clever talk and smooth beauty. Intelligent but not more so than the producer, interesting but not weird – unless they're looking for weird, in which case truly weird is what she is – for Yana it is all an audition. And that is what she is scared of, the constant try-out, permanent trial.

Yana is afraid of being found out. We all are. No matter what we do, every one of us dreads the day when those we work for suddenly realise we've been bluffing all along. When Yana discovers I don't really care about her family enough to remember each of their birthdays, but I do have an alarm on my personal organiser that does it for me. When the students figure out the professor has been giving the same lecture for the past ten years and has nothing new to say about Sylvia Plath. When the doctor can't find a specialist to refer you to and must make a life-changing decision all by herself. When the mother admits her children really aren't all that interesting to her. The bus driver, the airline pilot, the traffic cop. We all suffer from performance anxiety. But Yana hurts more than most. What if this time she really can't do the job, not just emotionally, but physically as well? What if her body won't stand up to the punishing round of exercise and nutritional denial required to maintain the skeletal figure this character so desperately needs? What if she just can't get her Russian lips round those South London vowels? What if, when the set is cleared and the lights dimmed, the room hushed for the sex scene, she finds he smells dreadful up close and she cannot bear to kiss him after all? Or worse, he tastes so good that she cannot stop? Yana keeps her sexuality a secret because it is good box office to do so. Because it is necessary for her, if she wants to stay at the top of the ladder, to appear to be both entirely ordinary and yet utterly beyond reach of everyman, anywoman. Her real fear has nothing to do with whoever she wraps her limbs around at night, it is that those with power over her life might see she can't do it – can't do the job. And if they see this fear made flesh, it will not be like it is for you and me. The boss notices we have screwed up, a favourite teacher gives us a low grade, our parents and children sigh in disappointment. When Yana fucks up, it will be all over all the papers. Truly, half the world will know she has failed. And yes, the news will be fish-and-chip paper tomorrow, to anyone else, anyone not directly connected with her work. But it will taint her.

My job then, once I understood, was to stop her failing, falling, floundering. It is not a lack of confidence that makes Yana scared, not some crappy actress psychosis. It is simply the nature of the beast. If Yana fucks up, everyone here will know about it within a day. And her career, that which she has worked for so long and so hard, will be over. Monroe died at thirty-six. She was lucky, caught out on the way down, preserved beautiful and doomed. We quite like our celebrities doomed. But only once they are dead. Celluloid is long-lasting and entirely unforgiving. Brando stayed too long. Yana is celebrated now, tomorrow the public who adore her will quickly switch to hate if the scent is there. Their interest level may remain the same, or even increase, the appetite for dirt and nastiness feeds itself, but once the people have turned, there is no going back. Yana needs to keep them in love with her. And to do this, she needs to keep being good. Not just gorgeous (which she is, and will continue to be as she ages, the bones are there, she is safe) but properly good. Simple stardom isn't enough any more. We demand more from our highest paid, most indulged. We need Yana to deserve her success. And she is scared that she doesn't. Though she does not quite know it, it is this fear that makes her vulnerable, keeps her approachable. This hint of not-quite-impervious armour that has them hanging on her every word. But it only works because it is real. Vulnerability cannot be manufactured, and once established it must also be contained. That is what I do. I keep a lid on her pain.

I do it by rising an hour before she does so I can get to her email first and check there are none she won't want to see immediately, despite the fact that only the closest of friends and associates have her private address. She reads them all eventually, but not until she is ready. I do it by leaving her in silence until she has finished her yoga or Pilates or five-mile heavy sweating run – whatever is on the body maintenance schedule for the morning. I do it by making coffee the way she likes it. Decaff, organic, free trade. And incredibly strong. With half an After Dinner mint to follow so her breath won't smell and she gets the chocolate rush without the chocolate fat. I do it by keeping Jimmy's women far from her presence. She knows she needs them, doesn't want to have to meet them. I do it by lying to Felix, he who is master to both of them, the man who really controls their careers. My inability to answer a message from Felix gives Yana a day off every now and then when he would have her attend a charity lunch with the wife of a useful director, go to a new class where he knows she will sweat alongside some hot new writer, happen to bump into an up-and-coming baby producer. I don't lie to Felix, I merely ease into slight incompetence for an hour or so – I fail to give her the message until it is too late. It's all my fault, I'm the best PA any of them have ever known, but sometimes even I forget. He shouts at me, she pretends to mind, and her kisses are warmer in gratitude. I do it by mothering and sistering and lovering her. I do it by putting her needs before mine, before Jimmy, before her family, before it all. Which leaves Yana free to concentrate on the job. Whatever it may be. A day's cameo, four months' filming, a fortnight of intensive voice training, three hours a day hiking to totally change the contours of her legs for one shot that will take two minutes of film time. And I do it all very well. But Yana is still scared. Which is, as long as it is kept at the right level, perfectly OK. More than OK. It is ideal. That touch of fragility is why they like her. They may not know it exactly, but they – the directors and writers and producers and the vast insatiable public – can sense it. The merest hint of insecurity, placing her slap bang between the twin excesses of flaky Monroe and steely Madonna, means she's exactly like the big stars, yet just one of us. And perfect with it.

Five

I do it like this:

She is getting dressed. I am in the next room. The room next to her bedroom, our bedroom, is my office. There is a dressing room between the two, running the length of the dividing wall, one door from the bedroom, the other to the office. The bedroom is huge, white, smooth, cool. With dark red sheets and no TV. The office is perfectly proportioned, looks out on to the small walled garden that leads up to the pool and has everything I could ever want in a workroom; everything I have asked for, I have received. This house is classic American excess, Hollywood-wide: Yana's dressing room is easily as large as the Essex sitting room in which I happily wasted teenage evenings watching package holiday shows with my mother, natural history with my father. Until I turned eighteen I had no ambition, for years I was remarkably content to eat chocolate digestives and read the local paper, imagining that two weeks a year in the Canaries might be just about enough, going 'up to London' twice a year for shopping and a show, Sunday lunches with Mum and Dad at their local. And then, with no warning, the contentment left me, I grew bored and I left too. Yana doesn't discuss it if she can help it, but from her brothers' letters I gather the combined dressing room and office is close to the exact size of the entire apartment she was raised in. Neither of us talks a great deal about our childhoods. We were just different people then, there is no frame of reference to explain what we have become. Yana and I are very much products of the American-possible; immigrant dreamers, each of us looks to the now and the future. The past is rarely relevant.

Her dressing room is well-organised. She paid someone to make it so. We both laughed until we cried over the bill. The idea that she might actually pay a woman to stack her shoes, fold her T-shirts, arrange a system for putting away. And then I signed the cheque anyway. There are racks of dresses, layers of drawers, boxes of neatly labelled shoes. These are spring and summer clothes only, autumn and winter wear is in storage. For someone who is quiet about her past, hangs on to the privacy of those stories, Yana is not very good at throwing things out. I am, I love to clear, to empty – desks, drawers, in-trays, cupboards – it feels like achievement. But she won't let me touch her clothes, they are a weakness for her. It's a poor-girl thing I think. I have it as well, to a lesser degree. My passion, though, is not clothes but stationery. I am perfectly happy in her cast-offs, those that fit me. Sometimes those that don't. Fresh paper and clean notebooks and just-bought pens on the other hand, these my fingers itch for, hand-delivered, internet-ordered. On her account. Allowable expenses, accountant excesses. I think it's from the care-nothing nights of my teens, when working in an office seemed a perfectly good use of the rest of my life. I always wanted my own stapler, different-coloured pens, a desk with a view. Lucky me.

This morning Yana cannot decide which T-shirt to wear. She is dressing for coffee with an old friend. Though of course there is no such thing as an old friend, as just coffee. The old friend now works with a new pro-ducer. She is a friend from Yana's first year, not-yet-successful year in LA, and she has moved to and from New York, had another child since they last met. Of course Yana is more interested in the friend than the clothes she chooses to wear this morning. Honestly. But both of us know that every time she leaves the house it is a presentation. The photographers and the café waitresses and the touring passers-by make it so, want it so. Yana must look as if she does not care what she wears, as if she has just thrown on any old thing and yet is still startlingly, casually gorgeous. Yana knows how ordinarily beautiful she is. And she also knows the effort it takes to maintain that state. When any of us dress to meet an old friend we have the same agonies, we want to be slimmer, prettier, lovelier than we were before, years apart or not, male or female – for Yana, the importance of first-glance perfection is hugely magnified.

'Wear the white one.'

I keep typing, fingernails tap-dancing on shining, translucent keyboard. A letter to one of her favourite charities, a shelter for homeless young women. Thick paper, imported from France, signed in Chinese ink. Politely and regretfully letting them down. Yana cannot make the ball the board are planning, offers signed photos instead. And a private visit to one of their centres to encourage the real workers, those who actually work in the shelter, as opposed to the thin women doing good while pushing an uneaten lunch around a too large plate, before paying with their husband's money.

'Which white one?'

Yana's accent is sharp this mid-morning. Sharply undefined. It is what she really sounds like. A smattering of nowhere-in-particular UK, smudged Californian drawl, a twisted vowel or three from her mother tongue.

'Agnes B.'

'Not a bigger label?'

'For a T-shirt? You'd be better off in Marks and Spencer's.'

'Do I have any Marks and Spencer's?'

Letter printed, signed. Her signature, my hand. Folded in the neat four-corner-meet I have made her trademark, stuffed into the square envelope, slow lick sealed.

'No. You don't.'

'Do you?'

'Nope.'

'Then you said that for why?'

More irritation. Sentence deconstruction.

'To remind myself we should get some for you. They don't last all that long, won't hold their shape.'

'So what is the point?'

Clothes hangers rattle, doors slam shut.

'They're cheap and fine to wear just a few times. The English love you in M and S, Americans think it's cute. Non-pretentious without having to resort to K-Mart.'

'Fine, later, fine. But it doesn't help me now.'

I slice another tatty envelope with the razor-sharp letter opener her brother sent last New Year.

'Penny! Now!'

'Second drawer down. On the left.'

'I looked there already.'

'No you didn't.'

I answer three more letters, each one signed and sealed by my hand in Yana's manicured flourish.

She comes through to the office. Stands at the door.

'Well?'

I cross off two more things from this morning's to-do list, save the file I am working on, and then turn to look at her.

Flat lapis-beaded sandals, pale blue cotton trousers low and soft just on her hip-bones, small white T-shirt almost too tight across high natural breasts, long hair loose against her shoulders. No make-up. Not even the unnaturally natural look so favoured this season.

'Yeah, that's fine. You could do your hair up though.'

'But I just washed it. Doesn't it look OK?'

It does look OK. Smooth, shiny, naturally straight with no need of ceramics. But: 'Mandy had hers cut last month. It's quite short now. Your long hair will make her feel unfeminine.'

'Mandy has just given birth to her third child, how could she possibly feel unfeminine?'

'Tired, overweight, tired. Unfeminine.'

I am shuffling papers, tidying my beautiful desk.

'Oh. OK.'

'And put on some mascara. You'll look washed out in the sun.'

Yana does as she is told, comes back for her goodbye kiss. Neither of us mention that she is nervous, that this coffee feels like it matters. She tells me when she expects to be back for lunch, I agree to eat with her. If I've finished sorting the correspondence, arranging her appointments. I will have, of course, but I want to maintain some hold over my own hours. Yana owns all my hours, pays for them with a monthly salary and soft skin beneath my fingers, but I need to claim something back, every now and then. I come out to the car with her, saying I want to pick some flowers for the kitchen table. I wave her goodbye. I have a slight frown on my face, am preoccupied with the question of hibiscus or bougainvillaea and whether the gardener is taking enough care with this border. Later over lunch she will tell me how the coffee went and I will tell her how beautiful she was as she drove out. This evening in bed I will stroke her long heavy hair and lift it to my mouth, the scent of her shampoo lingers into the night. When her

36

room is again our room, when her time is also mine, then I will address her loveliness with the praise it deserves, then I will be open, interested, attentive. While she is parcelling herself out, dressing her body not for me but for the work that is every other occasion in her life, then I am businesslike and detached. Her body is the tool of her trade. My distance keeps it sharp, gives her a layer of protection. Allows her to access the valuable vulnerability, but saves her from drowning in it.

And the distance gives me a little power too.

Six

Jimmy, meanwhile, sleeps through the entire morning. His room, equally large, just as perfectly presented, is at the other end of the house, away from my suite of rooms and her stretch of space that has become ours. His is the part of the house where they play happy families on the rare occasions someone comes here who doesn't know where we all stand. Sit. Lie. It isn't merely his distance from our domain that keeps him happily snoring though, at this time of year, Jimmy sleeps through most things. Last night he was out drinking, as much as he is able to drink in this twelve-stepped town. And while his good ole boy reputation allows him to drink more than most, it often isn't enough for Jimmy. So he came home and drank too. With a few of the guys from his show. Cast and crew, out by the pool until well after three. While Yana and I protected our privacy with closed doors, pulled blinds, dimmed lights and the certain knowledge that none of Jimmy's friends wanted to see Yana Ivanova in a bad mood in the middle of the night. They all like her, enjoy her company when she is free to offer it, but Yana is more successful than the crew, more famous than Jimmy's other actor buddies, and that scares them.

So they smoke soft joints, drinking and swimming in the orange sky night light, but their voices are muted and the water cools their excess. They are polite party animals, these men who work fifteen-hour days, nine months of the year. At least the crew work those hours, Jimmy and the actors have it easier. Were he to have achieved his dream of movie fame, or even TV drama stardom, he'd be working those hours as well, whenever he had a job – and hoping he always had a job. Instead, when his show is filming, Jimmy works just four or five hours a day, and gets every fifth week off to allow the writers time to write. All the sitcom stars know it, but few of them admit it, theirs is the sweetest job in town. They are paid to play, offering up other people's funny lines and then taking the laughs – and from a live studio audience who remind you your first love was always theatre anyway. He couldn't have it easier, though of course, the big screen siren lures him on, will steal him away eventually. Whatever, filming is done now, the endless months of four-thirty rising for the crew are over until the new season – school's out for summer. Jimmy and his lost boys play happily in the gently graded pool, concrete version of seabed beneath their feet, slipping from shallow water kissing their chests to deep water over their heads. In the semi-darkness the pool's dark indigo base hides traps for unwary visitors, Jimmy laughing from the side. And down in the quiet house, Yana and I count our blessings, we know we are safe in bed. None of those guys want to piss her off – not Yana Ivanova – they might be loud, but rarely rowdy. And anyway, the sound-proofing in this house is very good.

Jimmy's lucky. He was up for three different shows when he got this one. The sitcom was his job of choice, partly what he knew of the hours, mostly what he knew of himself. Jimmy does innate comedy timing with the best of them. The second on his list was a cop show. He didn't get it, that part went to a younger, prettier man. Jimmy snarled through the audition in what he thought was a good version of the bad cop, snarled and spoiled his own good looks. Not having heard back from the sitcom, he was just about to give in to a six-month contract of fake blood, tricky acronyms and stormy brooding (Jimmy may not be good cop pretty, but he does a fine line in angry young men, always useful for sensitive medics), when his real dream came through. He got the sitcom, perfect sitcom, bright young show. Jimmy NcNeish as bad boy next door made comedy god. Every woman loves a man who can make her laugh, Jimmy McNeish loved the writers who gave him the lines. Not only was Jimmy ideal for the part, but the part was ideal for him. Jimmy likes to play hard, party fast – albeit with an inhaler hidden in his back pocket – this town's summer smog does his asthma no good at all, but then, neither does the beer. Or the coke. Pretty TV policemen and brooding young drama-doctors with serious career prospects tend not to get kicked out of bars at 3 a.m., shooting off their smart mouths with a perfectly placed quip and a just-saved pratfall. Whereas dirty-mouthed and cute-smile young men with a tight twist on taut lines of bathos-to-pathos, are perfectly entitled to let off steam every now and then. It goes with the comedy territory, it's practically expected. And Jimmy wouldn't want to let down his fans.

Series one took off after a first slightly shaky episode, the second series did great business with a slew of Emmy nominations – no wins, but they tried – and now Jimmy has the green light for the all-important third. So while Yana works with her voice coach and attends class and works out every day before starting on a new project, Jimmy gets to take the summer off, lie by the pool, eat what he likes, and binge when he wants to. Given next season's storylines, this doesn't do his character image any harm – Felix has, of course, checked. If there was any danger in Jimmy's behaviour, any chance of his bad boy character coming back a reformed man, Felix would stop him immediately. And Jimmy's behaviour doesn't do Yana any harm either. Deep in the all-American psyche there is a residual yearning for the tough guy, the bear-hugging, bitch-baiting real man. Even from a man with perfect comedy timing and the best of deadpan deliveries, it's still wanted. From a comedy genius, it's expected. And this particular incarnation of the real man lives with the very lovely Yana Ivanova. Which must make her all-woman.

For his summer break playtime, Jimmy parties with the other guys from his cast and several of the crew, one or two of the writers. The girls from his cast don't party. Partying isn't conducive to thin. Yana and I mostly stay in. He gets to look like one of the lads, she gets to be loyal girlfriend and hard-working, serious actress. I get what I like best. Yana and me: happy couple at home together, whole days where neither of us leaves the house except to eat in the garden, swim away the close afternoon. Good girlfriends sometimes dining with other good girlfriends while their menfolk go out to play. When the holiday ends, I go about my business with the appropriate people, Yana and Jimmy are seen at the most public of private restaurants, hurrying home for early nights, going to the right parties in perfect clothes and staying just long enough to be polite before coming on home for an early night and a good day's work tomorrow. All three of us enjoy the summer.

So Jimmy McNeish wanders from his bed late in the morning, just as I'm finishing with the letters, signing the fan photos, tidying my immaculate desk, and dealing with my last phone call before I start on lunch. Yana has a new job starting soon. She is on her pre-filming diet. Marina the housekeeper is a brilliant cook, but not even vaguely interested in thin. I've become a perfectly adequate creator of beautiful salads with just about no nutritional value whatsoever. As I stand and push in my ergonomically ideal chair, Jimmy slides back the door from his bedroom that leads up to the pool, jogs up the twenty-three wide stone steps and throws himself in. Naked as usual. The gardener is used to it, the pool man, Marina too, though I don't doubt any one of the regularly visiting staff will sell the pictures one day. Jimmy wouldn't mind, he's very happy with his naked body.

I go to the kitchen, make coffee, he walks past me, grunts something like good morning, picking up cigarettes and wallet, dripping chlorine-free, organically cleaned pool water as he goes. Half an hour later he comes back for his coffee.

'Hey.'

Jimmy looks like shit.

'Hi.'

This does not mean he doesn't look good. He looks great. If you like stubbled, baggy-eyed, dirty-haired men who haven't yet bothered to clean their teeth this morning. Many of the female viewing public appear to, quite a few of the men. And I do too. I think Jimmy McNeish is gorgeous. Really, absolutely, my type of guy. When I have to have a type. I've always been drawn to the bastard cliché, it's one of my weaknesses, why I'm better off with girls. For some reason I only ever picked nasty guys. Difficult girls maybe, high-maintenance women like Yana, but not mean. Never cruel like Jimmy can be. Not cruel to Yana, he wouldn't dare. Those two play nice. Mostly. But to the women he employs for himself sometimes. And one of the girls on his show – the one he says likes it that way, keeps her on her comedy toes. And me. Sometimes. When I let him. Like today.

'You were out late?'

'Fuck off.'

I pour him a cup, add warm milk.

'I'm sorry?'

'Fuck off.'

'Why?'

'I don't want to talk yet.'

'That was hello, Jimmy. I wasn't starting a deeply meaningful.'

'Good. I don't feel like chatting with the staff this morning.' He sips at his drink, shakes his head. 'What's wrong with this?'

'Nothing's wrong with it. It's the same as always.'

'No. It tastes like shit.'

'Might be the milk. I made it with the fat free.'

'For fuck's sake, Penny. Christ. God. Fuck.'

And he's off his chair and out of the kitchen, slamming doors and kicking chairs behind him. And though I know his moods change with whatever chemical he imbibed an hour or so earlier, probably the remnants of last night's coke which he will have taken to get himself out of bed and into the pool, and although I know I make great coffee – half the time he tells me so, at length – and though I am not at all concerned about my true position in this house, I am stung. Because he's hurt me and because he wanted to hurt me. Maybe I spent too long with Yana yesterday afternoon in the sun, or maybe he didn't get the shag he wanted last night when he knows I did, or maybe – as all of us do at times – he feels the constraints of our three-person life too tight. Too tight today, when the sun is fierce and anyone in their right mind would want to walk the streets, lie on the beach, swim for hours freely holding hands with the one they truly love – for whatever reason Jimmy is pissed off and he's taking it out on me.

And he will continue to do so until he chooses not to. And I'll take it from him. Because that's part of my job too. Keeping the peace, making it nice for Yana, placating Jimmy whenever I can, not rocking the boat. Never rocking the boat. Which he knows. All of us do, we all know way too much, know each other far too well.

So I open a carton of half-fat milk and make fresh coffee and I take it into his disarrayed room and he doesn't say thank you and his beautiful grumpy face and stunning unwashed body are turned away from me. And I think he's delicious. And I really don't like him.

Seven

That evening we ate together. The four of us who make up our little family of liars. Yana, Jimmy, Felix and me. Jimmy was on good form, had slept all afternoon, was looking rested and ready to party. As usual when he was feeling happy with his world, he started teasing and flirting with me, trying to annoy Yana. And I admit to flirting back just a little as well. Though I wasn't flirting to annoy Yana, not exactly, just to make her notice me more. It's all very well being the one who knows all, cares for all, caters all — sometimes what I really want is just to be wanted back. On an even footing and with equal desire. And sometimes Jimmy's games are great for making Yana look up from her own complicated life and out to me. And I do like that look. I like everything about her look. Always have, always will. From the first day we met I was hooked into her, drawn into her, wanted more of her. Yes, there was the star quality thing, but something else as well. Something as crude and as simple as knowing she was my one. Deciding she was the one. And wanting to keep my place.

We sat outside by the pool drinking good wine — three of us were occasionally still amazed by the fact that we were able to sit by a pool, and such a very lovely and unusual pool, in these hills at all, astonished that our lives had access to this opulence. Felix though, born into easy luxury, remained blissfully unaware that anyone would even consider questioning this much pleasure, let alone think themselves lucky to sit at a cedar table, stepped herb garden at their back, wide view in front and dark blue water at their toes. The doorbell rang, I walked through the house, returned with dinner. Four different meals. Ordered from four different restaurants, delivered fresh and hot-tipped to the door. A protein-only selection of well-styled Japanese offerings for Yana, a creamy Italian concoction for me, Mexican for Felix. Jimmy had ribs and potatoes, beans and beer – though he made sure not to finish the whole order while Felix was around, it may have been the summer break, but the boss, whose genetic wealth extended to his own perfectly regulated weight, kept a watchful eye on his product's intake. The careful product sipped wine by the pool, guzzled beer in the kitchen.

We make a nice-looking dinner party, quite often we go out as a foursome. Plenty of people have suggested that maybe Felix and I should get together, have been together, are secretly together. Plenty of people who don't know either of us well. Felix is wealthy, late thirties, successful and a great catch. I'm a little younger and while I don't have the family money he does, I'm not that bad a catch myself. Sure I don't have the star looks Yana possesses, but I live here – I'm very well groomed, work just enough at my body to be able to get through the parties without running screaming from the room calling for a plastic surgeon, have pretty good upper-body strength if I say so myself – while hiding less successful legwork with extremely successful designer jeans. Anyway, I'm foreign. Which makes me already-interesting. Best of all my attributes, though, is that I'm not an actress. So while I'm never likely to bring world-class fame and fortune to the equation, I don't carry the concomitant neuroses either.

However, great match though we might be, Felix and I couldn't do it. American men have always seemed a little clean for me, but Felix also has that peculiarly sanitised aura that only men from truly wealthy families possess – even those who've worked for themselves, built their own careers as he has. (Naturally, he built the career with family capital, but he had to do the daily work himself, take the risks, make the breaks, make the stars.) Felix, unlike Jimmy, is not my type. I, meanwhile, am way too old for him. About half my life too old. Felix likes young girls. Not children exactly, but definitely young. If he could get away with it, his occasional lovers (they never last long) would be closer to high school than college. Seeing as he can't get away with it, seeing as who Felix Berger fucks is almost as interesting as if he were one of the stars himself, our overseer simply confines himself to very young-looking women. Girl-women. None of them my type or Yana's. Or even Jimmy's – and his tastes are way more eclectic than any of ours. All three of us prefer women who can hold a conversation. And a glass of wine without breaking their stick-thin little-girl arms.

Lack of desire aside though, Felix and I get on very well indeed. We respect each other's work and practice. Since I came to the job we have helped each other out with Yana and, to a lesser extent, with Jimmy. Felix talks to me two, three, four times a day. I advise him on how to approach Yana with whatever new project he has lined up. In summer-time, when his studio spies are not in use, I occasionally report to him on Jimmy's behaviour. Is he getting too raucous, are his fun times too close to the edge of no-longer-funny? Jimmy is allowed to play, he is allowed to suggest a hint of problems, inner turbulence – that's all part of the attraction. But a hint only. Anything more and Felix is on the phone, Jimmy ostentatiously on the wagon. In the hierarchy of this city, Felix and I have very different jobs, in reality we do pretty much the same – we tidy up our people. Package the stars and the lives they live. It's what I've trained myself to do, both because I turned out to be good at it and because it keeps me even closer to Yana. Felix, though, simply loves it.

He started off at nineteen working for his mother, a simultaneously feared and fêted casting director. After eighteen months with her he went off to college but a year on he decided there was nothing he could learn about this business from school, switched to his father's production company for another two years, and then set himself up as a personal manager. It was an audacious move for a young man of twenty-four. But it worked. He poached two hugely famous clients from his mother's best friend – both of them looking for new challenges to revive stalled careers – and took on just three new unknowns. The unknowns became well-knowns, the old stars regained some heat. Two years later he discovered Yana, decided it was high time the screen had a new icon – someone foreign and enigmatic, someone viewers would find different enough to dream themselves into – and set about making her career.

Felix thinks he discovered Yana Ivanova. The fact that Yana paid his assistant, Will, a thousand dollars for a month-long copy of his diary, and then made sure she was at every second event he attended, remains a secret between Yana and Will. The fact that she dressed as little-girl as she could get away with merely enhanced her attraction. It suits Yana to let Felix think he made the moves, it suits Will that Felix never found out how dishonest he can be. And Will isn't stupid, he'd never have agreed the deal with Yana if he didn't also think she had something worth buying – he's studied Felix well.

*

Plates empty bar the traditional side-relegated three mouthfuls, we moved on to dessert, fat-free sorbet all round, and talked about Yana's new job. She was to start shooting in three weeks, a month of six-day weeks on location up the coast, followed by a few less hectic months back home, with extra time optioned at the end if need be. If her notoriously demanding co-star needed it. How she would be tied up pretty much until the end of the year. How Mike Scarling was known to be something of a handful, but he would be the perfect foil to Yana's outing this time as clean-cut all-American girl verging on all-bad woman. How working with Scarling was a great move for her. How excited Felix was that she got the part, that the effort they'd put in to make this happen, to make Scarling demand her for the job, had been well worth it. How they were totally delighted that she would be working with the sharpest, coolest, baby director in several years. Jimmy had a few smart things to say about child-labour laws and on-set tutors – Lou Cerbonit was French-Algerian and good-looking and very clever and way too successful and too different for any of his peers to like him all that much. But everyone loved his work, wanted to be involved in his work, and being first choice for this role proved Yana had climbed another rung, made a new leap. She'd done Felix proud, fulfilled his plans to this stage and far more. We toasted her new success.

Then we moved on to Jimmy's show. How this year he was tipped not merely for Emmy nomination, but already holding more than one statue in the palm of his hand. That it was Jimmy's time now, his turn for recognition. How Felix's pet story-liner had spent the summer working on a few great ideas for Jimmy's character, and Jimmy got on so well with this guy, they would have lunch in the next week or so. It was all going perfectly according to plan. They were even bringing in a hot new love interest for Jimmy's character, which could only do them all good. Felix was so delighted with himself that he actually turned off his cell phone for the rest of the night and we opened another bottle on the strength of Jimmy's brilliance. And no one turned down a new glass.

Finally, Felix brought my job into the conversation. Whether I should go on location with Yana or not. I was surprised he even asked. Of course I would go. I wanted to be with her, Yana wanted me with her. It was what we always did, it would seem weird not to go. I was not wanted merely for love, though that was there, always there, but because she needed me. Yana is way stronger and braver when she is actually doing the job, as opposed to the tedious rigmarole she has to go through to make herself amenable and wanted, to get the job in the first place. The necessary tricks and carefully-disguised showing-off make her uncomfortable and self-questioning, once she starts work, she's far more self-assured. But she still likes having me around. I am a barrier, her safety net. Someone who really knows her. And Felix had always agreed I was vital to Yana's abilities. This time, though, he was not sure. He wondered if me being on location with her was not too close to the truth.

'What? Everyone who takes their assistant away with them is a fucking queer? Christ, this town must be even more full of fucking perverts than I thought.'

Yana and I smiled, Felix did not; he ran a nail-bitten hand through his carefully tousled hair. 'Shut up, Jimmy. It isn't about that.'

'Then what is it about, Felix?'

Yana was interested, I was starting to get concerned.

Felix looked uncomfortable. 'I don't quite know how to say this.'

'Just say it . . . unless this is some private little girlie thing? I'll hop in the water if you like? Swim way down deep and blow bubbles so I can't hear?'

Jimmy was having way too good a time and I didn't like it. I could endure his twisting dances with me, play at he and I against Yana, give myself more status by joining in with him. If I wanted to, when I wanted to. This was about me though. This was edgy.

'OK look, it's just, well . . . here's the thing.' Felix sighed, Jimmy stopped grinning long enough to listen. 'Mike Scarling would like to go out with Penny. He called yesterday and asked me for her number.' Felix turned, directing his comments to me. 'He likes you, Penny.'

Yana's face fell, I was stunned.

Jimmy burst out laughing. 'Wooh! Go girl! Mike Scarling – yes! Fucking A-list, fucking A!'

'Jimmy, piss off.'

All three of us at once. He pushed away from the table, threw himself backwards into the pool, laughter bubbles floating to the surface as he swam the curving width underwater.

Yana's top-of-the-range co-star wanted to date me. I looked at her face and saw all the emotions there at once – jealousy over me, jealousy to do with Scarling, irritation at Jimmy, fear of loss of control, and the one emotion Yana so rarely allows herself to feel, let alone show, anger.

'He can just fuck off.'

Felix was quiet, bit on a chunk of dead skin at the side of his thumbnail. 'Of course. I thought that's what you'd say.'

'What else would I say? Felix, this is stupid!'

He ignored her, continued, 'So I figured it might be best if we find a reason to keep Penny here at home, then there wouldn't be a problem with Mike seeing her on set every day.'

'Me, me! I need Penny! Give her to me!' Jimmy was still laughing, reached a wet hand up for his glass, received a stab from Yana's heel instead. 'I must have Penny, I'm not funny without Penny, please, she's all I want, all I desire, she is, she is . . .'

He winked at me, blew a kiss, and was up and out of the water, down into the kitchen to sneak a few more beans and a lot more beer while Felix dealt with Yana.

'How the hell am I supposed to work with this man – this film has two sex scenes for God's sake – when he really wants to be fucking Penny? Christ, Felix, I thought you said this was all going to work out just fine?'

Felix shook his head. 'I know what Scarling's like. He sees someone new and he wants her straight off. It's why his last relationship broke up. Remember, he'd never met Penny until you two came to that party at my place, I introduced you to him.'

'I was new. Didn't he want me?'

'Yana, you're likely to do as well out of this movie as he is, if not better. You're the perfect match for him right now, but he isn't stupid, you're a threat. Penny isn't. She's not on the same level, he doesn't even think of her in that way.'

'Thanks so much.'

'Come on, Pen, you know what I mean.'

'I do. And I don't appreciate it.'

Felix reached out for his cellphone as if it might have a solution for him – it usually did – and then realised he'd foolishly turned it off too soon. He sighed, empty hands spread wide in appeal. 'Girls, look, we can handle this. Yana, you go off on location, we'll make up something about Jimmy needing Penny in the home office right now, you're so hot with this part that you don't need any help at all, whatever . . . Penny stays here for the month, you get on with the job, make Scarling like you so much that he forgets all about Penny, come home, finish the rest of the shoot, and it's all over.'

Yana wasn't convinced. 'You think it's that easy? This man wants to fuck my girlfriend and I get on with behaving like he's all I've ever wanted?'

'Well, yes, that is what I think. It's acting, Yana. It's what you're good at.'

'I don't want your flattery right now.'

'I'm not flattering you.' A hint of anger from Felix now, slow speech, measured words. 'I'm just telling you what's going to happen. I know this guy, Mike's brilliant at the job and a total fuck-up at home. He thinks he's found the ideal girl, gets all worked up about it and then another one comes along, and he's all confused, chases her instead. He changes his mind as fast as he changes his sheets. Faster actually, I think he's a bit of a slob. Don't worry, sweetie, it'll be fine.'

Jimmy was back at the table now, still grinning. 'Sure it will. Sweetie.' Extra cheese with the sweetie, wider grin that suggested a line or two of kitchen coke with his beer. 'Either that or Penny could go fuck him and turn him right off her. You can do that, can't you Pen? Be bad in bed? I mean I know you haven't had all that much practice, but surely even you can be bad at it? Be a really bad fuck? Just this once, just for Yana?'

I couldn't stop myself, knew better, but had to reply. 'Oh, I don't know, Jimmy. Maybe you fancy teaching me?'

Felix and Yana glaring at each other, Jimmy's smile wide now, and happy, straight back at me. 'Any time you want, babe, my door is always wide open. You know that, right?'

Eight

Things got messy then. Clearly we'd all taken too happily to the second bottle of wine. Jimmy kept up his threats about how much he was going to need me, how he just had to use me, it was so definitely his turn to have me all to himself. Yana ignored him and insisted she wouldn't go on location without me, would pull out of filming, would tell Mike Scarling to go to hell. Felix dragged me aside and told me I had no option. I knew he was right and was perfectly prepared to go along with what he'd suggested. Though I wasn't in the least bit happy about it, nor did I intend to pretend I was. At least not until Yana had given in as well. I knew Felix needed me to agree with him but it didn't hurt my position to hold out a little longer. Though Yana and Jimmy paid him, Felix was really in charge of their careers. Of course I could always get another job, though it was unlikely to be one that would have so many pleasurable perks, and without a reason for being near Yana day in day out, it would be almost impossible to maintain our relationship. Felix knew this and so did I. He didn't have the same control over my career as he did over Yana and Jimmy's, but he had it over my life. Which was his main bargaining tool whenever he had to deal with me, and it usually worked. In this moment, though, I had some sway with Yana. What I did and said in the next hour or two would make all the difference to how she approached her new job. She wasn't going to throw over the film, she had no intention of not doing it to the best of her ability, but right now, the option to quit was all she had to hold on to. And so we carried on biting and bickering, each one of us knowing exactly the outcome we were headed to, each one of us bartering as long as we could. When there is no choice at all, we are most likely to bargain as if we hold all the cards.

Against Felix's better judgement, Yana lurched over to the small pool-house fridge and pulled out a third bottle of wine, poured herself a large glass, drank most of it in one and launched into a tirade about how tired she was of Jimmy's passive-aggressive flirting with me. By now I was tired of it too. It had lost its allure pretty much exactly at the moment Felix demanded I spend the next month full of Jimmy. I can do play-flirting, half-fancying Jimmy. But it's way easier to do at a distance. Too close and I see clearly what I might have been. And that victim-girl is not a sight I value greatly. Felix was just gearing himself up to launch in and read the riot act to his loudly bickering children – I could see the signs: wine refused, toe-tapping, shirt collar fingered, cellphone picked up, put down, turned on and off repeatedly – when the doorbell rang again. Jimmy whooped a hello that would be heard round the front of the house and halfway up the hill, and Yana immediately threw what was left in her glass on to the grass and poured herself water instead. She smoothed her hair, fired a warning look at me, and hissed 'You're not leaving until we're through with this,' at Felix. Who had no intention of moving until everything was sorted, but allowed Yana her moment of power. It was her house after all. Her garden, her pool, her water, her wine.

Jimmy's best drinking buddy Dan, chief sound guy on his series, had turned up to watch a late-night match on the

TV Jimmy usually commandeered as his own. With beers in his bag and grass in his pocket no doubt. Jimmy brought him up to the pool, explained while popping a can that we were having a family domestic, gave Yana a lingering kiss for Dan's sake – and mine – and then whispered loud enough for all of us to hear, 'It's just like fighting over the dog really, isn't it baby?'

Dan, who had seen Jimmy and Yana argue before, who was clearly hoping to see another hot war between the two of them, sat down on the mosaic edge of the pool and reached out for a glass. Yana slapped his hand away, Felix bit deeper into his thumbnail in agitation.

Despite her desire to look the part, Yana was in no mood to entertain Jimmy's buddy. The image she had to maintain was one of typical hetero-girlfriend, an image any of us accept just as well while the woman is slagging off her bloke – and his mates – as when she's playing hand-holding happy.

'Fuck off, Dan. You're not welcome right now. This is a private fight. Jimmy and I don't need spectators.'

'Yana!'

Felix spat out her name and raised a single censoring finger. He didn't need Yana to be Jimmy's lover-girlfriend all the time, but with a week to go until she was away for a month on location, he didn't need her to start any estrangement rumours either. And like anyone in this business, he knew the biggest and best rumours came direct from the crew.

Dan grinned into his beer, and Jimmy laughed out loud. Felix pulled at his collar and spoke clearly to Dan.

'Actually, we are in the middle of something.' He lowered his voice and leant down to Dan on the grass, 'You know what these two are like, Yana's about to go off on location and neither of them are happy about the day-breaks deal I've got for her. And I do need to get it sorted before tomorrow morning, so if you wouldn't mind . . . we won't take long. An hour maybe? I'll be gone by then, I need to get back to the office tonight anyway . . . '

Felix smiled his 'all-actors-are-hell' smile – which made perfect sense to a crew member – and Dan lifted his feet from the pool, waved goodbye to Jimmy. 'I'll be back in a while. The first half is crap anyway.'

He knew Jimmy would fill him in on all the details later – even with the restrictions Jimmy always kept to, there was usually some gossip to catch up on. And Dan had a girlfriend who would just love to hear that Jimmy McNeish and Yana Ivanova were having a not-quite-perfect-couple evening. Passing on that juice might even get Dan forgiveness for giving up their Saturday night to sports and another guy.

Jimmy made a show of kissing Yana yet again. Kissing her even though she didn't want him to, running his hands across her thighs, ensuring Dan saw exactly what he was doing. One guy to another, each bloke as aware as the next of how difficult the little woman can be – especially when she's as gorgeous as Yana. And, knowing Dan was taking it all in, Yana played up to Jimmy this time. Her body moving of its own accord, against my wishes, betrayal of her flesh. Just another couple who would let their rampant sexuality overtake their bitter irritation with each other. Dan saw it and smiled. So did Felix. I didn't. Not while Jimmy was staring at me over Yana's bare shoulder.

I saw Dan out of the house and walked slowly back to the pool. It was time to move on. We all knew that. The three of us were ready, waiting to agree. We'd had our playtime, Yana's tantrum, Jimmy's teasing, my proud reticence, now it was time to do what we had to do. Each one giving in, not just because we really had no choice as a threesome, but very much for our individual needs as well. The sake of all of us, magnified by each of us. We were ready to be good kids. And Felix knew it. But it didn't stop him launching into a lecture first. Felix gives good lecture. The actors love it.

Jimmy's irresponsibility, his proximity to the line. How Felix could – and would – pack him off to rehab, whether he needed it or not, just to get him back in shape and keep him there until the series started filming, or at least until his big mouth and his ludicrous appetites could do no more harm this break. A spot of public humility never hurt anyone's career and if Jimmy didn't watch it, then Jimmy would damn well be getting it. Jimmy didn't speak or answer back. Kept his eyes on the beer in his hand, slowly turning the now-warm bottle, nodding at appropriate moments, not shamefaced, but hidden-faced. Not agreeing with the words, but allowing that they be said. Jimmy and Felix each content to go along with the charade; big daddy and his wayward son, wounded partner and the headstrong lover – a proper old-fashioned telling-off from the boss. It was what Jimmy's day had been heading towards, it was what the night wanted.

Felix's tack with Yana was different. Softer-spoken and yet harsher at the same time. No role-playing necessary for this version, Felix was simply putting the bare facts on the table. Yana's choice, Yana's lifestyle, Yana's romantic inclinations. Yana's obligation to make the greater sacrifice. It was not true really, any of it. Yana had no more chosen to fall in love with me, than Felix chose his predilection for late-teenage girls, or Jimmy preferred his bedmates brunette and shapely. Like anyone else, Yana had come through the confusion of her youth and eventually grew to understand the form of her desire – she had not chosen it, merely acknowledged it existed. Women were her prime desire. I was her prime desire. But Yana had chosen this life, her work. She knew the sacrifices it entailed. And, as Felix pointed out, if she didn't know them thoroughly when she started, she certainly did now. We'd all seen enough careers derailed through injudicious gossip, lack of forethought, careless execution. If Yana was superb at anything, it was planning. It was one of the things that first convinced Felix he could work with her. It was one of the reasons she had chosen to trust him. And now she had to trust him again. He was doing his best for her, we all knew it. But it wouldn't happen without her assistance. He needed her co-operation. He needed all our co-operation.

Felix let his words hang over the table, the pool. Carefully timed, no doubt part-written as he was driving out to the house that night. He couldn't have known for sure that Jimmy would be near-pissed when he arrived and he certainly couldn't have guessed Dan would turn up on the doorstep at exactly the wrong moment, but he must have been expecting Yana's reaction, my anger, Jimmy's glee. These two little speeches were simply statements of what we already knew. Sometimes, most times, none of us want to do the difficult thing. Even when we know it is the only option, we still don't want to choose it for ourselves. Felix's lecture gave Yana and Jimmy an opportunity to do the right thing and yet tell themselves they were only doing as they were told, accepting the inevitable. Jimmy shrugged, left his unfinished beer, went inside to call Dan and watch the match as planned. Yana picked up the dishes, tidied away the bottles, cleared our dinner rubbish. Felix sat back in his chair, watching the compliant clients proving his twenty-five per cent value in their inevitable acquiescence.

*

I hate being told off. Have always hated it. It's why I try to never fail, I can't stand being in the wrong. I particularly can't stand being in the right and getting told off anyway. I knew it worked for Jimmy and Felix, could see that the role-playing was as valid a part of their relationship as the deals and negotiations. Lad stuff, bloke stuff, that both of them got off on. I understood that Yana sometimes followed a dangerous line. That as much as she was incredibly controlling about her career and her plans, her volatility and her fear bubbled up occasionally and needed placating, soothing. Yana needed talking down. Half the time Felix took on that role, very often it was what I did for her. I don't believe it's to do with her being an artist – I have never bought into the bullshit that says creative people are somehow entitled to behave worse than everyone else. I've left jobs within a week when people have tried that crap on me. I've known volatile data inputters and troubled librarians and have no doubt there are sensitive-soul, creative-genius, sheep herders out there in Mongolia somewhere. It's just the kind of person Yana is. Felix handled her really well. And, given she was holding so much together most of the time, she quite liked being handled; tucked into bed, told just do this one thing and all the nasties will go away. But I don't like to be placated and I don't like to be handled and I especially don't like to be told off. I was never one of those kids who misbehaved just to get attention. I hate the squirming, the apologies, the giving in. I've made a very successful career out of being brilliant at what I do, which frees me from ever having to make up for fucking up.

So when Yana went inside to load the dishwasher and Felix finally put down his cellphone to start on me, I shook my head. 'Not with me you don't.'

'What?'

He was smiling. I could have smiled too, made it easier on him. But I'd had enough. He'd spoiled my nice evening by the pool.

'You are not going to bully or flatter or threaten me into making this happen. I'll do what needs doing. You do it. I do it too. You know I always do it.'

'But?'

'But I'm not going to give you the satisfaction of thinking you've worked me in the same way you've handled the two of them.'

'Oh right. You're the only one who can handle them. Is that it, Penny?'

'Fuck off. We all play each other. Every one of us. It's what relationships are. We three – no, we four – just have a more involved version, that's all.'

'Wow, your British cynicism is so refreshing.'

'Yours works just fine for me.'

We sat in silence then, Jimmy and Yana lit silhouettes in the house below us, travelling from room to room, window to window.

Felix spoke first. 'I'm just doing my best to hold all this together.'

'And you do it really well. What I'm saying is, I don't need the game-playing. Not between you and me. It just makes me cringe.'

This time he grinned. 'I love it.'

'Yeah, I know.'

We were both watching the pool, thin wind ripples spreading across the surface, the dark blue tiles at the bottom almost black as the sun finally settled.

I explained, 'I've always hated the idea of being in the army.'

'What?'

'The army. Any of the forces. All that hierarchy crap.

Grown adults behaving as if one person's rank gives them any kind of inherent status over another. I hate that shit.'

'And what's that got to do with what happened this evening?'

'I don't get off on being told what to do.'

'Not at work anyway?'

'That's right. You're not my boss, Felix. You don't employ me. And even if you did, I still wouldn't recognise that as giving you any rights over me.'

'But what I do for Yana allows her to employ you.'

'Yep. She's officially my boss and I don't let her tell me what to do either.'

Felix nodded, studied his fingernails for a moment. 'OK. Point taken. But you will see Mike?'

'Yes.'

'And you'll be nice to him?'

'Very.'

'It is important, Penny.'

'I know it is, Felix.'

'Thank you.'

'You're welcome.'

Negotiations over, Felix was anxious to close the deal. 'I'll give him your number? You could meet up with him this week before they go on location, so he's nice to Yana when they start shooting?'

'OK.'

'And you'll go out with him once or twice up on set, maybe?'

'She'll hate that.'

'Probably, but it will give you a chance to stay up there with her.'

'Fair enough.' The wind was stronger now, I wanted to go back inside, be beside Yana, but we still needed to sort the little details. 'Do I need to fuck him?'

Felix couldn't help himself. 'I thought you didn't like being told what to do?'

'I'm asking your advice, not your permission.'

'Maybe not. Not just yet. And it might be best to hold off any sex while they're on location anyway.'

'Good. That should put him off.'

'But gently, yeah?'

'Fine. I'm great at gentle.'

'So they say.'

The next afternoon Mike Scarling called to ask me out.

Nine

He was sweet actually. Surprisingly so. Short – as they so often are, nowhere near as tough guy as his image. Polite. Good at talking – and not only about himself. Interested in politics and geography. Not just travel, everyone's interested in travel, even people who go nowhere say they are interested in travel, beauty queens say they are interested in travel. Half the world knows about or wants to know about Africa and India and South America. Half the world that can afford to visit, that is, the rest already live there and haven't got the money to go anywhere else. Scarling talked about proper geography, the real thing. Igneous and metamorphic rock, mountain ranges, water courses on desert plains. We had dinner and talked about rocks. Scarling talked, I listened. I like listening to that stuff. I liked learning it at school. Briefly. Before my late-onset teenage arrogance meant I had to pretend I knew everything in order to cover up the little I did know and the very much more I didn't yet understand.

Surprise number one – Mike Scarling knew about rocks. Surprise number two – he was vegetarian. Surprise number three – it seemed he didn't want to have sex with me. Actually, by the time I'd been impressed with surprises numbers one and two, I was almost disappointed by surprise number three. Not that I particularly wanted to have sex with him. He was way too nice and easy a bloke to excite me all that much. But I wouldn't have minded letting him down gently. As it turned out, he was still mourning his ex. Not that he knew himself to be in mourning, and not that I blamed his lack of attraction to me solely on the spectre of his ex. He clearly was attracted to me, had been quite honest with Felix when he'd said so. He just didn't know that he still wanted his ex-girlfriend way too much to move on yet. I could tell he fancied me – and that he fancied her still – by the nice things he said. All the many nice things he said which related me back to her.

'Melissa really likes green curry as well.'

'Yeah, that's exactly what Melissa said when I first told her about those rock formations.'

'Melissa never wanted to be an actor either. I think that's why we worked out. It's very hard to be two people working in an insecure field at the same time.'

Melissa did, Melissa didn't, Melissa could, Melissa couldn't. Melissa was – now Melissa wasn't. Melissa had clearly fucked up. This guy – this nice, good-looking, slightly weird geography guy – was still in love with her. Melissa, on the other hand, had dumped him for time to herself, some space to get her head clear and a place to think for a while. Obviously Melissa wasn't quite as brilliant as me, despite Mike's certainty that she and I would so have got along. I worked out long ago that when dumping someone, always make them think there is a successor. Even when there isn't. The silly bitch hadn't even given him the option of hating his usurper. Which meant Mike didn't realise – or didn't want to realise – that he was still infatuated with her.

So I happily played my part, safe in the knowledge that while Mike Scarling might well have fancied me, he was too into his ex-girlfriend to do enough about it to disturb my life with Yana. We talked about his work, his routine,

I found out all the things it would be useful for Yana to know. And a few it wouldn't – he knew far more, for example, about the Russian steppes than she herself did – or cared to. I talked Yana up and played down Jimmy's summer excesses. Mike, like everyone else, had read several gossip column inches about Mr McNeish that year, as Felix had pointed out, that was close to enough. I told him how much Yana was looking forward to the job, how I'd be travelling up a few times to the shoot, maybe we could get together then. It was all way easier than the argument with Felix had suggested, much less of a hassle than I'd expected, and there didn't even seem to be the likelihood that I'd need to worry about letting him down sexually. Not for a while anyway. And I was sure that once he'd spent another few dates with me as his alternative Melissa he might even want to look at other women, real women, not ones who mirrored the pinnacle-figments of his imagination. I would set him up to love working with Yana and let some other woman reap the benefits of my sexual preparation. How generous of me.

And then we bumped into Melissa. It was the night of our second date. I'd left a grumpy Yana at home, not impressed that I'd got on well with Mike earlier in the week, and less impressed that with five days until she went on location, I'd agreed to spend another evening away from her side.

'You could have said no.'

Jimmy said nothing, but nodded his agreement with Yana.

'I thought the point was I say yes and get him to be nice to you?'

'You could have had lunch instead. You could have spent the evening with me.'

Jimmy nodded again. Silent and bloody annoying.

'You're working with your dialogue coach this evening and anyway, Mike asked me to dinner.'

'You didn't have to say yes.'

'Yana, you told me to say yes.'

'Ah, but she didn't really mean it. She was just being a good girl for Felix. She wanted you to put up the fight she wasn't allowed to. Right, sweetie?'

Jimmy was enjoying this conversation way too much, we both rounded on him and he left the room, a happy smile on his face. Yana left the room too. Furious and slamming doors as she went. And much as I wasn't looking forward to my month to come with Jimmy, or all that time away from Yana, I dressed quickly and left the house not a little relieved. Being genuinely interested in someone else's stories, someone who at least behaved as if he were genuinely interested in me, seemed like a pleasant way to spend an evening. Especially when compared to the egos I had to deal with at home. At least it did until Melissa joined us.

Officially she was just passing. But as Mike said, Melissa had never wanted to be an actor, which was lucky, because she was really bad at it. We were sitting in the window of the restaurant, which I thought was odd when we first went in, odder still when Mike didn't seem to care that most people did a double take as they walked past us in the street. But it all made sense when Melissa walked by. And tried a triple take. Badly. She came in, kissed Mike, smiled a dazzling array of teeth down on me, and then pulled up a chair for coffee. And bourbon. And another coffee. A second bourbon. Then she asked if I wanted to accompany her to the bathroom. I don't really do that girlie thing of make-up and gossip, certainly not with a woman I've only just met who is the ex of the guy I'm officially dating, and

about to be the on-screen lover of the woman I'm unoffi-
cially fucking. Factor in the shared mascara and it all gets
way too messy. Not to mention that, being British, I call a
toilet a toilet. But I went with her anyway. I had a feeling
I was being offered more than just mirror-bonding. I was.
Two lines of coke. One threesome with her and Mike.

'Ah – I thought you guys broke up?'

'We did. We are. I just needed a change. Only Mike still
wants me. And when he and I talked earlier, after you two
had dinner the other night, I figured that maybe this was
the kind of change I could do with. Look, don't tell Mike
I asked you yet? He wanted me to take it slower. I was just
excited by the possibility. OK?'

I was polite, flattered, played little English-girl-shocked,
hoovered up the lines, made promises of possibly-maybes
later on, another time, maybe when Mike and Yana were
on location. And got the hell out of there.

They were waiting for me in the kitchen. My beautiful
brother-sister lovers in the white-tiled kitchen light, waiting for my post-match report. Jimmy would not usually
have been waiting for me, not usually have spent a night in
with Yana, he was obviously way too interested in what
was going on for my own good.

Unfortunately what I had to tell made him even happier.

Yana was visibly horrified. Jimmy's shoulders began
shaking and then the laugh burst from him. 'Oh, but this
is so cool. Mike fucking Scarling! How brilliant is this?
Christ, Penny, you have to do it. Please?'

'Piss off, Jimmy.'

'But think of the gossip value. Think of Yana.' He
turned to our silent partner.

'Babe, come on. You're on set, having a quiet chat about

68

the next scene, you find a way to let him know Penny's told you everything – he'll bend over backwards to be nice to you.'

Yana shook her head. 'Yeah, or decide he can't work with me at all.'

Jimmy opened another can of Coke, brown sticky drops spilling on to his fist, quick lick to the crease of his palm. 'Maybe not, but he certainly thinks he can work with our little Penny . . . perhaps it's some pheromone thing you give off? Ready and willing to fit into any sordid little threesome as long as the pay is good enough? They did offer pay, didn't they?'

'You're an arsehole, Jimmy.'

'We all have our price, Penny.'

He left the room then, leaving me to deal with Yana. And think about Jimmy. His reaction was weird. Not that it was out of character. Jimmy was a classic lad, ordinary actor. This was perfect gossip fodder for him. But even he wasn't usually this gleefully nasty.

I unloaded plates and glasses from the dishwasher, tried to engage Yana in my problems, draw her away from her own. 'I hate the idea of you going away without me. I hate that I have to stay here and be with him all the time. He's being such a bastard at the moment.'

Yana wasn't to be distracted, managing not to chew the fingernails she needed long and perfect for the shoot, by chewing the cuff of her T-shirt instead. 'Mike's being a bastard?'

'Jimmy, Yana. It's not all about Mike. Or all about your new job. This is about Jimmy, how he keeps being such a cunt to me. Or hadn't you noticed?'

'Sure I noticed. Jimmy's jealous, Pen.'

'Yeah, but he knew you had this job lined up. It won't do him any harm to be associated with Mike Scarling either. And he starts shooting himself in another six weeks.'

'Not jealous of me, stupid. Of you. And Scarling. He doesn't want some other man sniffing around you.'

She was right. And I was an idiot not to have known it.

I tried to backtrack. 'Jimmy doesn't think about me like that. Not really. It's just part of his game-playing.'

'That might be how it started, but of course there's something. It's obvious. He just won't ever act on it – not openly anyway – Jimmy knows where his money comes from. We all do. We're all doing it.' She sighed then, and got up from the table. 'All doing the same thing. The lies and the cheating and pretending. You going off and screwing some stranger every new season.'

I hated her talking like this. Making it about me. Blaming me. 'I do it for you.'

'Sure you do. And you do it for yourself too. No wonder Mike picked up on something in you. I'm surprised everyone else can't smell it on us as well – all three of us stink with lying. I'm going to bed. I'm sick of this. Sick of it all.'

I turned off the lights and set the alarms, then sat in the dark in our bedroom. It was horrible. Our perfect little set-up, our scheme that had worked so well all this time, thrown out of orbit by some short, sweet geology major and his inability to get over his ex. Yana lying in bed, paranoid that Scarling had only asked Felix about me in the first place because he knew or had guessed something about us. Me upset that Yana was right and Jimmy was jealous for me – and that maybe I'd also been tripped up by my feelings for him. Jimmy enjoying both our discomfort way too much. And Mike Scarling calling me twice a day, asking when I was planning to come and join them on set. I tried so hard – all three of us did – to make this work. I'd given such a lot to be with Yana, chosen to be with her, chosen to keep loving her even once I'd realised most of our true life would have to be hidden, understood I would have to seem always not to really matter to her. I decided way back that she was worth it to me and I would make it OK, whatever it took. I lay awake beside her, hating how it had all got so messy in only a week. And there was something else too, something that made me uncomfortable even though I wasn't sure what it was. To do with Mike and Melissa maybe, her eagerness to get together with me. Something I didn't trust about her, beyond the big hair and the excessive make-up and the fake tits. Something else I didn't like the feeling of.

We had an uncomfortable last few days at home, Yana distant, Jimmy watching his words, if not his sly glances, and me sick with uncertainty over what was coming. I wanted to be with Yana, curled up in bed, warm in the pool, cool in her arms, preparing to spend too long without her, too long with her back in the world where I was so very much her assistant and she my distant boss. I wanted to store up slow kisses against our separation. Instead she worked out and studied her script, I sat in my office, and Jimmy had the pool all to himself.

The morning she left we woke early, I finished her packing, threw out the 'Looking forward to working with you!' flowers Scarling had sent her the day before, then we made love, urgent and scared. Scared that with this departure something might come between us, that somehow Melissa's blundering attempt at seduction might achieve what five years of secrecy and well-hidden truths had not. We promised each other that no one else mattered, she promised me that none of the fake-fucks had mattered, despite what she'd said the other night. I agreed she was all

I needed, she was, I was telling the truth. When her driver arrived Jimmy and I lined up in the doorway to wave goodbye. He went inside. I went inside. We carried on.

The first letter arrived three days later.

Ten

I had no idea it would matter. I threw it out. I always throw them out. She gets so many letters. The begging letters, the pleading letters, the angry letters, the marry-me/adopt-me/fuck-me letters. The daily dribble, seeking attention, demanding Yana.

The marry-me letters are dumped immediately. She doesn't deem them worthy of a laugh. The adopt-me ones she refuses to look at, not even the sad-eyed photos. Though admittedly half of them are from people twice her age. The angry ones she asks me not to show her. They are the bitter recriminations of anyone else who might have been her – had they met the same agent/director/producer. And slept with them, of course. Or the ex-communist emigrés who believe in hard work and study and taking the new life seriously, not basking in the shallow wealth of an adopted land. Or the still-communist Americans to whom Yana is the epitome of all that is Western and decadent, betraying with her every action their hopes and dreams. It is ludicrous that total strangers believe they have anything to do with her at all. But that she talks to them in the dark, her face magnified a dozen times, her eyes open only for them. She shares their popcorn and shares herself. They think they have a stake.

I kept the fuck-me letters from her at first as well. I thought they were likely to be the most disturbing ones, the pieces of crumpled paper she'd least want to see. I got it wrong quite often in those first few months. Not for long though. She loves the fuck-me letters, they make her laugh. Even the nasty, dirty ones. Yana finds it properly funny that complete strangers choose to send her photos of themselves – or their body parts, often their body parts – postal auditions in hard card envelopes. I hate them. I found them disturbing in the beginning before there was anything definite between us, like them far less now that she is mine, that it is my body craving her attention. There's something about the intimacy of these letters that touches me too close. To her, though, that's the best bit. The fact that these people are so far from reality they really think they know anything about her, could possibly understand her. They go about their day jobs as mechanics and teachers and plumbers and surgeons and belly dancers and in the evenings they write to her.

But it's the begging letters she really hates. It took me a while to work it out. I used to show them to her every now and then. Those I thought might be deserving causes. Some little Southern belle, eldest of five children, desperate to make that first lucky acting break and needing just five thousand dollars to cover her first year's tuition at the amazing, incredible drama school where she just knows she'll be discovered. And it's true, to Yana – hell, even to me in a good year – five thousand dollars isn't that much. Not much at all. Which is why the little girl is asking in the first place. Yana came from nothing too, Yana knows how hard it is to get started, Yana must surely want to help those who are back where she once was. Those who know they can yet save the world with their mercurial talent, astonishing abilities. But no, she doesn't. One: Yana doesn't believe in drama school. On-the-job training didn't do her any harm. Two: Yana thinks there are way too many actors as it is, the drop-out rate is incredible, why doesn't the kid just give up now and do something sensible? Who needs more actors? Three: Yana's read that in South Africa there is an acute shortage of medical staff willing to tackle the AIDS epidemic. Why the hell is it only the would-be artists who think they can save the world? And need her money to help them do so? Why doesn't anyone ever write and ask her to help them fund their way through medical school and into Médecins Sans Frontières? She's got a point. And we're still waiting for the first of those med-school letters. Maybe they get sent to the doctors.

I have no idea how many of these letters she actually gets. I know Felix's office gets way more of them than we do. He's in the papers with her, people read he is her manager, they know to write to her care of him. And his assistants know to bin the letters, unopened. Anyone who wanted to contact Yana with legitimate business would either have Felix's number, or know how to get it. At the house, though, I am more careful. Of course, there are those times when the hopeful tourist leans from a supposedly private car and cranes his or her neck to see if this driveway or that is the one that leads to Yana's house. Drives up and down the street twenty or thirty times hoping to catch her on her way out to pick up a pint of milk. She doesn't drink milk and I do the picking up. The tourist who is a fan who just knows that all Yana needs to do is set eyes on him and he will metamorphose from stranger to trusted friend, from nobody to someone who matters, that mere proximity will close the yawning gap between their two lives. It never happens, but it's the stuff that dreams are sold on. And maps of stars' houses in the hills. So people drive by and some of them work out the house number and some fewer of them send letters. But of course the letters might be from someone real. Someone who does matter. Someone Yana does want to be in touch with. Because even now, some people will still send letters. And so I read them, just in case.

I love letters. I think they are so much better than email. Email for me is for work purposes only. For keeping in touch with my friends at home I write letters. Real ones. On real paper, with pen and ink. I think it pisses my mother off actually. She'd much rather I emailed her every day, phoned twice a week. I phone once a week and write once a month. Posting the LA version of the long newsy letter I'd love to get back from her. It never comes, but I figure if I don't send what I want in the first place, I have no right to ask for it in return.

And because some people still send letters, and because I respect the form, I open them all. Her last assistant didn't bother. But there are a few good ones every now and then, and she does like to read the fuck-me's. I open them because I have to, because one of them might contain something important and because I find the writing interesting. How it is that someone who recounts the 'serendipitous elation' of seeing Yana's picture on a poster while he was driving to work is simultaneously unable to tell the difference between its and it's. Why a woman mentions her chest of draws. They are an opening into otherwise-closed lives. That's the part I like. I have no intention of getting into their lives. But I like to look at them sometimes.

And then there are the letters like this. They tend not to come on very good paper. Sometimes they don't come on paper at all. The sender rarely uses a good quality ink. The sender often uses crayon. Or pencil. Rubber stamps. Potato prints once. Or, tediously, cut-outs from newspapers. I deplore the lack of imagination, expect the appalling spelling. This one, that I didn't keep, just as I didn't keep any of them at first, this one was typed. Centred. Correctly spaced. It looked like a Lonely Hearts ad. And it said nasty things about Yana. That's all. Just nasty things. I'm not even sure now what they were exactly. Something about her not being as pretty as she looks. Or as clever. Something like that. Not a big deal, but not one to show her and not one to keep either. So it went in the bin. And I thought no more of it. That was my choice. Sometimes choices can seem really small in the moment. And yet they change everything.

Eleven

Yana was staring at the ceiling. The ceiling at Sheremetyevo Airport seemed to be made of cake tins. Copper cake tins. Yana thought it was the silliest thing she'd ever seen. Modern and shiny and bright. Taxi drivers pushed against her, their bleating the plaintive cry of abattoir-herded sheep, and she held her small handbag even closer. This was it, the longest journey she'd ever undertaken. She was doing it. The possibility her mother had prepared her for since the day Yana first moved her mouth from nipple to a mama-mumble. Yana was going to England. Home of Shakespeare and Milton and Blake. Land of poetry and strange modern theatre and dark Dickensian streets. Yana was staring at the ceiling, thinking about flying and whether or not she was nervous and wondering if there might be any English boys she would find attractive. At home in the small empty apartment, Masha was holding her daughter's photo, crying, wishing herself in her baby's place.

The day Yana came home from school with the invitation Masha jumped at the chance for her daughter. In Masha's head, the journey her daughter was undertaking had none of the decadent Western overtones some of the other parents fussed over. Yana was not, after all, going to America. This was a pilgrimage of high art and true culture, delicious language and real hope all mixed into one. Manchester, England. England. Five Russian schoolgirls invited on spec, the host school not actually expecting anything might come of their offer, not really believing they'd need to find host families for these girls, just a social history module, the invitation offered as much an exercise in Western expectations of Soviet bureaucracy as it was in the slender hope of acceptance. Five Russian girls invited and politely accepted and then, shockingly, granted permission, travelling on the astonishing visa Serge and Pavel could only finger in wonder.

A school party Yana and her friends knew was special, everyone said was special, but any one of these five would have been just as happy to be part of last year's privileged group travelling to Yalta, they simply wanted a few days away from home. They might have been the brightest and the best from their class, hence the first permission, but they were still teenage girls. Five days and no interfering mothers, pushy big brothers, sulky little sisters, overbearing fathers. Of course they were excited. Five days somewhere else. A school party that would never have been considered in Masha's youth, a school party Masha was perfectly happy to give up four years of her savings for her daughter to achieve. Perestroika was kicking in, glasnost was a new and delicious possibility, made true for five extended families in this moment. And a handful of teenage schoolgirls were jostled by taxi drivers and giggled at the bad Russian accent of the British woman who was to chaperone them and marvelled at the weird ceiling and it didn't once occur to any of them to think they were incredibly lucky. Not once. Russian or not, the girls were seventeen, eighteen. And the world owed them everything.

They had flown from home too, from the small airport,

one large cold hangar and the lone plane waiting for them on the tarmac in the snow. They'd carried their cases up the short steps and on board into the belly of the aircraft, small cases, just a few days. Yana's case was the one her mother had taken away to university twenty-five years earlier, Valeria had her father's from the same time, Irina and Yelena had the cast-offs of big brothers, older sisters. Only Tatyana had a new case – and that was because her uncle now lived in Moscow. Did something in Moscow. Some occupation that was not to be spoken of, merely enjoyed as a provider of shiny new things. They placed their cases side by side in the hold, and then walked up the narrow internal staircase to the seats. Six seats in a row, the aisle between them, and their teacher already fussing. Probably because she was to hand them over to the Englishwoman in Moscow, probably because she so wanted to go with these girls herself, wanted to see what they would see. The girls had drawn lots to agree who sat by the window. Yana had a window seat on this leg, home-to-Moscow, but had drawn aisle or middle seats all the rest of the way there and back. So now she sat determinedly in the window seat, her face turned the whole way to the right. Whatever view there was, Yana would see.

When the plane finally took off, the rattling increased and the girls squealed and were shushed by their teacher. Other passengers, more used to flying, were already trying to sleep again, their bags and small cases, books and newspapers, piled on their laps, spilling over into the seats and floor space around them. Sweets and drinks were handed out, Valeria and Yelena started humming along to their favourite song, a verse each and then the chorus, just loud enough to annoy their teacher, just quiet enough for it to be impossible for her to complain. And Yana ignored it all. She left her beef sandwich to the ever-hungry Tatyana, her tea-with-lemon to Irina and stared out blankly, into the rising day.

It was the beginning of March, and while it had been a soft winter at home, spring had been slow to start. On the street outside their apartment Masha picked her way to work over solid ice, eight, ten inches thick. The man who ran the little coffee kiosk where she stopped every morning before joining the bus queue was digging deep into the ice, just able to sink his shovel into the solid grey material, digging it away from the front of his kiosk where it had built up over the past five months, a static glacier pavement, almost a foot above the real one. Spring would come soon enough and with it the thaw and longer days and warmer nights and green trees and bright flowers and bare-shouldered women. But before then they would suffer a fortnight or more of the streets gushing with water, dirty, fast-running melted ice. The more he moved from before his little shop now, the less he'd have to mop out every morning. He smiled at Masha and put down his spade to hand her a coffee. They talked about the girls – little Yelena was his sister-in-law's cousin's daughter – the school trip and the huge changes it embodied. Four sentences to say what it all might mean. A different future from the same past. And then the bus came and Masha handed him her half-full cup to join the scrum already climbing aboard even as the bus driver tested his brakes on the breaking ice. Konstantin returned to his spade.

In the air, Yana craned her neck back as far as she could and saw what might have been her own town or maybe the next closest, the one nearer the airport where they'd spent the night, guests of yet another school, hard to tell at this distance, hard to tell which direction they were travelling in just yet. The lights were still on below, cars and streets and apartments becoming ever less distinct as the aircraft moved on upwards, and then the world shifted beneath them, the pilot turned fifty, sixty degrees, they were above fields. Cold fields, still monochrome in the half-light. A thin, winding river cutting through fields and forests, twisting back on where it had already come from, telling the same water story from different points of view, meeting itself and travelling on. Light arriving over the distant curve of the earth and everything warmer now, brighter below. Still snow, but the white lessening, the green more distinct, then another dark patch, a forest dotted throughout with open specks, toy-town roofs, tiny dachas maybe, and now a smooth disc of silver, too bright to stare at directly as it reflected morning into her shielded eyes, then the plane moved on another fifty miles and the disc became a lake. Definitely dachas then, like the one her extended family share, one large space divided into two rooms for the hottest months of summer when her mother's brother and his family come out to join them, and there is no one else for another mile or two, all the lake and trees any girl could possibly want.

Flying on, the forests sparser, fields filled her vision, long straight roads and train tracks cutting through flat land. Closer to Moscow and now beginning their descent there were forests again, but smaller, and the dachas hidden in them were many, densely packed. Yana knew about this, that people here went out on their days off and rubbed shoulders with exactly the same men and women they'd left behind in the city. They had heard the city stories. Provincial girls, they knew them well. But it still looked strange to her, defeating the purpose, leaving the paved city for a forested same. And then the city itself and a ripple of excitement across their six seats, Yelena pushing into Yana's shoulder to look out as well, and there, that was one of them, Stalin's seven skyscrapers that never made it to nine. Yana looking where her friend was pointing but not seeing in time, Yana looking and seeing nothing but buildings and streets and cars and trucks and buses and trams and too many apartment blocks and all too the same and so much and suddenly she was scared. This was Masha's dream, not hers. Yana wanted to be in her real life, in an over-heated classroom, conjugating the perfect verb, longing for spring to crack open the tight windows. Yana was homesick and she wanted her mother and she didn't want to go to England after all.

And then there was the cake-tin ceiling and goodbye to their teacher and the new Englishwoman with her stilted language and their own tickets and a British aircraft and hardly any other Russians boarding with them and odd food, different food, no sweets. An in-flight movie Irina's English wasn't good enough to understand, and another cup of coffee, and then it was Heathrow and they were so tired. The tube, King's Cross, a train, and finally Manchester Piccadilly. Smiling host family and the father offering her a glass of vodka because he thought maybe he ought to. Tea and cakes to welcome the little Russian girl. (Not so little, she was tall this girl, much taller than their own daughters. And so striking the father thought. Incredibly beautiful. Though he didn't say it. Not to his wife.) Tea and cakes and hello, how was the flight, and here's the bathroom, this is your room, this is what we'll do tomorrow. All the same and all so different, such a big house – three up, three down, enormous to Yana. And cold, what heating there was turned way down low, too low. A bedroom to herself, host sisters sharing for the greater comfort of their foreign guest. Pink walls, pink sheets, dark red carpet, Sinead O'Connor crying down above her head, New Kids on the Block at the foot of her bed. Then sleep and morning and another day all new and then meeting up with the English girl and that model agency woman in the shopping mall, the one who thought she and Kathy had looked so good together and then that was it. The end of that part of her life and the beginning of this. No more homesickness. No more home. Yana's adventure and Masha still wishing it was her own.

Twelve

The house without Yana is noisy. Jimmy plays his music way louder when our partner is away, he stays up later, takes more drugs, puts out more beer bottles for the recycling collection. I put out more bottles for the recycling collection. I don't want Marina counting his intake and passing the story along. His old lady's left him alone and he's going to party. For the first week anyway. Then he calms down, goes back to the gym, drinks water for three days, de-toxes, de-tenses. Jimmy's image is all loud and party. But he is not that through and through. Felix would never have chosen him if that were the case. And Felix had several to choose from when he was looking for Yana's perfect man. Several young and eager actors, each one willing to do whatever it took – they usually thought it would take doing Felix. But that they were too old and too male. So Felix dined the prospective suitors, met with them, looked into their references, and found out their secrets. Everyone has secrets. Something back in the dark they don't want mentioned. Or if they do want it mentioned, it is to be only in the most positive terms. There are some things that can't be kept quiet, not even by a master like Felix. Criminal convictions, mad mothers, ex-lovers with a grudge. But criminal convictions can be spun into wild youth and penitent, lesson-learned age. Mad mothers can be cared for, if rarely visited. And ex-lovers can usually be paid off, paid up, shut up. Jimmy's secret was of the ex-lover variety. Something he came to the city hoping to ignore, then found – as Felix could have told him all along – that the better known he became, the thinner the ice between his past and present. For Jimmy, it was Carla. The drunken high-school fuck. The ex who didn't want him. The son he barely knew.

Now Carla and her son are no longer secrets. Felix found a way to tell the story and make it look not only good but positively glowing. They were just kids themselves, Jimmy and Carla, passion impossible to hold back, little Sammy the product of the union. In truth Jimmy didn't want Carla to keep the baby, did everything he could to persuade her to get rid of it – Carla didn't want it either, but by the time she finally admitted to herself that she was pregnant it was six weeks too late. In Felix's story, Jimmy and Carla would never have contemplated an abortion, they were young, but they accepted their responsibilities. In truth, Jimmy and Carla barely knew each other, studied different classes, were in different school years, and found themselves pregnant with the second drunken fuck. In Felix's story, they were childhood sweethearts, destined for ultimate union. In truth, when Sammy was five months old, Carla left the screaming kid with her parents and ran off with Jimmy's best friend. She didn't come back until winter. By then she was pregnant again and wanted nothing to do with Jimmy. In Felix's story, Carla knew Jimmy had a great destiny and persuaded him to follow his dream, while she settled for small-town life with her two little boys and the next best thing to a movie star, the local mechanic. In truth, Jimmy sends money to Carla and Rob and the boys, giving them way more than he has to, way more than Rob could ever earn – mostly to rub it in. He sees Sammy only once a year because they have nothing to talk about and he doesn't know what to do with the kid. In Felix's story, Jimmy helps out Carla and Rob and the boys because it is the right thing to do. He sees Sammy only occasionally because he doesn't want to disrupt his son's happy, traditional childhood, doesn't want little Sam tainted by the rich kid values Jimmy sees all around him in LA. Felix makes up a good story. Carla and Rob loved the outcome – and the income – for themselves. Jimmy loved that it got him off the hook – needing neither a pure past, nor to lie about his son. Carla doesn't know the whole story, but then she has no need to. As far as she's concerned, Jimmy finally got that lucky break. And so did she. Sammy may kick up a fuss later, may well rebel when he's older and understands some of the truth behind his father's distance. But what would be strange about that? His father is a star. Surely he's supposed to rebel?

Four years ago Felix had Jimmy over to his house for dinner. Jimmy was offered the solution to his home-town problem. And then, carefully, feeling the way, gently reaching out, always keeping back a get-out clause, making sure Jimmy knew exactly what Felix already had on him – Jimmy was offered Yana. Yana and me. They signed long and very binding contracts that night and the next morning Felix accepted, on Jimmy's behalf, his new client's first guest star role in a major and already-successful series, rushed through by a producer who owed Felix a favour. Of course it was important that Jimmy be able to do the job. Fortunately he was good at it. Jimmy is a good actor. But there are thousands of good actors, in this town and everywhere else. This good actor happened to meet Felix. And at that moment, Felix needed him and knew how to use him. Not who you know, but what they know about you.

We all know such a lot.

*

I hate it when Yana's away. Of course I am used to it. Her personal assistant, however efficient and utterly reliable, cannot possibly be needed on every press trip, each out-of-town meeting. I have grown accustomed to sleeping alone. But I don't like it and I don't sleep very well. I don't like that I cannot see her, watch her, keep an eye on her. I have trained myself to anticipate her needs. I work at being ready for her, she is my love and my occupation, vocation, liberation. Like an amputee I feel the itch of her desires when she is away from me. And I know she will get used to me being out of range. Will miss me terribly at first, crave all that I do for her, am for her, but then, as time passes, a week, ten days, Yana will realise she doesn't need me as much as she thought she did. I don't just mean in terms of the work I do for her – though there is that of course – but more as her partner. She will stop noticing I am not there and begin to see herself as a single entity again. I know this because it happens to me too.

The first nights without Yana are broken sleep and early rising, crumpled sheets folding creases into my skin. I need her to touch my shoulder, my lips. And then, as soon as a few days later, while I am still aching for her, I know too that my edges are smoothing over again, the places where I have reshaped myself to fit her round out to become all and only me. The spaces that I have shrunk or changed or adapted myself to suit Yana-and-Penny fill out and I am only-Penny. This is normal, and right, and for myself, I like it. Even in the moment of still missing Yana, I like to feel only-Penny. Except that I know the same is happening to her. Each of us shapes ourselves to the jigsaw of this relationship and, away from the need to fit in with Jimmy and me, she too becomes more and only Yana for every day that we are apart. And I don't like that at all. Yana is my proper true love. Better than any of the others, deeper than any before, she is my One. I know this. I have chosen this. Even with the hassles we have to maintain our lives, I want this. I do not want her happy being only-Yana, I need her to know the necessity of me.

Jimmy changes as well when Yana is missing. He spreads himself wider somehow, takes up more room. It is not as if he is confined to his side of the house when Yana is around, never has been, we each have free access, all areas, with a degree of polite closed-door knocking just in case. But there is always the unspoken awareness that Jimmy is actually in this house because of Yana. Because of Yana and me. It is paid for with her money, graced with her presence. While I too live in Yana's house, I am her real partner, Jimmy is in our place. But when she is gone, Jimmy becomes king of the castle. Walks naked through rooms, ties up phone lines for hours, plays interminable computer games. And gets in my way. I think he tries to get in my way. He comes into the office for no real reason. Insists I go out for dinner with him and his friends and won't leave me alone until I agree. Wants to stay up late drinking and talking. In a way I like it, enjoy Jimmy's attention. Like that he needs me to notice him. I have worked for other people and know that their partners truly have seen me as nothing more than a glorified housekeeper. I like that Jimmy's attention means he acknowledges my true position in our hierarchy, even if in public he makes an equally obvious effort to hold me down in my assumed place. But Jimmy's attention to me only reminds me more forcefully of Yana's absence. And my need to maintain pole position in her life.

The third night away she called me. It was very late, I'd already been dozing for a couple of hours, she was worried about a scene, things she'd need to do with Mike the next day. We talked for an hour and she calmed down, I listened to her voice soften as she spoke about the scene they'd shot that day. I heard the pleasure in her tones when she repeated the director's approval, the DoP's joy in lighting her perfect bones. And I wanted to be there with her. Playing with her, lighting those bones myself. We talked about nothing then. What I'd had for dinner, the computer games Jimmy had been playing all morning, how she was missing our house, wanted to rest by the pool, swim beside me. Missing us. Missing me. Me too.

I got off the phone and went outside. The walled garden by my office was too hot, so I walked up to the pool, looking for a cool breeze, finding the thyme path and stoned Jimmy instead.

'You want some?'

'No. Thanks.'

'Yana OK?'

'She's fine.'

'You missing her?'

'Of course. Are you?'

'Fuck no. This little mouse likes to play.'

'You play when she's here.'

'Yeah, but she always makes me feel guilty.'

'You don't look it.'

'I'm very good at not looking it.'

'Guilty about what?'

'Christ. I don't know. Everything. Not working as hard as she does. Not taking it all so seriously. Not getting up and exercising every damn morning. Drinking too much. Taking drugs. Fucking around. Whatever. Yana's attention to detail, to every step of her fucking career, makes me feel bad.'

'I don't think she means to.'

'I don't either. I don't think she even notices it affects me. But I do. And it grates. She holds it in all the time.

Don't you ever want her to just go crazy? Let it all out?'

I thought about Yana, her anger, her passion, her fears – and her total control of them all.

'She lets it out. All that fuss with Felix about Mike Scarling and me?'

Jimmy smiled, enjoying the memory. 'Yeah, but that's about work again. I mean properly let it all out. Get really pissed or stoned and say things she shouldn't, embarrass herself, make an idiot of herself.'

'What, like you?'

'Yeah. Why not?'

'It's different for girls, Jimmy. Different here anyway. It adds to your image, but it's the kind of thing a girl's career can take years to come back from.'

He began to roll another joint. 'Yeah, I know all the double standard crap, all you women go on about it all the time. But I don't mean that. I don't mean she has to be a cunt in public – though hey, it might be funny – but she never even lets go in private. With us, you know? Not really.'

'True. Mostly. I suppose it might be good. For her, for us. I mean, not that she's always so controlled, absolutely . . . '

Jimmy smiled. 'Not in bed anyway, eh Pen?'

'I was thinking more of her dressing tantrums actually. But there too, yeah. You're right though. She certainly holds it all together. Really tight.'

Jimmy held out the new joint, I took it this time. He got up and walked down towards the house. 'You want a beer?'

'At three in the morning?'

'Do you want a beer?'

'I'd love one. Thanks.'

We drank and smoked a little more until the sun was on its way back. We talked about Yana and the garden and

Jimmy's unrealised (more likely unrealisable) Shakespearean dreams. And it was a soft and quiet way to kill the insomniac hours. Then Jimmy went to bed and I went to the office.

I sat at my desk and thought about Jimmy, if our set-up really was working for him. He seemed lonely. Part of the plan, vital to it, but not really at the centre of it. Knowing so much and yet unable to talk about any of it except to me or Yana or Felix. All of us were in the same position, but to Felix it was a job, and to me and Yana it was our life. I think that was the first time I realised it might be hard for Jimmy too. He was definitely growing up. Some of the things he'd said made me think he might even want a proper partner of his own eventually. We'd be in trouble when he did.

And then the post arrived and with it the second letter. Only it was among half a dozen other nutter scribbles so I didn't give it a second thought. Even while I noted it was another Lonely Hearts parody, I still didn't pay much attention. Whoever had sent it wanted to know the secrets of Yana's heart. Hell, we all wanted that, even Jimmy wanted that, if his stoned night's musings were to be believed. The crazy letters went in the bin, the nice ones had replies signed by me in her hand. I booked a few appointments, turned down a bunch of requests, left a coded love-you message on Yana's cellphone and went to bed. I was lonely there myself. Jimmy would cope. Just as we all did.

Thirteen

Yana on location is concentrated attention. All effort given unreservedly to the job in hand. Whether that job be two hours in make-up, four more waiting for the lights and camera and action to finally be ready for her, or the single thirty-second scene she shoots ten, eleven, twelve times in a row. Twenty-three on one memorable occasion before her co-star – a five-year-old precocity – broke out in hives and the director had to be forced to call a halt while the stage mother performed instead. Once the child had been cleared Yana carried on with her own shots, a crouching stand-in at her knee. Take thirty-four was the one they finally used. Critics said it was the best scene in the film.

Establishing scene: Yana Ivanova wakes up, reaches for her alarm clock, scrunches up her beautiful, not-quite-American face at the red light flashing. Time: 5 a.m. We see her rushing around the rented house. She is clearly not sure where things are yet. She mutters lines as she gets herself ready for work. In half an hour she is at the door and ready to greet her driver. The driver is an old black guy. He is cheery and expansive. Chats to her all the way to the set. Her face is no longer scrunched. Forty minutes later she is in make-up. She greets the hot young director, the breakfasting crew, and saves an especially warm hug for her co-star. As she passes, we see looks exchanged behind her back. People have been nervous about meeting her. She is the female lead after all. Their looks suggest relief and pleasure. They think they might like working with Yana. The director asks Mike and Yana to come over for a chat. Yana is relaxed, smiling, and ready to work. It's a good start.

When she is at work, Yana engages only with the moment that is currently happening. I think this is the secret of her success. One breed of actors ignore the make-up girl entirely, being way too in-character already to enjoy the morning chat before the mirror. Opposing-camp actors break out in the middle of a scene when something makes them laugh, or cry, or forget their lines – something other than being too lazy to learn them properly in the first place. Not Yana. In front of the bright-bulb mirror she is the complete charm offensive, but with no undertone of manipulation, happy to turn this way and that, quietly interested in the make-up woman's affair with the guy play-ing second lead and totally disinterested in being beautiful unless the part requires it. Or the make-up artist's vanity. In front of the camera she is totally present for that eternal moment. For most people – and I've watched quite a few – there is only one route or the other. The totally in-character actors, the Method-emoters, who cannot get into the part without becoming it, and cannot get out of it for a month or two after. Always a good excuse for the on-screen romance that became an off-screen fuck – or yet another brawl in yet another bar. Then there are those with limited attention span but maximum camera-grace. The actors who drive the crew crazy, not least because while they are on set all the time, the most they actually do the job for is about half an hour a day, giggling between, screwing up long-planned shots with a single lapse in concentration – and then they have the public eating out of their hand when the luminescence shines through the dark. That indefinable something that turns a fuck-up into a star. At least until they get around to burning out or killing themselves. Or both.

Yana belongs in neither category. She simply attaches herself to the moment she inhabits. She does it all the time, to a lesser degree – from loading the dishwasher to buying shoes – but it's an especially useful skill in her chosen career. It makes her easy to organise – dressing tantrums notwithstanding – and it makes her brilliant to work with, she will always be ready for exactly the right moment. It also means I found her difficult to read until I got to know her better, when I worked out how she does it – that she changes according to the circumstance she finds herself in. At base, Yana's directed interest is all about making herself liked. And wanted. And trusted. Kind of like being the perfect PA really. Or the perfect dog. And she's very good at it. I've seen her do it hundreds of times. Sometimes I wonder if she's doing it to me. I know I did it to her. At least in the beginning.

This location shoot was no exception. Within a week she had the crew eating out of her hand. Being ready and willing, on time and in position doesn't sound like a lot, but for a lighting cameraman who's taken two hours to set up and then finds the subject of the scene has disappeared to have a long cellphone conversation with their loved one, it makes all the difference. The catering guys were hers from the moment she walked up to their truck on the first day's lunch break and ordered direct from the menu, no star-lite fussing with dietary requirements. The fact that the whole menu conformed to both her and Mike's eating requests put in weeks earlier by their managers – and that Yana had to know this – was irrelevant. Just to watch the lead girl actually eat their food at all was a joy to the caterers. They weren't to know Yana ate nothing else the rest of that day. Though they probably guessed. Five days on set and even Mike Scarling was prepared to concede he'd made a brilliant choice in wanting her for the part, agreeing to Felix's request that he push for Yana for the role. Mike, being the main man, never had to actually ask for help, wouldn't have known how to ask even if he wanted it. But Yana always knew when to give it.

MIKE

OK Yana?

YANA

Yes. Thank you. You?

MIKE

Yeah. Fine.

(*Beat*)

YANA

Actually, Mike, you know this scene here? You have so much to do and I'm just not sure I know what Dan wants from me.

MIKE

Oh. Right. Would you like me to go over it with you? If it would make you feel more comfortable . . . ?

YANA

Thanks Mike. I'd really appreciate that.

And Yana was having a good time. It was a great part, one she knew she could do well. Mike – for all his interest in me – was a good actor. They worked well together, enjoyed each other's company in the breaks. By the end of the first ten days everything was on schedule and happy and all was right with their insular world. And that was when Mike called and said he'd already told Yana I should come up to visit – he and I, Jimmy and Yana had a double date planned that weekend. The way Mike told it, Jimmy would be all in favour of the idea, Yana couldn't wait for the two of us to get up the coast.

Jimmy wasn't so sure. 'Do we have to?'

'I'd really like to see Yana. And you know it looks good if you're on set too. Felix thinks we should.'

He shook his head. 'Fuck Felix. Can't I be sick? Have pneumonia? Syphilis maybe? What a cunt.'

'Who?'

'Scarling. Double date. Jesus, are we in high school or what?'

Jimmy wasn't normally quite so reluctant to swan around on Yana's sets, but I understood his lack of enthusiasm for the double-date concept. It wouldn't do either of us any favours.

When I explained we really had no choice Jimmy tried his other method of attack.

'Oh well, at least I'll get to spend time with my darling Yana. The love of my life, Russian princess, my adored, adorable sweetheart. Wouldn't be at all surprised if she and I just have to run off to her little beach house for the whole weekend, we'll be so desperate to get our hands all over each other. Eh, Pen? That smooth skin of hers, the big dark eyes, all directed to my gorgeous manly body?'

As if it was up to me to let him off the hook anyway.

'Yeah, well, as you say, Jimmy. What a cunt.'

Yana wasn't much happier. 'I told Mike not to do that. He was talking about asking you up the other day and I said I'd speak to you first, but I said I thought you'd be busy this weekend and I knew Jimmy had things to do. Mike was going on about how much he wanted to get to know you better. Some crap about you being all mysterious and interesting.'

'Hey! Why is that crap? I am interesting.'

'I just had the feeling he was only doing it to annoy me. I like him, to work with I mean. He's good. But I don't think I trust him.'

'He's an actor, Yana. In competition for screen-time with you. What's to trust?'

'Anyway, I said to wait until I'd talked to you, and then you go and tell him you're fine to come up.'

'He told me you wanted us to.'

'Yeah, well he's a lying shit. I told him I wanted to spend this weekend working alone.'

'So you don't want to see me either?'

'Of course I do. I just don't want to see you with Mike Scarling.'

'I have to watch you and Jimmy all over each other all the time. And I'll have to watch you and Mike fucking in this movie.'

'For God's sake, Penny, that's different.'

'How?'

'You're used to it.'

'Right, Yana. And familiarity breeds contempt.'

So it was a truly joyful journey Jimmy and I made that Saturday afternoon, almost three hours up the coast to the location, all the way in heavy traffic. He offering me tales of what he would do with Yana's body the minute he saw her – 'So much the better to convince the world of our mutual heterosexuality, my dear' – she calling every half-hour to see where we were and how soon the two of us could get away from our planned evening with Jimmy and Mike – the double-date high-school desire and no virginal conclusion.

We arrived and Jimmy was all over Yana. But that was only in public. Mike had made a booking, despite Yana's requests for a quiet night in after a week of work, we were going out to eat that night. The four of us out to dinner at the local high-class restaurant and not one of us expecting anything tastier than a grilled chicken breast over-stuffed with an inappropriate cheese. But with dinner arranged we did at least have an excuse to prise Jimmy from Yana's flesh. After all, she couldn't spend all her time with Jimmy, on the steps of the make-up van, in the corner of her caravan, on set as she introduced him to her favourite runner – even if they had been apart for ten whole days and nights, there was the evening ahead and we had an important date to get ready for. Good for us, good for the movie. The unit publicist couldn't have been happier, it was all she could do not to send a photographer out to eat with us. I'd been driving all afternoon, Yana had been on set, clearly we had to get dressed up, we needed girl-time in front of the mirror. We needed girl-time in front of each other. I have often wondered about the men in our position, how they get away with their lies. Women always have the opportunity to grab an intimate conversation, share important diet tips, exchange bodily fluids in the bathroom. Perhaps that's why so many of the guys claim to have coke habits. How else to get a stolen moment alone in a bathroom cubicle with the object of desire?

Montage: two women, two men, dressing for dinner. The men, in two different venues, take their time, slow grooming, cock preening. The women shower together, make up together, dress together. Undress to dress again. One woman dries the other's hair, one woman kisses the other's hair. New links are formed and quickly remade as the first man joins the two women, and then the second man waits at the front door of the house, pairs mutate through triangles into fresh geometry. Clear coupling becomes uncertain doubling. A car is made ready, doors opened, a woman's bare legs folding into the passenger seat, strong man's hand possessive on the back of her long neck, ocean drive, setting sun.

Cut to the restaurant.

Fourteen

Dinner with the famous is not the same as a normal meal. When I dine alone I eat. Mostly I do so while watching TV or a movie, I forget that I could go outdoors. You can take the girl out of Essex, but you can't make her remember LA sunshine isn't really trick photography. When I dine with Yana at home we also eat. We might drink some wine, certainly water. We talk to each other. More often than not, we sit outside by the pool, the garden reflected in the dark water, topaz mosaic picking up the last of the sunshine. I remember the water when she is with me. It doesn't have to be really hot, we just like to be outside together. We didn't come from here, she or I. We like the sun, the comforting assurance of constant shine. We're careful of it — she has that perfect complexion to maintain — but we like it. Above all, though, we eat the food. That's what we're there for. That's why we are sitting together at a table or in front of the TV with plates on our knees or on leather and chrome carefully protected poolside 'outdoor room' furnishings. That's why the plates have food on them and our hands hold knives and forks. Or just a napkin if Jimmy gets his way. The point is the eating. Even for Yana and her perfectly proportioned screen-star's body. That's why it's called a meal. But this definition exists only for private dining. In-house dining, poolside dining. Out at a restaurant, dinner is a very different thing.

The door is pushed aside, we enter the room and are, in a single glance, shuffled into place in the hierarchy of the current clientele. Yana's status is lowered slightly by my nonentity presence, mine raised exponentially by hers. Both of us enhanced by Jimmy – not only added star quality, but at least one of the two women is potentially hetero-sexualised as well. Though it's true his presence does relegate me to assistant. Without Jimmy, I am as likely to be defined as friend as I am assumed to be her attendant servant. Still, having the man around raises Yana's status and therefore mine too – whether as friend of the famous or simply slave. I could taste her food to check for poisons. I might as well. Unlike most eating paranoiacs, she eats larger quantities at home than when out. In the current upward curve of Yana's career, it is more appropriate for her to appear to be starving herself than to care about the anorexia rumours. They are rare in her case anyway, she has a good body, honed body, but the only bones that shine through her skin are cheekbones. The rest have a perfect few millimetres of yellow fat smoothed over them. Yana is like the rest of us but better, very fine but not too thin, it's one of the reasons we love her.

We are greeted at the door, normal diner or five star, and now the meal has nothing to do with food and everything to do with where we sit, which table is made free for us, how long we wait until the chef and the manager come to greet us. I say us, I mean Yana, maybe Jimmy. And how very irrelevant the menu immediately becomes. Even in a burger bar the chef wants to offer his or her speciality, the manager wants us to have it for free. And no one expects us to eat. Not really, not properly, not so the plate is emptied and the perfectly fresh bread is employed to soak up a rich thick sauce. We taste, we nibble, we exclaim. And we drink water. Bottle after bottle of bloody water. With maybe half a glass of wine. God it's dull. And yet, to everyone else in the room, making extra trips to the restroom, peeking from behind embossed card menus, taking an especial interest in their own reflection in the mirror behind our table – we are so fucking fascinating. She mainly, he next, but me too. Because the hand of fame is close to me – they don't know how close – and the passers-by, carefully positioned extras, want to know what it feels like to hold my secret knowledge, be who I am, to get so near. In restaurants like that, the ones where we are nice enough to refuse the offer of a private room, where we like to show just how down-home normal we really are by eating out there with the ordinary people and ordering straight off the menu, much of the time what dinner is like is just plain hungry.

The addition of further celebrity to our mix, however, adjusts the geometry of attention. Being on location even more so. There is both more gratitude that we are gracing the establishment with our out-of-town presence and less attention. Less attention, expressly pointed, to remind us that out of LA we're just normal people after all. That night on the demanded double date with Mike and me, Yana and Jimmy, much of our evening passed off as a perfectly ordinary night out. Of course there was still the fawning-while-pretending-not-to-care maître'd, and the head waiter suddenly abandoning his usual Saturday-night tippers to cater to us. And, after consultation with the chef, there were one or two more specials announced at our table than were listed on the chalkboard. But we were almost ordinary. Something about the double-dating ideal, something about two boys and two girls, seemed to normalise our situation. Made us look, at first glance, just like any other couple of couples. The girlfriends might be old friends, the guys Saturday football buddies, our kids at home with a shared babysitter maybe. Four looks more ordinary than three, the square is safer than the triangle. Equilateral, isosceles, scalene – there are too many names for three.

We had a perfectly pleasant meal. It was the first evening off all week for Yana and Mike. There would be a day free tomorrow, time to sleep well beyond the rest-of-the-week five o'clock alarm, and several spare hours to spend in the gym, allowing space for a whole bread roll instead of just half, two glasses of wine as opposed to one or none. There was plenty to talk about without needing to go anywhere near the tricky area of who would kiss whom good night. Not that early in the evening anyway. And when we came to order I found that with four of us there, I was asked for my meal choice second. Normally the girl/boy politeness goes right out of the waiter's head. It's Yana first, then Jimmy, then me. Strict pecking order of who's who. But with Mike sitting beside me, and he officially surpassing Yana in fame gain, she and I were addressed first. I may have been a nobody, but I was a lady-nobody. Nice. And it was no doubt something to do with our geographical positioning up the coast as well. The further we are from the centre of production, the greater the chance that I will be seen as well as Yana, her radiance is somehow less blinding with the dilution of distance. It was easy to keep the chat flowing between us too. Yana and Jimmy had been apart for a week and needed to catch up, Mike needed to talk about how much he enjoyed working with Yana – code for how well his own scenes were going. There was a week's worth of new shoot gossip to relate and both of them wanted to talk about the brilliant young director they were working with, a chance to fill us in on the stories and bond as co-stars should they ever need to fight together, or fight the director together. Jimmy had received a fresh batch of story-liner's notes and series secrets, always good for half an hour's tales. I'd spent my week working in Yana's home office, no news there. But I'm good at listening. Especially good at listening to Yana tell Jimmy her new secrets and hearing them as if they are being offered to me, dividing my brain between the conversation I am having and the one I'm listening to, the one that truly involves me. And then, we are girls. We go to the bathroom together. To share lipstick and powder and kisses. She'd been away from me for ten days. We'd done it before, we'd be doing it again, but I never got used to how good it was to hold her angled bones first in my gaze, then in my hands. The shock of her skin, all the more delicious for it being a stolen touch.

The meal was easy and Mike was fine company, Jimmy enjoyed himself, watching him watching me, watching me watching her. Touching her leg under the tablecloth. Feeling the stretch of her body reaching out for mine. And even Jimmy pushing us apart, kissing her in front of Mike and me, fingering her fingers while talking intently to me, intentionally to me, even that was fine. Mike was cute, and funny, not a bad dinner companion at all. He ordered good food and was surprisingly happy to drink the wine. I figured Yana could kiss Jimmy now and I'd kiss Mike later, give him a sweet good night that lined up his expectations and covered all our backs. As I would cover hers. It was all way easier than I'd been expecting and much more comfortable and ten o'clock came quickly. Soon I'd be back with Jimmy and Yana at her rented beach house, in a borrowed bed, owning our bodies.

Fifteen

And then Melissa arrived. She turned up looking incredible, smelling incredible, being incredible. I was incredulous. Truly. I couldn't believe any woman was prepared to be this obvious and wasn't also dying inside with utter shame. Any woman who isn't me. I'm used to whoring myself for the right moment, right cause, I'm just not used to seeing other people in my position. Or doing it so well. Melissa did it really well. Was charming and beautiful, her surprise that we were there, coupled with her delight when Mike asked her to join us, were in perfect proportion to the slight hesitancy she employed in working out where she should sit. She sat between Yana and me, joined in the conversation, explained her presence in the restaurant: 'Oh yeah, I lived up here as a teenager? I knew Mike was filming? So I called his place and they told me where you were? Mike, you should so sort out security arrangements with that housekeeper! Anyway, here I am, you don't mind me joining you? It's not too late?'

The rising inflection of each coy and slow-delivered phrase prevented any interruption – and any suggestion that what she spoke could be anything but fact. She settled in and made herself comfortable – while in no way undermining the status of any of the chief guests. It was very impressive, on another night I'd have taken notes, Yana would have wanted to video the performance and see if there wasn't something there that would work for her. This night, though, Yana and I were too stunned to pay attention to Melissa's work methods, we were both so distracted by the excesses of her hair, manicure, make-up, clothes and the constant waft of some perfume that smelled both very expensive and very, very cheap. Jimmy was intrigued and clearly enjoying my discomfort way too much. Mike was delighted. Melissa was just in time for coffee.

And a bourbon. Another bourbon. A second coffee. Melissa showed no signs of wanting to go home and sleep. Despite his obvious desire to stay and watch the floor show, Jimmy knew his job as well as I knew mine. He started making noises about how nice it would be to get to bed after the drive up here. Yana joined in to agree that we must all be tired, she certainly knew she was, long week at work and all that – yawning, stretching, and rubbing her eyes. Careful rubbing that didn't disturb the nearly nude make-up. Mike and Melissa agreed yes, it had been a hard week, and just as I started to relax into the possibility of getting away from the two of them, finally alone with Yana, Melissa opened her wide, toothy mouth:

'Why don't Jimmy and Yana head on back to her place for a good night in? I'm sure you two want one after a whole week apart?' No need to double the entendre. 'We'll show Penny round town.'

Mike thought this was a great idea, a brand-new idea, one that clearly hadn't occurred to him before. 'Fantastic, Mel! I mean Mel knows this area really well, she was at school here.'

All of three years ago then.

'Just because Jimmy and Yana are too tired to handle a night on the coast, you won't disappoint us as well, will you? That's not what I've heard about the staying power of British girls?'

I was stuck.

*

107

Jimmy simply couldn't help himself, he told me to go out and enjoy, Melissa was so right – he and Yana could really use some time alone anyway. He said it with a smile and a kiss to Yana's cheek and a special bastard wink, just for me. It didn't help that Mike paid the bill and ordered an extra car to take the two of them home and the three of us out. It didn't help that Yana, instead of suddenly remembering some vital job she had for me to do back at the house, decided instead that now was exactly the time to play along with Jimmy's in-love farce, and urged me to go out and have a good time. It didn't help that a tiny part of me actually wanted to go out and have a good time with Melissa – just to see if she really was as transparently obvious as she made out to be.

Yana and I grabbed a whispered conversation in the restroom, but it didn't get either of us very far:

'You really want to go home with Jimmy, do you?'

'Don't be stupid. I was looking forward to getting you home with me. That woman has amazing timing.'

'I imagine it's not all she's got that's amazing. Sure you can trust me with her?'

'I don't know, Pen, it's a hard one. I know how much you fancy fake hair, fake tits and fake laugh.'

'Then save me.'

'How? We knew this was possible.'

'That she'd turn up?'

'No, that Mike would want to spend longer with you. At least with her around there's less chance of it developing into something.'

'Sometimes, Yana, you're incredibly naive.'

She sighed and turned to the mirror. 'I don't know what you think I can do about it. We've got all day tomorrow. You and me. Just go out with them for now and get it over with.'

I didn't like the sound of that. 'Get what over with? You want me to fuck him?'

'Of course I don't, I never like it when you fuck anyone else. Not to mention that I have to work with the guy for the next month and that would only complicate matters.'

'Yeah. God forbid that should happen.'

'You know what I mean.'

'So?'

'So be nice to him, help get them back together. That's obviously what he wants. She likes you . . . '

'She doesn't know me. She just likes the idea of me. Those girls in *Buffy* have a lot to answer for.'

'OK. But he's still in love with her. You said so yourself. They'll get tired of the games soon enough. Come on, babe, I need this job to work out. Mike's a big coup for me.' Her hand on my arm, cool, reassuring; her perfume close to me, soft, light. 'We need to keep him sweet. Just play along for now.'

'Like you and Jimmy?'

'What do you mean?'

'He's been all over you the whole bloody night.'

'Playing his part.' Kissing me. 'Like you. Like me.' Kissing me. 'There's no point in getting jealous. This is what we do.' Opening the door, holding out her hand, just another girlfriend leading her slightly more pissed girl-friend from the ladies', whispering secrets like any other. 'And you have to admit . . . Jimmy is being a darling tonight.'

Back to the table. Kissing him. She was right. He was. Bastard.

She was right. This is what we do. What we did. The waiter came over to say the cars had arrived, Yana went home with Jimmy, I went out dancing to some local dive with the too-sweet M and M. He couldn't stop touching my shoulders and her thighs, while she maintained a steady flow of inane chatter and pearly pink fingernail-waving that threatened to take out the eye of any passing local. I became progressively more drunk. And then Melissa produced some coke. Hence the chatter. And the thigh-stroking, I guess. It certainly helped my reticence. Didn't make me fancy her any more though. Too young, too loud, too pink, too blonde. Too good at it.

What followed was a long dark night of drink and dancing and drugs and when I finally got back to Yana's bed at four-fifteen, she was fast asleep and not talking to me anyway. She'd encouraged me to do the business and now she was cutting me out because I had done as I was told. Rigid body firmly clamped to the far side of the ocean-wide bed, cold back to me, nothing bending my way. The next morning there was an hour of recrimination and shouting, before a surf-pounding swim and some sorry, followed by brunch and better. Much better. She didn't like that she'd sent me out and she didn't like that I'd gone. I told her there was sex. Between them. And me as a sort of stand-in to allow him to get it on with her. Which was, after all, what Yana guessed Mike had wanted all along. I didn't care what Melissa really wanted. She was a brainy Barbie who was playing him too damn well. And me too by the looks of it. Yana wasn't fussed about the sex. Hoped that now Mike had revealed he still wanted Melissa, he'd be too embarrassed to push the Mike-loves-Penny possibility any further. We put the wasted night down to experience. And moved on.

Yana and I had a slow, simple Sunday. Jimmy stayed in his room, out of our way. He'd made his point the night before; with Yana cuddling up to his loveliness and me appropriately jealous, now he was sated for the weekend. Jimmy closed the curtains, shut out the lovely sun, the lovelier sea, ordered rental movies and pizza. His position in our lives provided perfect permission to be a slob. We stayed in bed too. The bed that was sofa, floor, sheets, kitchen and bath. A private deck. All with surround-sound sea views. Mike called twice and left messages. He didn't sound as shamefaced as Yana might have hoped. But then again, he didn't sound quite so eager either. Maybe he was tired, maybe Melissa had more staying power than you'd expect from a hundred-pound blow-up doll. Yana didn't quite understand. I didn't quite explain.

On Monday morning Yana was up early and driven off to the set. Jimmy and I stumbled out a little later and went home. I left her love-notes beneath the pillow. Mike left a message on my cellphone. I called her in make-up from the car and again as soon as I got back to our own bedroom. I called her wanting another weekend, another day, more time with her warmth in our sheets. She said Mike wanted me to know he thought I was great. She said Melissa had left that afternoon and, contrary to expectations, Mike was even worse than before. Kept going on about what a great dancer I was. She was pissed off and jealous. I was sorry she was pissed off and happy she was jealous. I persuaded her that Mike would calm down. He had no reason to think I was so brilliant, all I'd done most of the night was watch him and Melissa, and it really hadn't been that great a view. And once I found a way of letting him know that's what I thought, Mike would soon back off. I hoped.

Truth was, I'd fucked them. Both of them. Willingly in the end. Coke is a fine manufacturer of willing. Mike was OK actually. I'd do him again, if I had to. Though it's true he was way more interested in Melissa than me. Whereas I found her beach-baby accent, fake body and entire manner just incredibly irritating. I had to do something to shut her up, and sex can be a very effective gag. Truth was not what Yana needed to hear right then.

I assured her and reassured her and eventually she was placated. A nice role-switch given our restroom conversation of Saturday night, and one I would take time to savour later. I left a message for Mike saying I didn't think it was going to work between us, pointing out that he really was still in love with Melissa, his actions throughout the previous evening had made that very clear to me. And that Yana had mentioned it was a little difficult acting in love with him, while he was talking in lust with me. That she had a problem with the male-lead-and-PA thing. I was sure he'd understand her difficulty with the status discrepancy, maybe we should give it a rest for now, at least until they had another few weeks in the can. And that anyway, finally, actually, threesomes weren't really my thing. I was very convincing. I was telling the truth.

Then I made dinner for Jimmy and me. We ate in silence, with trays on our knees in front of the TV, watching *High Society*. For all his brute-boy pose, Jimmy loves his musicals. I prefer *The Philadelphia Story*. I like my lies at least pretending to be real.

Sixteen

Mike and Melissa are very pleased with themselves. Stretched out on a cool-sheet bed, sunshine flowing through the window, bodies flowing together, his perfume and her perfume perfect top notes together. They are warm fur Cheshire cats with fat creamy moustaches. They got just what they wanted. Melissa wanted Penny, Mike wanted Melissa. And if the two of them weren't exactly Penny's top choice for a good night in, then she was a better actor than either of them. (Not hard to be a better actor than Melissa, but Mike's pretty damn good. All the awards ceremonies say so.) Mike hasn't done this before, the two-girl thing. Mike is very much the ordinary bloke he's often made out to be. Sex god of course, superstar actor, but ordinary bloke with that special magic something. He's only ever been a one-girl man, one at a time anyway. But this opportunity has given him a new link with Melissa. He wants all the links with Melissa he can manufacture. He is prepared to do it all, anything she wants. He is in love with Melissa and, sadly for Mike, Melissa is in love with any other offer. Easily bored, his blonde siren, she needs constant change, weather-vane girl, vain girl, glorious girl. Melissa had heard things about Penny, rumours that she was more exciting than her job title might suggest. Had heard more than that as well, pieces of maybe-stories a 'close friend' whispered to her, things she hasn't mentioned to Mike, doesn't yet want to tell. Melissa prefers to parcel out her secrets, stay in charge of the truth, it's a reason to hang around Mike for a little longer. That and the money, his rub-off fame. She was bored before, now she is awake. Was awake most of the night. Melissa doesn't really enjoy sleeping. This is fun.

Penny is annoyed. She did not want to have sex with Mike and Melissa on Saturday night. She did not want to enjoy having sex with Mike and Melissa on Saturday night. But she did. Both enjoy and enjoy both of them. Penny wants to not like having sex with other people. She wants to be only Yana's one and only. She wants to be wanted in the way she wants Yana. Totally, jealously. She wants Yana to truly mind that Penny fucks around. Whether she is doing it for their greater good or not, Penny is tired of the expedience. She wants to be true love, good girl love. But Penny has a job to do, and she can't help her body helping herself. She is good at the job and her body is good at the job and sometimes, often, her body likes the job, the extras. Her body feels like a traitor. Penny thinks perhaps good old-fashioned purity would be easier to attain, simpler to stick to, cleaner than this coming-and-going uncertainty, the attendant jealousies, the fall from in-love to fury to lust and back again. There is a part of her that gets off on all the secrets and enjoys the jigsawing that the hiding involves, plays the status games with ease and interest. And there is a part of her that wants it all done and out in the open and over. Most days Penny just gets on with it and knows that everyone, in any relationship, not just the famous, not just the hidden, but everyone, makes compromises and bends and suffers silently and complains loudly and just gets on with it. That people do what they can for a happy life, because they would rather be with someone than not, because being with someone means giving up some of yourself, because that is what a relationship is. Most days Penny doesn't really mind. And then, some days, she feels like a whore.

Jimmy is tired and bored. Bored with the pretending. Tired of wanting and not quite getting. He knows this is what it's like, living here, being in this environment, having his career, he knows this is the life he has chosen. A place of always chasing after more and wondering when any of it will ever feel like enough. And he does like his job – both his jobs – and he is good at them and the career is certainly happening and the house is amazing and his prospects are good and all his past worries are taken care of. But but but. There is something missing. He still wants more. More success, more fame, more love. Yana has it all and he lives right next to her, stands constantly beside her tight grasp on the handle of adulation and gets to see it up close. Jimmy likes what he sees. Sure it's scary and constantly being in the public eye can be disturbing and needing to maintain that status is definitely hard work, but it looks good anyway. And Jimmy has a better view than most. Yana has the better job, the more success, the greater fame, the woman in love. She has it all, nicely wrapped up, under wraps. And her manicured hand holding his reminds him of what he hasn't, what he isn't. Always present in his life – even in her absence, still here, he's still hers – Yana rubs it in. Not always knowingly – though sometimes, not always wanting to underscore his losses – though sometimes. And Jimmy doesn't even want a partner of his own, not really, not yet, not again. He was pretty hopeless at his last attempt. But he does want something else, something more, something more exciting. No ideas what, but he wants it. Jimmy is bored. Not very, not especially, the new season starts shooting soon, he has to get back into shape, get his things ready for the new school term, and he knows once he starts work again he'll be too busy to mind much, too busy to notice much. But, right now, he is a little bored. And a little jealous. Settled resident in the envy culture capital, Jimmy cannot but mind. Just sometimes. Just now.

Yana is fine. The shoot is going well. She likes working with Mike. She can tell she is doing good work with him in the moment, and his response shows she is right. As Felix suggested and Yana had hoped, Mike Scarling brings out the better in her. Sharp, quick, easy to learn and adapt, Yana Ivanova offers clean lines, nothing extraneous, pure and simple. Pure looks good on film. And it takes so much work to do nothing. Mike is a good partner. He makes Yana look better than she is, she does the same for him. They reflect back at each other, build on the image and are way more than the sum of their two parts. That's what happens when it all works well. And the rushes prove it is working well. The set is easy, comfortable, a happy place to work, and that's no mean achievement. Yana doesn't even mind about the sex, not really. She knows Penny does what she has to, what they both need her to do, will make whatever is the appropriate choice in the inappropriate moment. Yana trusts Penny to do it right, to give only as much as she needs to – and never more than that. She knows that underneath any of Penny's fuck-forays there is real and proper love for Yana. She is not insecure there, just everywhere else. But for now, even those everywheres are taken care of. The job is happening, the good workplace is happening, the loving boyfriend is happening. Jimmy could not have been better behaved at dinner with Mike and Melissa, she remembered all over again why she liked him in the first place, why he was her first choice. Why she likes him now. That actually, when Jimmy makes Penny jealous, Yana doesn't mind at all. It's all in place and coming along very nicely. And part of her wonders how long this ease can possibly last.

Felix is in the counting house counting out his money. And his past success, his potential triumphs, his marvellous present. He is counting out Yana and Jimmy's money, and counting out his own. He is counting out Yana's secrets and Jimmy's complicity and his own involvement. It is quite an achievement. Felix has lovely clients, he is a lovely manager, Penny is a lovely PA. It is all very lovely. Like the young woman waiting for him at home. Looks sixteen, admits to twenty-two, quite possibly closer to a quarter-century if he asked for the truth. Or twelve. But he doesn't ask, Felix doesn't like to ask. Asking makes it seem as if there is something he doesn't yet know. And Felix likes to be seen to know, biting his nails, talking on the cellphone, keeping it all together.

Marina who comes in every day to clean Yana's house, cook up some little treat, take care of anything Penny leaves behind, is at the post office. Sending money home to her sister in Puerto Rico. She sends letters too, long juicy letters. She could fill these epistles with the stories she picks up as she makes her way round Yana and Jimmy's house, Penny's house, her Monday-to-Friday daily house. The well-thumbed Russian novel – in English – just the one, read and re-read. The clean sheets and the dirty sheets, the pillows that have not been touched by a messy head for several nights in a row. The uncounted beer cans and badly disguised cocaine bags and used condoms – in his room only. Marina does not need to look through cupboards to pick up secrets. Though she does wash and fold

117

the clothes, open the drawers, put away the clean laundry, smooth and so very fine. The hidden paths are there for anyone who has eyes to see – in the open-page diaries on the office desk, the labyrinth of messages on the notice-board, the tangle of knickers in the laundry basket, the hieroglyphs of intimacy lining the rubbish bins she empties every morning. Marina could say so much in her weekly letters. Except that for the past three years she has been having an affair with the local pool man and since the second week of their coupling she has been contemplating leaving not only her husband, but also her three children for this glorious, delicious boy, barely nineteen and so good, so tasty, so utterly fine. And her sister Serafina is the only person in the world she can tell, does tell. Serafina is shocked, every single week, shocked and amazed. But she loves the letters, devours the fear and possibility. And the money is useful too of course. Marina's letters are full of lust and hope and crisp clean dollars. Other people's secrets are just so much household waste to her, Marina has a bed of her own to lie in.

The pool guy can't believe his luck. Marina is beautiful and generous and brings him gifts, food and new clothes, and loves him and wants him and Armando was never charmed before, never much wanted before. Now he has it all. Marina is the best lover he has ever had, she is the only lover he has ever had. He didn't know he was saving him-self, but he was, and it was worth it, and one day she will be all his, only his. For now, good enough is close to best. And the rosemary-scented pool house at Yana Ivanova's place is a fine spot for hidden coupling, closer touch.

In Moscow, Yana's brother Serge is about to take the plane back home after a week in the city on business. He hates the city, it stretches too wide, rises too high. Even though early autumn has finally arrived and swept away the last of the summer fug, revealing dusty buildings in their true pink and yellow and green, soft pastels to surprise the grey-anticipating tourists, he does not like it here. There are too many people, too many buildings, all those beggars in the metro, demanding his money and sympathy for their one-legged, one-armed, aged and infirm plight. He saves his coins for the old lady at the entrance to his apartment building. Sweeping the stairs and footpath in what was supposed to be the pension-easy days of her Party-loyal life. At the airport he sees the glossy sheen of foreign magazine covers. His sister is on two of them. He smiles. He and Pavel had little time for her as a small girl, she was the wailing baby to their world-weary teens. But they are proud of her now. Serge fingers the change in his pocket and figures he is lucky too. Yana will take care of their retirement, he and his brother. Their families, her family. She has promised, he chooses to believe her. His plane is late.

In London, eight hundred thousand, six hundred and eleven people read the latest headlines as they travel to work on the tube. Civil unrest in Nigeria. Government crackdown on unlicensed music venues. Hit-and-run body found on the North Circular. Yana Ivanova and Mike Scarling getting a little too close on their new movie set.

And out there, in a darkening evening, concentric ripples make heart-shaped patterns in kidney-shaped pools. And someone is writing a letter. Picking the font, spacing the page, printing it up, making the form of a Lonely Hearts ad from some neatly placed secrets. Folding it gently, placing it into a clean white envelope, gloved hand free of fingerprints and self-sealing envelope saved from sampling DNA. Someone is playing games. And enjoying it.

Seventeen

I know how to deal with things that aren't going my way.
I have always been good at it. I know how to take a situation and turn it to my advantage. Not always obviously,
not always immediately, some things take time and
thought. But usually, in the end, I get what I want. Often
a compromised gain, but a gain none the less. It's what I
did when I realised my boss before Yana wasn't going to
make it – for either of us – and helped her see the error of
her wanting, waiting ways. It's what I did when I chose to
move to LA rather than stay in London, when I moved to
London from Southend, when I stood up to the third-year
bullies in the second-year playground. It's what I did when
I told my little brother he was adopted – he was five weeks
old at the time, I don't suppose he remembers. Made me
feel better though. I was four years older and not allowed
to hug my mum in case I hurt the caesarean scar he had
ripped into her. Clearly it was all his fault, cuckoo baby,
mother-thief child.

Later I told him there were alligators under the bed as
well. I know he remembers that, he got in trouble for wet-
ting the bed. But I'd already persuaded him that he'd lose
his toes – or worse – if his feet touched the floorboards,
swimming with sharpened teeth. It wasn't very nice, certainly not an action people who saw me lovingly take care
of my little brother would ever suspect possible, but it did

get me a bedroom of my own. It also meant my Aunty Anne (newly divorced, fashionably dressed, incredibly self-possessed, and openly rude to my stay-at-home mum) couldn't come to stay as much. Success for both us kids who outgrew the shared bath/shared bedroom routine long before our parents noticed. Success too for my dad who had never much liked his pushy sister-in-law. Secret success for my mum as well, who had spent thirty-one years thinking her sister Anne was unbearably arrogant and had never had the courage to tell her. They got on much better once visiting rights were limited to alternate Christmases with my maternal grandparents.

It's what I've always done. I take my time, work out what's going on, what's going wrong, and then – minute adjustment, major disruption – make it right. Whatever it takes. I'm better in the background, not taking centre-stage, directing from the wings. There's so much more to be done when you're actually pulling the strings, not being held up by them. Of course I'd been in love before, many times, many people. But none of them were Yana, nothing like as special as Yana. And none of them had ever loved me back like she did. She was the real thing. My real thing. Once I knew Yana meant it, honestly and totally wanted me, I gave myself over to her, to everything it would take to keep her. We had a contract, mostly unspoken, largely unsaid, but absolutely real. I was hers and she mine. Partnership, friendship, need, desire – reciprocated often, selfishly demanded sometimes – classic relationship, the whole package. On top of that, none of my previous lovers ever had Yana's lifestyle either – the house, the pool, the wealth – not everything associated with her career was a problem.

I wasn't happy about what had happened with Mike and Melissa. Much as the sex had been fine – and it was fine, I find almost all sex is fine – I just didn't like the way I'd been coerced into it. I like any coercion to be on my own terms. I was even less happy about Mike's continued insistence to Yana that he and I were a good option – a statement Yana relayed to me regularly in our phone calls. However, given that these were the circumstances in which we found ourselves, I decided to work them to my best advantage. Yana wasn't happy about me seeing Mike again, therefore she would need to come home to me on her next day off.

Yana gives her all to a shoot. Will take the union-regulated day off, she will even enjoy the imposed holiday as we'd had the Sunday earlier, but when she is forced to play, Yana prefers the playing to come to her. Yana wants the set, the location, to become her real life for the duration, any outside distractions can only be visitors into what she has made her new daily truth. When she's happy with how the work is going, and in this case she was delighted, she doesn't want reminders of reality to intrude. The house, the pool, the messages, bills, phone calls, laundry, Marina, the pool guy, emails from her brothers, cards from the nephews and nieces – all the things I deal with anyway – encroach on her psyche when she is working. So she says.

Of course this is artist bullshit. I know that. She knows it too. There are plenty of artists who've created great works and lived in the real world because they had to, because they had no choice and no blissful income to protect them from the rigours of daily life and getting the kids off to school in the morning. But Yana lives in a culture that does give her permission to play the artist-as-monk and it's a great way of taking permission to be selfish. As if the film shoot truly requires one hundred per cent concentration. As if the celluloid lies really are vital and true and essential, and Yana is a heart surgeon, daily saving lives. She's really not. We both know that. But the world that buys into celebrity-deity allows her, and the rest of them, to get away with taking themselves too seriously. So seriously. This seriously. Which in turn allows her to get away with not having to come home and admit to any real life while she's working. The film comes first and the rest of us follow along behind.

And normally I don't mind. She pays my wages after all. And more. Yana's passionate commitment to the job in hand makes it possible for me to have the lifestyle – and the life partner – I have grown accustomed to. The one I always wanted to grow accustomed to. But this time, with the unremitting hunter-gatherer attitude from Mike and Melissa, with the arrival of the third letter, with Jimmy and I rattling around that sprawling house all alone – he not yet back at work and demanding I provide his distraction – I didn't feel like allowing Yana her customary cushioning. I had no intention of telling her about the letters – I threw away the third just as I had the other two – I didn't mean to involve her in how manipulated I'd felt by Mike and Melissa. I wasn't going to let her know that Jimmy and I were veering between getting on extra well and extra bad, childish will you/won't you married games, uncomfortably coupled with teenage fuck me/don't. I just wanted her home for a bit. Yana as part of my life, instead of me having to always make myself part of hers. Yana didn't want me to see Mike or Melissa, not so soon after last weekend's fuck anyway. In that case she would have to come home instead, if she wanted to see me. And she did. And I did. I loved making her come home to me. Tricky situation, a little homework, my advantage.

Though there's always a price in the end.

*

She didn't come home that first weekend. The weather forced a shift to night shoots and everyone's body clock was fucked, the spare Sunday became Monday and was spent toss-turning in a fitful flight-free jet lag. On the Tuesday they went back to day shoots. Wednesday, Thursday and Friday we spoke two, three and four times a day. On Saturday a car pulled into the driveway and she arrived home to me. Swim, bath, bed. Yana and I, easy and cool. Water on my skin, cream on my skin, Yana on my skin. Jimmy out with his friends, away for the weekend, he wouldn't be back until late Sunday afternoon, she and I had almost twenty-four hours for just the two of us. No Jimmy, no Mike, no Melissa, no Felix, no camera. Our own home, phones switched off. My ideal. It should have been hers.

Midnight magic long gone, sheets twisted hot with agitation. Yana sighing, not sleeping, irritable.

'What's wrong?'

'I can't relax. My legs want to get up and run, I'm all fidgety.'

Pulling sheets back over both of us.

'I noticed.'

'You know I find it hard to come home in the middle of work.'

'You're not working. It's seven-fifteen on Sunday morning. You wouldn't be working if you were up the coast either.'

'You know what I mean. I think I'm bored.'

'Thank you.'

'No, it's just that it's all been so full. We've been going for fourteen-hour days, some of them longer.'

'I know.'

Most of the past fortnight I could never get hold of her

at the right moment, when I needed, wanted to speak to her. Had to be by my phone until she called me, had to not mind that it was six in the morning and Yana wanted to chat while in make-up. I gave her chat back. Loving chat, sweet chat, calming chat. Then she went off to play make believe and I lay alone in our too-big bed.

'So let's do something. Go for a drive? See someone else's movie? I'll take you out for lunch.'

Yana winced. 'I don't think I should eat. The nude scenes are coming up soon.'

'They're the week after next. You're not going to eat for ten days?'

'No. I'm going to eat less for ten days.'

I looked at her body beside mine, ran my hands over her abacus ribs. 'You're already eating less. You're already less.'

'I'm working. I always lose weight when I'm working. You don't like how I look?'

Not fair. Have to say yes she's lovely, want to say stay and be taken care of, fed up, smoothed out, brought back to her normal state which is truly lovely. Have to collude with the celluloid powers that decree she becomes properly thin when filming, to appear merely slim on screen. Want to tell her to take more care, be more loving of herself. Let me be more loving of herself. Don't.

'Of course I like how you look. I love you.'

'I love you.'

And we did. And we do. We stayed in, swam a little more, ate almost nothing. I looked at the papers, she studied her scenes for the week to come. I tried not to let the thought of their love scenes invade my head, she tried the same. Didn't work for either of us, but we kept it at bay. Her and Mike fucking but not fucking, loving but not loving. We played together, happy couples together, touched and held and sucked and bit and licked and dismissed Mike and Melissa from the places, the spaces, they still resided in my body. Even when Jimmy came home it was fine. He was in a good mood, content to leave us be, she and I the couple, he our lodger. Her car was coming at four-thirty in the morning. At nine we went to bed. A different agitation now.

'You're excited, aren't you?'

'What?'

'You're excited. You can't wait to get back to work.'

'Don't start, Pen.'

'I'm not starting. I'm stating a truth. Being at home isn't enough for you. I'm not enough for you.'

'I have to go to work. Going to work is how I afford to be at home with you. In this home. This lovely home.'

'And you like it.'

'Shouldn't I? Would you rather I stopped work, did nothing?'

'We could live more honestly if you didn't work.'

'Oh yeah. We could definitely live more honestly. We could move back to England if you like? You could get a job in some office, travel in on the tube every day? I'm sure I could find some theatre work. If I took off enough of my clothes. And no one anywhere would be interested in our relationship or sell the story to the tabloids or think we were worth a second glance. You're right, babe, I've had well over my fifteen minutes, it is that easy to turn it off. There's a whole heap of options open to us.'

'I miss you.'

'I know. But it's not like I had a different job when I met you. My work makes me happy. I know how lucky I am to have work that actually makes me happy. I'm sorry, but I don't want to give that up.'

'Fair enough. That's not what I meant. I just like it

better when I'm away with you. We're fine when I'm on location with you. I like my work too. But you are my work. And I miss doing it properly.'

In the morning we got up together, as late as possible, last seconds vital, she washed, dressed and was ready for the car in ten minutes flat. No need to prettify herself. There was someone waiting at the location whose only task was to make early-morning Yana look like late-evening Yana. And even after the night, after the sex, the sleeping side by side, finding a way back into each other's dreams, Yana was still pleased to leave. The set of her shoulders in the car, the way she relaxed as she drove away from me, the emptiness in the pit of my stomach. It is not that I had not felt any of this before, or that being with her hadn't been good, or even that I didn't know being with her only served to reinforce how lonely I was without her. I had my own routines and my own life and once she'd been away for another few days, I would be perfectly fine. Waiting, not pining. But I did mind her relaxing shoulders. She's a good actor, Yana. She could have made it look a little more like she didn't really want to leave.

I was pissed off with it all. With Felix for bringing up the whole Mike crap in the first place and making me have to stay in town away from her. With Mike for being so damn persistent, with Melissa for simply adding to my woes. And with Jimmy because he was sleeping on, oblivious to all this. I went back into the house and played Courtney Love. It's rubbish music, but it works as a loud alarm. Really very loud. Jimmy's face, his crumpled naked body, his pitiful angry bleats as he stumbled from his bedroom didn't make me feel a whole lot better. Just a little. Sometimes, a little is the best there is.

Eighteen

It was the fourth letter that finally made me take action. But by then the journey had already begun. Same as the others, same wide envelope, same careful folds, same centred Lonely Hearts ad. Different words though. More knowing, more obvious. This letter said it was time to get serious. Really. That's what it said.

Ready To Get Serious?
Famous gent seeks infamous lady to corner in perfect coastal triangle. Previous experience useful, Saturday night experience essential. NS. GSOH irrelevant. No time wasters.

This time there was a box number to reply to. The others had had the same format, same last line. Of course it might have meant anything but I had fucked Mike and Melissa two weekends earlier, I felt weird just looking at the page. I felt different about it. I thought back over the three earlier letters. They had all been addressed to Yana. Each one had ended with the same reference to time wasters, but the earlier ones had just been references to Yana's work, to her beauty, to the sender being the one true one for her. This one seemed to be talking about me as well. Or instead.

I knew there was no point contacting the sender's private

postbox company. To get them to take me seriously I'd have to tell them who I worked for, and why I was concerned, and even then, there was no guarantee that I'd get them to break confidentiality with a client. The most I could hope was that they would check out the box owner themselves. The worst would be they'd check me out. It wouldn't take much to find out where I lived and who with. It seemed the sender knew that. I thought about what else he or she might know. Most of Yana's weirder fan mail came from men; now, though, I wasn't so sure. After watching Melissa in action I wasn't entirely convinced of the saner-than-men attitudes of the average woman either. Not that Melissa was all that average. Except in bed.

I sat in the office and waited as the day became hotter, a late-summer-into-fall morning where it seemed summer might start all over again and the only sane place to be was in the shade by the pool, lavender drying on the bushes, fat clumps of mint planted in the close-mown lawn, scenting the steamy air. I sat at my desk. I didn't know what to do. Kept thinking something would come to me, a way to move forward, what to do next. And nothing did. I wasn't ready to share this letter with Jimmy; despite his most recent sweet-roommate behaviour, he was always so changeable that I wasn't sure he wouldn't just get off on my discomfort. I certainly didn't want to tell Yana; if she thought for a moment that any of our security had been compromised she'd totally lose it. With things going so well on set, and her love scenes with Mike coming up, now was not the time to upset her. There has never been a good time to upset her, just some worse than others. And it was true, this letter did seem to refer to me rather than her, and it wasn't as if we hadn't encouraged rumours about me in the past. Or that rumours about me and my amazing sex life hadn't been useful to us before now. But they'd always been totally straight rumours. Even the slightly too wild ones that pissed Yana off. Good time, shag-happy, straight-girl rumours. I lived with Yana and Jimmy. If there was any suggestion that I'd countenance a threesome, it wouldn't take long for someone to put one and two together and come up with the three of us. I considered telling Felix, after all, he had started the Melissa and Mike fiasco, but that just seemed to take it further from the house. Taking problems to Felix always meant things had gone too far for any of us to fix them. And I didn't want to give him the satisfaction of taking our troubles to Daddy. Now that the writer seemed to be talking to me, I really wanted to be the one to fix this. To make things better, not just for Yana, but for me as well.

I sat at that desk all morning trying to find my way out of the fear maze. I was furious with myself for fucking Melissa and Mike, furious with Felix for putting me in that position in the first place, and not very happy with Yana or Jimmy. I'd done what I'd done for all of them – though primarily Yana, my Yana – and now it looked like backfiring all over me. I thought of Melissa and her wide chattering mouth and could just imagine it spilling my secrets to anyone who happened to stop and listen. And with a body like that, even in this town, there would be plenty who'd stop, still more to listen. I didn't for a moment consider Marina or the pool guy or any one of the dozens of other hirelings we regularly came in contact with, from the staff in Felix's office to the make-up girl Yana had become so friendly with on this shoot. All these people knew some secrets, it was in the nature of their work. None of them knew all the secrets. And all of them had proved trustworthy – either with us or for other employers – in the past. Our whole life was a controlled experiment, Melissa and Mike were the only new variable.

I must have read the letter ten, twenty times. The page, the envelope, the page, the envelope. No clues. No hidden code. No stamp either, though this isn't unusual with our post. While we don't advertise Yana's home address, plenty of celebrity ghouls do, hand-delivered mail comes every day. I couldn't remember if any of the other letters had been stamped. I couldn't remember much, I couldn't even say for definite when the first one arrived, just that it had been a few weeks earlier, and I was fairly certain it had come some time after my first date with Mike. Though I'd happily thrown them out, along with all the other junk mail. I hadn't known to take them seriously. Not then. My brain was totally addled with excess adrenalin and that ghastly pit-sick feeling. The feeling when you get caught kissing your best friend's boyfriend, when the shop detective puts his hand on your shoulder, when you're caught in the mall by the very teacher whose class you're skipping. When you've fucked up and you know you've fucked up and there is absolutely nothing to be done.

Almost nothing to be done. There was the reply number. I wrote back.

Ready to get arrested?
```
Your letters have been kept. Your
postbox is under surveillance. You
are in breach of several State and
Federal laws. Stop wasting our time.
```

I made a copy of my reply, a copy of the envelope, sent it ordinary delivery – if this went much further we might have to get Felix or the police involved. Until then, I didn't want to run the risk of anything being traced back to me and from there to Yana. At the same time, when it all came to light — if it all came to light — I would want everyone involved to know I had been doing my best to make things better.

And then I waited. And tried to behave like I wasn't waiting. This involved working out for a frenzied two hours, and making three kinds of cookies — Marina's kids would eat them, someone else would eat them — for another two. That night, to Jimmy's surprise and apparent pleasure, I accepted his invitation to go out with him and some guys from his show and I drank way too much, even for a night out partying with his mates. I barely slept and at five-thirty I was up, reorganising my entire filing system. I called Yana four times that day and six times the next, each time getting her voice mail and each time hanging up, unable to leave a message in case she heard the fear in my voice. When she called me at night or in the early morning I pretended exhaustion or drunkenness so we didn't have to speak for long. She wasn't happy with me. I wasn't happy with myself, but I'd rather have that than let her know how I really felt. Not yet anyway. Not until I knew there was really something to worry about.

Two days later there was.

Who's we?

I deal in single spies not triple lies. My message was for the organ. Not her monkey. Though I am watching you. Grinding. And you look pretty good.

Which meant the writer really wasn't meaning these letters for me. Or said he wasn't. Hadn't been. Now he was. Assuming he was a he. And that kind of 'watching you' stuff seemed way more bloke than girl to me. Based on the letters I now had in front of me, and the earlier ones I remembered, there were two possibilities. Deranged fan, in which case I would have to at least tell Felix, if not Yana and the authorities. Or it was, as I feared, related to Melissa opening her big drunken, coked-up mouth to someone. In many ways this was the much more appealing possibility. It meant that no matter what the writer said, the letters really were more about me than Yana, so I wouldn't necessarily have to tell her about them and maybe I'd find a way of sorting it by myself without running the risk of exposing our lives still further. Just as soon as I stopped feeling sick to my stomach about what was going on.

I didn't reply to this letter. With no good ideas of my own, I decided to see what would happen next. When my heart-rate finally returned to normal I left the office empty and wasted a day up by the pool. I answered the phone when Yana rang and detailed her joy-of-filming today contrasted with her further fears of working on the love scenes to come. I listened and reassured and was calm and confident and loving. I didn't know what to do and so I decided not to move just yet. I realised there was a chance this had nothing to do with Melissa and she was just an easy straw to clutch at. Maybe we simply had a harmless nutter. There had been plenty of these letters in the past, they are the stray cats that go with the territory, there would no doubt be many more to come. And I was Yana's first line of defence against the mad people. That was part of my job. There was no point in me turning into one of the insane as well. I closed the door on my worries and hoped it might all go away. No chance.

Jimmy came home late and nasty, and the next morning Marina brought in the post. This was hiding at the back of a pile of bills and begging letters:

What? No smart reply?
Can nothing spoil the happy charms
of we three? Are you sure? Are you
safe? Aren't you talking to me?
Aren't you talking to her?

I'd had such a bad night's sleep and, sweat-stained scrap of
pure tension that I'd become, quite a lot of me simply
wanted to shoot the messenger. And I really liked Marina.

I don't have a gun. No one does in our house, Yana
hates guns. I'm not fond of them. Jimmy has been, in his
all-American past, but he keeps that history under wraps.
The right to bear arms perfectly fits a celluloid gloss, it's
way less attractive when coupled with designer dresses and
borrowed diamonds. Though a red carpet hides a whole
lot of spilled blood.

Nineteen

Three days later I told Yana. The timing was all wrong. It was the time off she'd been given to get her head around the sex scenes she and Mike were to film over the next week. It's different every time with this sort of work. Some directors do the scariest scenes – the love scenes, the big fights, the passionate declarations, very early on in the shoot, before the actors really know how the film is shaping up, before they get to know each other too well and the self-consciousness of self-knowledge slips in. Others take it step by step, shooting when and wherever is cheapest, taking the next scene on the schedule as just that, another scene, another day at work. Still others make it all into art. The actors must be ready, totally focused, prepared in every way possible. That was how Cerbonit had decided to work. Give the actors a couple of days off. Take that time to sort out everything to do with camera angles and lighting and sound, the stand-ins earning their wage. Meanwhile the actors make sure they are totally at ease with the lines, with their own bodies, with each other. It's a more pressured way to work, puts a huge amount of emphasis on the select scenes – and yet both Yana and Mike were delighted.

Film-making is a collaborative business, nothing can be achieved without the attention of the whole and even here, where the star system is so entrenched, everyone on set really does know their own worth. It's only out in the real world that people think actors make the movies. Because of that, anything that makes the actors feel more special – more artistic – is extremely welcome to them. And these scenes were, at least in the versions of the shooting script I'd seen, pretty damn heavy. Huge verbal fights blurring into violence from both partners merging with ferocious fucking. Graphic, violent, passionate fucking. A first for both Mike and Yana. Much of the public reaction to the film would no doubt stand or fall on the reception of these scenes when they formed the pivotal point of the movie. Sometimes the prime difference between pornography and art is how well the performers are treated. It shows on screen. Lou Cerbonit, the French wunderkind, was adamant that these performers were to be held with kid gloves – until the moment their choreographed fists turned into improvised lust – then they were to be let go, cock-fight free. He'd always worked this way before and it had paid off handsomely for him. It had got him here.

So there were several days cross-training in the gym and walking through the scenes, fully clothed with a fight director and a movement choreographer. There were long afternoons talking about what exactly they needed to convey. There were meals where people carefully left Yana and Mike alone to get to know each other better, create between them a crucible for what everyone hoped would be an alchemy of one-take wonders. Lou Cerbonit was a young guy, full of wonderful young ideas. Cross-cultural ideas – the producers hoped – from his Algerian parents and his Parisian childhood, ready to infuse this all-American film with some foreign magic. Not the least of Cerbonit's ideas being that as long as both Yana and Mike knew exactly what they were supposed to be doing, feeling and saying in each moment, then he would just let them go, trusting the actors to give him everything he wanted from their turning point. Mike and Yana trusted everyone else to do their jobs, Lou had given them all the support he could come up with, and on the day it would just be time to let them go for it. Whatever they did, everything they did, would be filmed. On a closed set with the bare minimum of crew necessary to capture what he was sure would be the nasty, beautiful magic of their scripted-into-truth desire.

For Mike it was all a bit European film school, not the kind of work he was used to, nor a style he especially valued. And more than a few of the long character conversations were just plain dull for Yana. But the two actors indulged the younger man because it was nice to have him indulging them for a change, giving them the attention he usually gave to his hand-picked crew, heroes of light and angles. Cerbonit knew, even if the viewing public had no idea, that the better his team, the finer the film. Mike was right, the young man did have lots of theories, but one of them was by far the wisest – clearly explain your wants, then shut up and let the experts fulfil them. Cerbonit hadn't always known this. But his first flop was a pretty good lesson. Failure always is, if only the student is prepared to learn. Mike and Yana went along with it all. If Cerbonit was right, and both of them decided to trust that he was, they would be brilliant. And if they were brilliant, there would be more work. Without the job to be brilliant in, an actor is just another person waiting at home for the phone to ring. Everything is an audition.

The choreography was over, the bonding had happened, the perfect-order involuntary mumblings and mutterings that constituted the script had been committed to memory. Yana was taking two days off to buff up her body and shine her confidence before filming began again. And then I arrived at her rented house, unannounced, with ten sheets of paper in

137

my hand. I'd made the three-hour drive in just under one hour fifty. I was still shaking, I'd been crying in the car. I didn't want to go to her. I certainly didn't want to do so yet, I wanted to get her through to the end of this week, after these next few days. But I didn't know what else to do. The last three days had brought five letters, each one more graphic than the last, each one more specific than the last. Until the final straw. By now the letters had given up all pretence of conforming to the Lonely Hearts pattern. It was clear from the very specific content of these latest missives that we no longer had our secrets. The sender knew Yana's schedule. Knew what was coming up this week. Knew about Mike and Melissa. Knew about Jimmy's women. They were short and to the point. And the last one most of all:

> Isn't it time the world knew the truth about the Russian peasant and the English rose? Maybe a closed set is just the place to tell the truth. Time to watch the fucking liars fucking.

The sender knew about me. About Yana and me.

Predictably, and understandably, Yana went crazy. Screamed at me for bringing the letters to her, now, when so much was going on, when so much rested on her concentration and attention. Screamed at me for not telling her sooner, when the first ones came. Screamed at me for telling her at all. She demanded I call Felix and make him fix it, then changed her mind and insisted I get Jimmy up here, bring Mike and Melissa into the room to explain themselves and find out who the fuck was behind this. And each time as I reached for the phone, no more sure than she of what to do next, Yana backed down. Like me, she couldn't be certain who these letters were coming from. Like me, she knew that whoever they were from was now watching us very closely. Like me, she knew the sender had to be very closely connected to one of four people she was screaming about.

Unlike me, after the fuss had died down a little, she came to a certain conclusion very quickly.

'It's Jimmy.'

'What is?'

'These letters. They're from him. He's trying to fuck me up.'

'Yana, that's insane.'

'Well yes, how could he not know I'd guess?'

'No. I mean it's insane to think it's Jimmy. There's no reason for him to do this.'

'He's jealous of me. Of my success.'

She wasn't wrong. I knew he was. Anyone would be.

'Maybe, but why should he suddenly start to act on it now? Nothing's changed. You've always done better than him, it's how Felix can afford to pay him so much from you. And anyway, his work's really taken off in the past year, he's doing really well. Now is not the time to fuck things up. Jimmy may be an idiot sometimes, but he certainly knows when he's on to a good thing.'

'And he likes playing games.'

'Yeah.'

'And he knows these letters would come to you first.'

'Yeah.'

'And he loves taunting you. So he has, what's the phrase? Both motive and opportunity.'

Yana groping for seventies cop show dialogue, me scared it was happening round us for real.

'Maybe, but I hardly think that's proof. There's thousands of people who have the opportunity to push a letter through our postbox. Half a dozen who know enough to make up these letters.'

'But only two who know about you and me. And somehow I don't really think this is Felix's style.'

'Yana, there's no style here.'

'There is. There's little bits of Shakespeare in a couple of these letters.'

'What?'

'See? You wouldn't know because you hate the theatre.'

An old argument between us, no place in this conversation, a diversionary tactic on her part.

'I don't hate theatre, it bores me.'

'Same thing. But Jimmy loves it. You know he does. He'd never be good enough, but he'd love to get to do all those big roles. He knows the plays.'

'Yes but . . . '

'You're not the only one to talk to him, we do have some things in common, Jimmy and me. He told me years ago how much he'd love to be asked to do that stuff.'

'He's told me that too. That doesn't mean anything.'

Yana was not to be deflected. 'And he knows it's never going to happen. He's not that kind of an actor. There are clues in the letters, maybe other ones too I just haven't noticed. Jimmy probably thinks this is a good joke.'

'Yes, or he didn't do it, and you're making up these clues because it's actually less scary to blame Jimmy than to think there's someone else out there who knows this much about us.'

'We'll have to find out then, won't we?'

We drove back down the coast. It was late in the afternoon and she was driving way too fast, hitting corners at speed and taking one hand off the wheel to shade the setting sun from her eyes. She was weird. Nothing like I'd expected. The drive was fast, frenetic, but Yana's speech was cold and detached. So certain she'd come to the right conclusion I almost ended up believing her myself.

Except that I couldn't work out why Jimmy would do this. Sure he'd been playing up recently, but he was always like that. He'd been so excited by the whole Mike and Melissa thing, getting his vicarious thrills from my discomfort, but this was a totally different matter. I knew Jimmy could be a difficult bastard, but this seemed just too nasty for him. And yet Yana was right. There was no one else, outside the four of us, who knew what had been said in these letters. No one else who knew how to get at Yana, and just when would be the worst possible timing. No one else we knew who might enjoy giving us a hard time.

Or if it wasn't Jimmy, if there was someone else who knew all that, then we were really in trouble.

She ran into the house screaming out his name. The house was empty, which was a huge relief to me, I didn't trust her not to hurt him. Then she went into his room and started turning it over. Books were pulled off shelves, drawers opened and slammed shut, his bed lifted off the floor to look underneath, beautiful clothes twisted and turned in his immaculate dressing room. Jimmy might mess up the rest of the house, but never his own clothes.

'Yana, please stop. We don't even know where he is, he might come back any time.'

'Good, then he can explain himself.'

I wrenched a pillow from her grip and tried to smooth out the bed cover. 'No, you'll be explaining. What the hell are you doing? You don't have any proof it's him and even if it is, you think he's going to leave rough copies of the letters under his pillow where Marina or me or anyone else might find them?'

'How often do you look under his pillow? Maybe it's both of you. Maybe you're doing this together?'

'Oh fuck off, Yana. This is shit. Of course it is. I'm scared too. But throwing accusations around isn't going to help.'

She sat down on the bed then, deep breaths, head in her shaking hands. 'I'm sorry. I'm so scared.'

'Yeah, I know you are. But Jimmy doesn't. And I don't think he's likely to be very forgiving when he gets home and sees this mess. Come on, let's put it back together and we'll get something to eat – when was the last time you ate?'

She shrugged, whispered, 'I don't know. Yesterday some time.'

'No wonder you're being so manic. You're probably starving. We'll tidy up together and have dinner – something light, don't panic, I'm not going to fatten you up – and then we'll find a way to talk to Jimmy about this when he gets in. If you're right, maybe he'll admit it. Say it was a stupid joke or something. If you are right, he might just have been trying to have a go at me, might not even have thought I'd show you the letters. I wouldn't have if I'd known it would be this bad . . . '

'And if I'm wrong? If it isn't him?'

'I have no bloody idea. In a way I hope you are right. At least Jimmy's the devil we know.'

And he was.

It was in his diary. I remade the bed and tidied the dressing room, directing Yana to sort out the bookshelves. I didn't trust her not to go wild again and decide his beautiful suits would look better with one arm missing from each jacket. Yana picked up the books she'd knocked to the floor and tried to put them back on the shelves in the right order. Jimmy's books and CDs and DVDs were all in perfect alphabetical order. Except the journal. Which didn't have a title. Didn't have the words KEEP OUT emblazoned across the front either. So Yana didn't.

I'd told her I thought the first letter came not long after I went out to dinner with Mike and was accosted by Melissa for the first time. I came back into the bedroom with a pile of T-shirts to fold and saw Yana swaying beside the bookcase, open journal in her hand.

'When did you go out for dinner with Mike?'

'I don't know, five weeks ago? Six?'

'Go and find out. Check your appointments book.'

'Why?'

'Do it.'

I went to the other end of the house and looked it up. When I came back she was still just standing there. 'July twenty-third. Why? What is it?'

'And the first letter came after that?'

'A day or so. I think.'

She held out the book. 'Have a look at June twentieth.'

'I really don't want to look in Jimmy's journal, Yana. I don't think you should either.'

'Look at it.'

It was an ordinary journal like the dozen or so others you'd see in any coffee shop round here, would-be writers sitting in cafés thinking somehow the ambience will write their books for them. I knew Jimmy kept a journal, saw him writing in it by the pool sometimes. Most of the actors we knew did. There'd been a craze a few years back for writing every day and some of them had stuck to it. Creative inspiration they said, though I wasn't sure it wasn't just a cheaper – and more private – version of therapy. Having tried it myself once, I was sure that what started out as journalling more often than not ended up as simply moaning. It's why I stopped, I didn't need to rehearse my life's grievances on paper. Besides, my only real complaint was then, and was still, that I couldn't have Yana all to myself. Writing it out was never going to make any difference. In Jimmy's case the problems seemed to be of a more primal nature:

> *God I'm fucking bored with them. All the kissing and cunting around. It's so fucking selfish when I have to stay single to keep her secrets hidden. I've had enough. Really. I'm not sure how much longer I can do this. I've told Felix already. He thinks it's just a phase and I'll be better once I start work again, but I don't know. All I have to keep me occupied are my little schemes. Kissing Y when we're out so I can get at P. Flirting with P when Y's around. (And checking out how quick she is to flirt back!) But it's such juvenile, high-school stuff. I'm bored with them and bored with myself. Bored bored fucking bored.*

A few lines later he wasn't bored any more:

> *Had a thought. A good one.*

'Yana, you get upset with Jimmy too. I mean, I had no idea he was so unhappy, but we both slag him off sometimes. I have you to complain to, who's he got? Him writing – privately writing – that he's pissed off with us is no evidence.'

She nodded at the book. 'Look at it.'

A week later:

Hey, this is good. I'm good. I think I'm going to like this.

And further on:

Brilliant! Penny's completely freaked. I wonder how she's going to tell Yana? Hope I'm around for the party! Ha fucking ha!

It was nasty. And hurtful and vindictive and it made me feel sick. I left the T-shirts on the bed and we closed the bedroom door behind us. We waited up for Jimmy. She was shaking. I was cold.

Twenty

For the first hour I tried to persuade her we should just go back up the coast. She needed the sleep, had to be on set in the morning – a morning which wasn't so far away now – Jimmy was only going to deny her accusation and anyway, a few vague, pissed-off references in his diary to something not especially specific were hardly proof he was the letter-writer. (Though they didn't exactly render him entirely blameless either.) But Yana wasn't listening and, after a bottle of wine, I was no longer arguing. Just waiting for him to come in and get it over with. And worried about the ending. Yana was so in the moment it didn't occur to her that accusing Jimmy might have consequences. All she could see to do was to confront him. I couldn't help thinking it wasn't going to be as easy as that.

Jimmy wasn't sober when he came home, but by then neither were we. Yana had his journal out on the kitchen bench between us. He walked in and saw it immediately.

'What the fuck?'

Succinct and to the point.

As was her reply, 'Yeah, what the fuck?'

It was hardly *Who's Afraid of Virginia Woolf?*, but then they'd only just started. There was plenty more where that came from.

About two hours' worth. Recrimination and insinuation, denial and fury. He said, she said, and every now and then, just occasionally, I said as well. Though mostly it was them. I poured drinks and moved glasses when they looked like being picked up and hurled, I tried to keep out of the way and to ensure that the fight stayed between the two of them without it being too much about me as well. Cowardly I know, but they both enjoy the anger way more than I do. And over my head the fight rang out:

'You've been trying to fuck me up ever since I got this film.'

'I don't care about your damn job.'

'Well you should. It's my damn job that keeps you fed.'

'I work for my money.'

'You work for my money.'

'We all do. We're all just your little toys to push around as you see fit.'

'Don't be so melodramatic.'

'And Penny's the worst of them, so tied up in you, so dependent on you, she can't even see what you're really like.'

'Leave her out of it.'

Yeah, leave me out of it. For a while, from the safety of my bunker next to the big red fridge, I almost enjoyed it. They were both saying things I knew they'd longed to say for ages. While we three were certainly in a relationship of sorts, neither Yana nor Jimmy had ever had the relief of a good old-fashioned lovers' fight to clear the air. There was almost five years of stale air to clear. I sat and watched and marvelled at their command of language, the ease with which they jumped from one allegation to another, the leaps of illogic that took them from the damning journal to his new season to working with Mike Scarling via a car

147

she'd bought me three years earlier and back to how many rooms in the house Jimmy felt he couldn't go into without knocking first. I wondered if this was what the directors and the writers felt like. Sitting in the middle of a whirlwind and watching it all go on around them, knowing you've made it happen, you've created this. Because I did feel responsible, I'd told her about the letters, and judging from the reaction I should have kept my fears to myself. I was some kind of puppet master but with no real power, I had no strings to rein them in. The two of them were pinball-rioting and it only took the slightest contribution from me to send them screaming in yet another direction.

'But Jimmy, come on, your journal does read like you're thinking about blackmailing Yana.'

I'd said it, but he ignored me and rounded on her.

'Why the hell would I want to blackmail you?'

'For the fun of it? Because you think it's funny to see me upset? Because you're such a bastard?'

'Yana, this is insane. Anyone could have written those letters.'

'So you do admit it?'

'What?'

'Half an hour ago you said you didn't know what I meant by the letters.'

'I didn't!'

'And now you do?'

'You just spent the past ten minutes ranting at me about them. Of course I know about them, now. But I didn't write them. Anyone could have. For all you know, Penny might have sent them.'

I didn't like that.

'Oh fuck off Jimmy.'

Yana was quiet, then, 'She wouldn't. She loves me.'

I did like that. That Yana knew, even in her fury and

148

fear, that I loved her. Love her. She could be certain of me. But not him any more.

'I can't trust you, Jimmy. I don't trust you.'

'Thanks. I really value your trust – the kind of woman who reads another person's journal.'

'This isn't a journal, it's a diatribe.'

'And it's private.'

'Nothing's private here.'

'Fucking right.'

'Anyway, it's about me. Your journal is about me!'

'You think everything's about you, Yana.'

He wasn't wrong. But he was getting good at this.

'So if I'm such a total bastard why keep me around? Or do you need me too much?'

'I don't need you.'

'Sure you do.'

'No.'

'Really?'

'Really.'

She couldn't hear it. She should have shut up. Bad matador not knowing when to stop the goading. There was an edge to Jimmy's tone, a waiting possibility, something forming as he spoke, a realisation. I don't think he expected to say the words that came next, or even considered that he might. But as he said them his eyes were wide, there was the beginning of a smile on his lips and he knew he meant it. I knew he meant it.

'OK then. I quit. I'm leaving you. Leaving the pair of you to your happy little love nest.'

Yana wasn't taking him seriously, was about to open her mouth to shout again, I stepped in between them. 'Come on Jimmy, we're all knackered. And not sober. You don't want to do this.'

I might have been able to talk him back then, he

hesitated, shook his head, looked ready to think, but Yana jumped in again. 'Yeah Jimmy. Don't be stupid.'

The realisation was all over his face and his shoulders dropped four inches in relinquished tension. 'I've never been more clever.'

He was moving away from us and she, too caught up in her own argument, couldn't see it.

'I should have left this lie behind ages ago.'

'Oh right, now that you've got what you wanted from me.'

He nodded. 'Yeah.'

'Now that you've used my success to kick start your career.'

He smiled. 'If you like.'

'Now that you've got where you want.'

She just didn't know when to stop.

He turned on her, speaking slowly and softly. 'Oh no. This is not where I want to be. This is nothing like what I hoped I'd get from my life. Sleeping alone unless I'm paying for it? Pretending to be your lover? Living out this great fucking lie that we're this happy couple while you get her and I get nothing? No, Yana, this is definitely not where I want to be.'

Jimmy knew when to stop.

Round and round and back and forward and it was getting later, Yana still less sober. And it was late. Really late. She was called for seven the next morning and already it was about two. At the best we'd get back up the coast in under two hours, but even then, she wasn't going to get any sleep now. I left the room and used my cellphone to call the PA, leaving an appropriately breathless message:

'Hi Lucy, it's Penny, look I've just made it to Yana's place, she called me this evening saying she didn't feel good and asked me to bring some things up for her, and I've just arrived and she's really not very well. Some sort of flu bug it looks like. I've got her off to sleep now – don't worry, no big drugs, just a homoeopathic remedy I brought up from her naturopath because we know it always works for her. But I think she'll be a little late starting in the morning. Two hours max. I'd just like her to have a slightly longer sleep. Please call me on my cellphone if there's any problem with that, I've turned off the phone here so it doesn't disturb her.'

I'd been lying for Yana for years. I knew Lucy would believe me. All the same, two hours was the most I could get her. Delaying shooting by any more than that might mean risking cancelling the morning, then insurance would have to be dealt with and they'd need the unit doctor's version of Yana's 'illness'. But Yana hadn't been late once and while a reputation for perfect punctuality endeared her to everyone on set, it also meant I needed to cover when she didn't make it. And when she turned up looking like shit. I went back to the kitchen determined to sort all this out and get her into the car and away from the wine bottle.

I'd bought her two hours but at the cost of leaving them alone together. Heavy price.

'Go on then, tell her.'

'Tell me what?'

Jimmy shook his head, Yana pointed at the journal. 'Go on.'

'You had no right to read any of that.'

'Yeah Jimmy, you are so hot on what's right and what's not.'

'Tell me what?'

Jimmy shook his head. 'It's not such a big fucking deal.

151

I think it's funny. You girls have got it all completely wrong. It was all just a joke. Really.'

The journal references to my being upset and how hard it would be for me to tell Yana weren't about the letters at all. At least Jimmy said they weren't, promised they weren't. And he had a good explanation. They were something else entirely. To do with me and Yana yes, but not the letters. Jimmy had been writing his nasty ranting raves about how he'd set me up with Mike and Melissa, how he'd heard from Felix that Mike fancied me and he'd also known Melissa for a while. Jimmy knew they had broken up and he knew Mike wanted to get back with her. He thought it might be funny to get me into a real threesome, thought it might add some spice to our otherwise dull lives, his otherwise dull life. Jimmy reckoned seeing me try to deal with having both Mike and Melissa after me would be a good laugh. It was just a joke. A gag. A personal little entertainment to fill his otherwise boring and lonely days. Something to pass the time, no real harm done. And it wasn't as if I didn't sleep around anyway, I could hardly claim to be the pure virgin of our relationship. Jimmy had had a brief thing with Melissa himself a couple of years earlier, a fling he hadn't told us about as it broke the bounds of our agreement. He thought my fucking both Mike and Melissa would pretty much round it all off quite nicely:

'You know, once Yana films her sex scenes with Mike there'll be just two fucks of separation between each of us. I think that's quite cool.'

I thought it was bad. Really very bad.

152

Twenty-one

Jimmy's heart was racing, his throat constricted and tight. Breathing quick quick slow, quick quick slow. He couldn't believe he'd done it, said it. Told the truth. Not the truth about Melissa, though that would have been enough to give him some of this reaction. But the whole truth, the can't-do-it-any-more truth. The truth he hadn't even known he wanted to tell. The leaving us he'd only dreamed about, made flesh in his retaliating mouth.

Yana on the other hand was trying to spin back time, half an hour would be good, twenty minutes might do it. Even ten if she took it all slowly enough, breathed through the forced farce, held her mouth and her words and made each one count for only its own value – the value of the single word, not all the time and hate and anger and lies it carried inside.

That awful moment when everything pent up and hidden comes out and reveals itself to be just as ghastly as expected, just as worth keeping down. Kitchen walls dripping with the bile of transgression.

Neither of them said anything. Neither of them confirmed this was their truth. But I could tell. They had both gone further than either expected and were now standing in a totally new place. That accidental leap from middle-of-relationship via a huge fight to suddenly all-over. It happens every day, every hour. Another couple bite the dust by letting the argument go on just that five minutes too long, those three hundred seconds that allow the withheld acid to spill out and corrode the shaky ground on which they stand. And then the free fall. It takes five minutes. Or less, much of the time. A true revelation might take weeks, months, even years in the building, but in the time it takes an Olympic athlete to run a mile and start their press conference, the truth is told and the competition over.

Everything about Jimmy expressed his shock, and his relief. Everything about Yana showed her fear. Pure fear. Even she, used as she was to other people making things better for her, could tell this was not just any other problem. For the first minute or so of silence I thought maybe, now Jimmy had said it, admitted his get-out desire and run-away clause, that perhaps he would still stay. He'd said all the words and made himself perfectly clear and maybe we could start again on a new, even keel. But very quickly I understood that wouldn't be the case. Jimmy had certainly shocked himself with what he'd said, had made a leap into an unknown he might have been contemplating for some time, though hadn't by any means meant to make yet – but now that it was done, he was ready to go for it. Everything about him, his relaxed shoulders, half-smile at the side of his mouth, the way he kept shaking his head in a combination of disbelief and startled joy, pointed out how certain he now was that he'd made the right leap.

Jimmy was the first-time-relationship lover who, in a moment of accidental anger, reveals he's been having an affair for ages and what's more he never liked his current partner and his new one loves him far more and by the way, he's leaving tomorrow. Whoo-fucking-hoo. Yana on the other hand was the abandoned girlfriend who'd only meant to complain that her mate had turned up ten minutes late for their date and, in voicing that small protest, unleashed the leave-me monster instead.

I was dealing with business.

I got Yana into the car and wrapped a blanket around her shivering shoulders. She wasn't speaking or crying. Not yet. I went back into the kitchen where Jimmy had sloped from table to armchair and told him to call Felix and tell him his plans as just revealed to us. Jimmy didn't have any plans, it wouldn't do him any harm to see that himself, to make the call now, middle of the night or not. I told him not to dare mention this to anyone else. It would all be sorted out, there was no doubt Jimmy could make an easy and careful exit. No one was in a state to arrange that just yet, we'd talk to Felix and get everything done in the right way. Slowly. Carefully. Jimmy was stunned and relieved, but he wasn't stupid. He nodded his agreement and reached for the telephone. At the door I told him what a cunt he was for the Melissa set-up.

He cricked his head to one side, shrugged his shoulders and nodded. 'Yeah. Sorry babe. Still, all's well, eh?'

Felix picked up on his end and I left the house.

I hated Jimmy then.

Not that I was particularly in love with Yana. After about twenty minutes she thawed out and started whining. Just noise, no words. Felix called me and I explained that all I was interested in doing right now was getting Yana back to her location and into bed. He agreed with me and promised to keep Jimmy quiet for now. We'd arrange a summit meeting once Yana was speaking in whole sentences again. Not tonight anyway, night rapidly opening up to day, me juggling the phone, steering wheel and her moaning. As we hit the coast road Yana started ranting about Jimmy's wickedness. Halfway there she decided it was all my fault and I should have stopped him. I should have stopped her. I should have known that it would all go too far tonight. I let her go on for about another fifteen minutes and then I pulled over hard.

'What? I have to get back. It's late. I've got to sleep!'

'No, Yana. You've got to shut up. You've got to be quiet and let me think about what's been going on. You've got to save your precious perfect voice and stop bloody crying so you don't look like shit in four hours' time. You've got to accept that you fucked up.' She started to protest but I wouldn't let her. 'Yes, Jimmy's behaved like a prize arsehole. And in the long run I have no doubt we'll be better off without him. Certainly without his nasty game-playing with the likes of Mike and Melissa, possibly without his letter-sending, assuming it was him. And maybe I shouldn't have shown you those letters tonight, just now, but I didn't know what else to do. I don't always know everything, not even me, OK? Sometimes you need to take responsibility too. Those letters might have been from anyone. I was scared, I am scared. But right now what's more important is getting you back in one piece. Staying on the road and letting me concentrate on driving. OK?'

She nodded agreement, understanding, and pulled the blanket tighter around her shoulders. I thought she might sleep then, but she didn't, just stared straight ahead into the not-quite-dark.

'Fuck it. I need him.'

Bette Davis and Celeste Holme stuck in the car in *All About Eve*. Neither of us smoking.

Felix sent his doctor to check on Yana, she bought Yana the morning off. Yana turned up on set that afternoon, immediately after lunch, exactly as promised, just another hard-to-start Monday worker. She was a little sleepy and needed a touch more light-refracting magic from her make-up artist, but was otherwise perfectly capable and controlled. She walked through three technicalities-only scenes, hit her marks perfectly each time, gave her undivided attention to all four of the one-line extras – the first of whom took six takes to get her one line out, the second tried a few words of Russian on Yana in the break and was promptly replaced, the other two hid their nerves and did the job – Yana was a consummate professional. There were a series of not-proper-acting, but still vital plot-point scenes to get through and then Yana could go. Cerbonit was holding her and Mike back from any real work for now, until they'd got through the big sex-and-violence scenes to come. She spent an hour with her dialect coach, an hour with Mike in his trailer talking through a few things they'd like to try when the love scenes shoot started, and then she came back to me. Rented house, rented bed, own me.

We lay together and I held her and stroked away the tension, the perfectionist cast she'd worn to get her through the afternoon. I kissed her frightened skin, made impossible promises that everything would be all right. Hold turned to touch became desire and we fucked into sleep.

Tuesday was another just-get-through-it twelve hours on set, and Yana did so brilliantly. She was delightfully charming to the lecherous member of ageing Hollywood royalty brought in for a cameo as her character's uncle. They shot three ten-line scenes before she whispered she'd break his fingers – individually – if he accidentally brushed her tits just one more time, and then a fourth slightly longer scene where he kept his distance and, in trying to regain his dignity, acting rather than salivating, he proved why he'd been a star in the first place, ability shining through the web of wrinkles masking his famous face.

There was an afternoon off scheduled on Wednesday and Felix drove up with Jimmy for a summit meeting. We were all nervous.

But Felix was good at this kind of thing. Twenty-five per cent good. They arrived, we talked, Yana cried, Jimmy sighed. Admitted the lesser charge, the greater denied. Too late. It was done. Jimmy was leaving. He couldn't be persuaded to stay, though he would hang on as consort-in-chief until Yana had finished filming, there would be no more interruptions to her need for concentration over the next two weeks on location, or the subsequent month in town. I would spend most of my time with Yana. I could pick up emails from the computer in her rented place and post would be forwarded up here. I could do my job anywhere Yana was. Yana was my job. Dealt with. Jimmy would receive a substantial payment when he moved out. The move would be timed to coincide with his mid-season filming break, giving his show's publicist plenty of time to use the story to their best advantage. Yana would keep the family home. Everyone would keep their mouths shut. Pressures of work, pressures of fame, pressures of telling the same break-up story that everyone else told. Sorted. Felix would have a word with Mike Scarling and make sure he was onside. He would be, the film – and his co-star's happiness – meant way too much to him. Mike didn't have his associate producer credit for nothing, and he was, after all, implicated in the build-up. Mike had things to keep quiet too. Done and dusted. We'd had a good run the three of us, four and three-quarter years, better than most. Jimmy had earned his benefits and Yana hers. Neither of them had anything to complain about, they'd both gained by association, would continue to do so as long as they behaved themselves.

Felix intended to keep both his clients happy and ensure everyone was well taken care of. This was not a problem, this was an opportunity. It would work for all of us because we needed it to.

And then we went out to dinner.

Very civilised, very adult, very nice. Ocean view. Private room. Five courses. Each one smaller than the last, so even Yana was willing to eat. Felix was buying. With Yana and Jimmy's money of course, but the very freedom of not having to lay down a credit card at the end of the meal sometimes makes all the difference. We ate and drank. We gossiped. Pleasantly. Yana didn't trust Jimmy and I didn't trust Jimmy and he certainly didn't trust either of us, but we all trusted Felix and believed him when he said it was going to be OK. And eventually it was. Jimmy's hunched shoulders dropped again and he remembered he was relieved to have made this decision. Yana had one glass of wine – and then another – and figured that if she didn't trust Jimmy not to have written the letters, no matter what he denied, then there was no point in trusting him to live with her. She'd be better off without him. Partnership had done this well for her career, now it was time to see how nicely she could do as a single girl. And I looked at Yana and realised she was mine. All mine. Only mine. I would-n't have to share her. Not in truth and not in lies. It was a revelation. I watched them flirting in character whenever the waiter came near and didn't mind in the least. Not that I expected her to start being honest about me – not at all – merely that she could soon stop lying about him. And Jimmy would move out, Yana and I would be only together. I hadn't known it would feel this good, hadn't known how hard the lying had been – until there was an end in sight. Each one of us now knew the end in sight and our meal was all the easier for it, we were all the easier for it. Felix paid and we left, Yana and I back to her rented house, Jimmy and Felix down to LA. I watched her kiss him goodbye – specially loving version for the locals gaping from the front window of the restaurant – and I didn't care. My Yana. Only my Yana.

In bed that night our fucking was freer than it had been in ages, simpler and deeper. Eyes wide open, hands held tight. She fell asleep in my arms and I lay on my back, astonished at the speed of events and how well everything had worked out and how lucky we all were. How lucky I was to have Yana Ivanova asleep on my breast.

In the morning Yana got up before her wake-up call and brought me coffee in bed. She kissed me and left me dozing. There were no letters that day. I answered some emails for her and a few for me, booked a couple of appointments for when filming was over, tidied the house, went for a slow walk on the beach. She came home in the late afternoon, long day made shorter by Yana Ivanova's perfect attention to filming detail, made love to me almost before she'd closed the door behind her. We went through her scenes for the next day, clarified some lines of dialogue and went to bed for an early night. Happy couple, happily coupling. Perfect company as two. The next morning Yana said she had something she needed me to do. I said of course, whatever you want, that's what I do.

I take care of her. I do things for her. I have made her my career, willingly and hungrily. I am eager to do the job, I love to go to work. I am Yana Ivanova's personal assistant. I assist. Personally. With whatever she wants.

Yana wanted me to kill Jimmy.

Twenty-two

I laughed. She wasn't joking. She told me a story.

'When I was a little girl there was a movie star. Russian movie star. Her name was Yana. She was in Red Riding Hood. And my brothers used to tease me about her, we had the same name. They thought she was exotic, Polish, Ukrainian. Not really Russian. She was beautiful and different and in their mouths her name sounded special. I wasn't special, I was just the little sister. The annoying extra, accident baby. I never saw the film, but I heard all about it. She was supposed to be very sexy. I was too young to understand that really, but I knew it mattered. They liked her, my brothers, my father too. In a way that they didn't like me. I don't mean I wanted them to like me sexually, but I was just the baby sister, mostly I was in the way. Sometimes they wanted to play with me, take me out with them, show me off – I was very good at showing off, being shown off – but mostly I was just a pain. The boys had to baby-sit me, put up with me, had to let me tag along with them. I wanted them to actually want to be with me. Like they do now. Except that it's too late now. Anyway, I must have been about thirteen. Pavel had finished his second year of graduate school and he'd come home for a break, brought a friend with him. And this friend, he was a few years younger than Pavel, he liked me, treated me differently. I was special. It was amazing, it was

161

a revelation. I'd always been special to my mother, of course, but I was bored with that. Masha was boring, just another mother. This guy, Dimi, was different. And I flirted with him, I didn't know that was what I was doing, not really, I was only thirteen and he was ten or eleven years older than me, but I knew it worked. Dimitri insisted Pavel take me out with them too. And when he spoke my name it sounded good. He was beautiful.'

I wanted to interrupt, ask what the hell this had to do with Jimmy, why now, why she was telling me this now. But I didn't. I waited and listened. Yana didn't tell many stories from her childhood, almost never spoke about it. I figured this must be important. I was waiting for the punch line.

'Well, you can guess the rest. He wasn't beautiful, not really. Not now I know what adults know. But at thirteen? You know that you like someone and they like you back. You know you are a girl who wants to be a woman and you have no idea how to negotiate the space between the two. Dimi went back to school with my brother and they finished their dissertations and then they came to visit again for the last time, the last break before they had to start work properly. And he brought me a cape. A red cape. Like Red Riding Hood. All the way from Moscow. A red cape. Dimitri said it was a cape like the women wore in Moscow. I didn't know any better. I believed him. And I was fourteen. My mother was married at seventeen, I didn't think I was that young. Sure he was a man and I was a girl, but he was my brother's friend, I was flattered. I thought it made perfect sense, I was that gorgeous, my brothers couldn't see it but he could.

'Dimitri and I fucked. And it was all right, not special. Not wonderful, not like in my books. And after that he didn't speak to me again. I hadn't understood. Hadn't

162

understood that the cape and the words and the specialness were all about priming me, setting me up for him. I'd believed him. And the truth is, I was part of it too, I wanted it too. I was certainly flirting with him, I was fourteen going on nineteen. We didn't talk about those things then, not like we do now, we just did them. Now it's all about pretending virginity until fifteen and then at sixteen girls are supposed to turn into world-weary whores overnight. Little kids get sent to therapy if they kiss in the junior school playground, and then they get sent to another therapist if they don't kiss in high school. We just did it then, when we were ready. I was ready. Actually, I expect they just do it now too, only they still don't tell their parents. And that was the problem. Pavel told my parents. He was furious with his friend. Thought Dimi had ruined me or something. They had a big fight and hurt each other and then Pavel told the story. My story. Because he couldn't help himself. There was an unspoken truth and he had to let it out. The truths always get let out in the end. My parents were furious. My mother raced over to my father's flat. And they took my cape away from me too.'

Yana was certain Jimmy would tell the truth eventually. She didn't believe he could keep it quiet. Didn't believe he wouldn't fall in love with some woman and want to tell her the truth. Or get in a fight, a drunken babble, a cocaine binge and just blurt it out. Or simply wake up one day and realise he had nothing to lose but maybe there was something new to gain.

'Jimmy won't let it go, Pen. I know he won't.'

'Felix trusts him.'

'Felix has to trust him. Felix thinks we have to trust him. Jimmy's made up his mind to leave, so Felix thinks there's nothing else to do. Felix is a pragmatist, he believes we have to make the best of a bad situation. But you and I know Jimmy better than that.'

'Yes.'

'We know what he's like. Don't we, Pen? Don't you know Jimmy better than that? After all this time?'

'Well . . . I . . . oh fuck, yeah . . . I do.'

'Felix is prepared to let Jimmy go because he can't see any other alternative.'

'And you can?'

She shrugged, 'Just the one.'

She had it all worked out. Apparently Jimmy was setting himself up nicely.

Marina had called a couple of times since the big fight to ask what she should do. Jimmy was passed out by the pool, or there was a young lady in the sitting room, should she leave the girl to sleep or move her out? There were things lying about the room. Bottles, glasses, mess. Jimmy was forgetting to put on the alarm at night; for three days in a row it hadn't been on when she came in at nine-thirty. Yana told her just to carry on as usual. Do what you always do, ignore Jimmy's excess. Clean around the mess. If the vacuum cleaner woke the young woman then fine, if not then lift her legs and dust underneath. Felix called too, to say that he'd tried speaking to Jimmy again, but Jimmy wasn't really talking. He begged Yana to apologise, to go back home and make it better, try to patch things up. But it was way too late. And I don't think even Felix believed it would work, for either of them, he just felt it was his duty to give it one last go. Yana had had enough. While she didn't know Jimmy was definitely to blame for the letters, she still thought he was more likely to have been responsible than anyone else. And even if he hadn't sent them, she was furious with him over the whole Mike and

Melissa thing. I wasn't too happy about it either, but Yana had taken it as a personal attack on her. My fucking other men occasionally was part of the deal, Jimmy setting up another woman to hunt me was one step too far. Jimmy was bored with our situation, but whatever games of distraction he'd been playing were way out of hand. Yana was fed up with the lies and the deceit and placating Jimmy. He'd shown how volatile he really was – and now he'd finally realised, admitted, how long he was prepared to stick around. We simply couldn't trust him any more.

Even as I listened to her explain herself, explain him away, I knew I would say yes. Yana was right. Jimmy might be fine for the first year or so. But the main problem was that while he would be as successful as Felix had persuaded him he might be, he was never going to be as successful as Jimmy had persuaded himself he might be. Jimmy McNeish was good and he was ambitious, but there was something missing, some extra spark. I don't mean talent, nothing as crass as that. I mean the kind of über-ambition that only the truly successful ever have. And mostly they try to hide it, keep it from public view, because it really doesn't look very nice. Even the young ones know it can come across as too much, too strong. But I never met a truly successful person that didn't have it; pure ambition allied to utter self-belief. Yana had it in spades. And while all that harnessed power can be daunting when you first catch sight of it, to many people it is also very attractive. You know you've been allowed in, and being shown a secret is always incredibly charming. But Jimmy didn't have that extra drive. He really was a good actor and he was ambitious and he would continue to be successful, but never at the level he wanted. So in two years, or five years, or even ten years' time, Jimmy would know he had reached his peak, and while to many people that peak would be a great achievement, it wouldn't be enough for him. Jimmy McNeish was never going to get where he wanted to be and eventually he would have to stop trying. In however many years it took, he would stop and he would see that Yana had gone on to accomplish exactly what she'd always wanted to and the jealousy – the tiny lacerations of envy we witnessed daily – would overtake him. He might have promised his loyalty to Felix and Yana, he probably meant those promises, but one day, when he finally accepted he'd come to the end of his road, Jimmy would want to bring her down too.

Yana sat in front of me, foretelling her own misfortune. Our misfortune. I knew she was right and I knew I would do what she'd asked. Because there was nothing else to do. And maybe because part of me wanted to. I have never believed in persuasion, everything is choice. It's just that often we don't want to accept responsibility for the choices we make, we want to blame the persuader, the propaganda. I let Yana persuade me, reason with me, make me see her version of sense. I would do it, just as she asked, but between the two of us, Yana could take the blame.

In the end it all came down to trust. She believed Jimmy had written the letters, but even if I didn't agree with her, even if she was being totally paranoid, he was still out of control. Way out of control. And she wanted to stop him before it was too late. Jimmy knew too much. A little knowledge may be a dangerous thing, but a lot of knowledge can be fatal. Yana never trusted anyone. Only me. She'd told Felix she'd go along with whatever he wanted and then told me to get on with the job. So I did.

We had reached a point that was simply a culmination of circumstances, that night there was an understanding that we had come so far and now there was only one way forward. At least, only one way Yana was prepared to try. And I loved her. I love her. I agreed to do as she asked, bound myself over to her desires. Jimmy was her problem, I make things better for her. It's in my job description, it's what I do.

Twenty-three

I always knew it would be wonderful. Kissing Jimmy, holding Jimmy, fucking Jimmy. Killing Jimmy.

The drive down the coast in the dark was easy. Smooth. Cool. The seasons were switching from summer to fall, the fall that doesn't really happen here, the fall that is measured by a drop in humidity, a slight lull in the air pollution rather than anything more mellow. We'd had high winds all day up the coast and even in the city valley, created by wind-tunnel buildings as much as geography, there had been breezes strong enough to wipe away the cloud cover, smog cover. Winds to whip fire into half the hillside homes, but that this was a good year, a safe year. For some. The wind had wiped the sky clean during the day and now the stars were presenting themselves against pristine black. They looked great. The night looked great. And I felt fine – having agreed, listened to her plans, adapted for further safety, assured myself of the necessity, the good sense, the no other option – I felt great. I drove fast, and safe. No traffic, no fear. Calm.

It was just gone midnight when I let myself out of Yana's trailer, no one around, everywhere quiet, half a dozen people locked in on the closed set, access restricted to only those who really needed to attend these night-filmed sex scenes, the rest of the cast and crew fast asleep in their rented homes down on the ocean front. Twelve-thirty by the time I'd walked halfway back through the little town to where Yana had left my hire car two nights earlier. Almost two-fifteen when I parked the same anonymous car several streets from our house, Yana's house, Jimmy's house, my house. I watched from outside the house, waited for the blinking lights that would show me if the alarm was on or not. Jimmy must have had a good night, four dark red lights winked at me through the dark. I deactivated the night alarm and let myself in the front door.

Your own home is a different world in the dark. Edges are sharper, corners darker. And I hadn't been there for ten days, had left with Yana in a fuss of fright and fury. Jimmy would have had friends over, women over, had women over his body. Now he would have me over his body.

Keeping in the moment. There was no way I could have driven down that coast road and let myself into the house and gone to Jimmy that night if I had thought it all through in one long piece, thought it out from the act of leaving her trailer to the culmination of the night to the drive back to Yana's side. I was doing what I had to do in each individual minute. That way it made sense. Separate scenes. Unedited.

The runner calling Yana from her trailer, they were ready for her now. Yana saying goodbye to me as she went, telling the runner I was dozing on the day bed, obviously Yana wanted me close, a safety-catch for the filming to come. The runner nodding, whatever it takes. Sex-scared baby runner, horrified and thrilled by the idea of what Yana was about to do, horrified and turned on by what she was about to witness.

Yana and Mike on the closed set. Naked, properly

naked. No modesty cloths or added divisions of flesh-coloured material. They have discussed this. The director's vision, the writer's dream. They have agreed to go with it. To allow themselves to be transported to something bigger than each of them, to take this idea and make it flesh. Real flesh. Skin and bone. No pretence. This is art after all. You can never do too much in the name of art. And anyway, there is always the cutting room for later, for safety, false modesty.

Jimmy was sleeping in his bed. Alone. I realised as I walked through the sitting room, the detritus of an evening – cans and pizza boxes all left out for Marina the next morning – that he would need to be alone. I don't know why it hadn't occurred to me on the drive down. What I would do with another woman there, how I would get rid of her, keep her quiet thereafter. I'd chosen to believe Yana. Jimmy had only a few free days left before he started work again, was heavily into preparing his body and soul to be beautiful on screen, but even with that pressure, Monday was football night. New season, new games, old Jimmy. He would have been drinking with the boys – organic beer maybe, gluten-free pizza, no cheese (fat-forming, mucus-forming, bad for the asthma) – and then gone to bed. Alone. I trusted Yana and she was right.

Yana and Mike finish a bottle of wine. They are naked. There is a fixed camera rolling at a distance, another shoulder-height skimming the room. It is all worked out. They know what to do here. The wine is real. The skin is real. Mike and Yana are acting. The alcohol is disinhibiting. It is an old Hollywood tradition, getting drunk to film the love scenes. It is an old life tradition too. Certainly my first love scenes were all carried out under the influence of wine or beer or vodka or dope. Any or all of the above. They are drinking and saying lines. Minds split in two. One half knows the situation, understands that the alcohol is there to ease the nakedness, the lights are half-bright to make the set seem dim, the words are not their own, though by now they know them as if they were. The other half-self is tricked into going along with the near-reality. Kisses. Skin. Warmth. Wine. Sweet words and tempting words and taunting words. They both know these words will turn later. They have read the script, know what comes next. For now though, it is soft and quiet, sound guy working extra hard to stay out of the way and yet pick up the softest rush of breath. It is all fake and feels real. The skin is real. The wine-warm kisses are real. Yana's long hair in Mike's hand, her soft fist on his hard belly, all true.

I stood for a while watching Jimmy; his light snore, the catch in his throat and nose made me think of my father. After a rare night out at the pub with my mum he would fill the house with the reverberation of nose and throat, warm beer smell in my parents' small bedroom. Jimmy was younger, and fitter, and his snores were way more elegant. Though the scent of beer was strong. After five minutes in the room, my eyes adjusted to the dark, I whispered his name. Several times. And he woke up. Maybe he wasn't surprised to see me. Maybe he'd been expecting a visit, one last plea on Yana's behalf. My behalf too, of course. I said I just wanted to talk, Yana was going crazy, I couldn't stand it up there with her for another night. That made sense to him. Would have made sense to me too. Jimmy pulled his naked body from the sheets and recommended a beer. It was a warm night. His skin was clammy. Mine too. He put on a robe and we walked into the kitchen, opening cans by cool fridge light. I told him I had coke

171

with me as well, that the unit publicist was every bit as useful as we'd hoped she might be, he was happy with the offer. Warned he wouldn't be swayed, that now was his time to go. Repeated his promise that he would stay quiet – in return for a good enough settlement, of course – but this departure was long overdue. Jimmy had made his mind up. He felt free and happy for the first time in ages. Meanwhile, though, his argument wasn't with me, I wasn't the one who'd gone crazy accusing him of blackmail. We had beers and Coke and Jack Daniels, he thought maybe one of the guys had left a little dope from earlier, in the sitting room maybe, or out on the patio. A warm night and a swimming pool and each other to play in it. I said it sounded like a party, Jimmy offered a wake for the threesome we'd been. I agreed. A wake was probably more in order.

Mike is holding Yana tight. Very tight. She has delicate skin, too little flesh, will bruise after this. Tomorrow there will be shadows of his touch beneath her skin. Her head is thrown back and she is laughing. The laughing began several minutes ago. She started and now she cannot stop. He cannot stop. He is trying to stop her. His fear is that she is laughing at him. Her fear is that she is not. He must stop her. Increases the pressure from hand to arm, finger to skin. Kisses to shut up the cackling mouth, his front teeth catch against hers, swift crack of perfect enamel, snarl on her upper lip. The sound guy nods and signals to the silent director, the tooth smash is in, clean, tight. They both like it, smile across the dark-lit set. Yana and Mike are not smiling. Spitting and fighting now, she hitting out at him, yelling words and phrases, sentences, whole paragraphs.

None of the subject-object-verb combinations make much sense, neither of the mouths entirely coherent right now. Yana is word-perfect in her biting hissing mumbling fury. The few permitted crew are impressed. She and Mike do know there are other people around, of course they do. But now the one-half there and one-half gone has slipped into two-thirds fighting and fucking and only one-third self-watching. Brain on automatic, words and movement drilled in and fully functional, character through fury into focus into frame. And the sound guy and the make-up woman and the director and the DoP and the extra camera operator and the lone excited runner are so privileged to watch these two people fighting, beating each other up, kissing the furious licks, fucking back the kicks. They have been going for fourteen minutes without a break. It is entirely real and totally captured. Mike hits Yana across the face, it hurts, she steps back in shock. Stares at him. Wondering. Cut. Well done. Great work. Take a break and then re-set as quickly as possible, people. Hang on to this, don't let it go, stay here, be here, don't lose this, hold it here. Fast forward and do it all over again.

I like cocaine. I like the sense of a controlled lack of control. But I didn't take any that night. I waited while Jimmy turned off the outside surveillance cameras. It wasn't a big deal, anyone checking our records would know we turned them off whenever any of us were in the garden for any length of time. The cameras were for when we were inside the house, away from the pool, not to record the activities that went on beside it. Both Yana and Jimmy knew too many people who'd been betrayed by their own safety systems or the security companies they paid vast retainers to. While stoned-Jimmy might forget to put on the alarm that would take care of his personal safety, sleeping off a heavy night, he never forgot to turn off the system that might later be used to incriminate him. He liked his drugs. And he liked the illicit buzz that went with them, the rituals of misbehaviour. Jimmy cut out lines for both of us and I watched as he hoovered them up. The first time I turned one down I explained I was still too annoyed with Yana and didn't want to go off on a rant about her, I should wait until I'd calmed down and then the coke wouldn't send my mouth away without me. He was happy enough to hear that. Still furious with Yana over the letters himself, he nevertheless wasn't interested in a long story all about her.

Jimmy had been tired of it all, completely fed up, but now his big decision had given him a new lease of life. He felt fantastic, strong and forward-looking. My moaning about Yana would only bring him down and Jimmy didn't want to be brought down, not any more. So I pushed away another line and after that he stopped offering them to me. Just cut and sniff, cut and sniff. And shot glasses of Jack – I had two. Cans of beer – I had three mouthfuls. But I held the can and lifted it to my lips and made a swallowing motion. I can swallow anything, look like I can swallow anything. That's the thing with actors, they forget the rest of us can lie as well. It was September. Still warm, comfortable outside. And we were having a party, Jimmy and I up at the poolside, wild lemon verbena bending in a soft breeze.

The make-up woman rushes to Yana's side, wants to check for marks, needs to make sure the slap didn't bruise, at least not yet. Yana understands her own skin, knows that no matter what Mike has done in the past hour, there will be no signs for another twenty-four. The make-up woman is not convinced. And anyway, she needs to look useful or they'll ask her to leave the set, and this is way too much fun to be banished to her trailer. So there are creams and lotions and more fine, light-reflecting powder and all the while Mike is listening to Lou Cerbonit, nodding at the accented encouragement, breathing deep, cocooned in the held fury of the rage he has been creating, and watching Yana. More interested in Yana than he has been at any time in the preceding weeks. There was an adrenalin between them in that scene, something he's not felt from her before. Yana Ivanova is always technically adept, everyone knows that, and she has given some great performances up until now, but this is something else. This is really it. Mike catches an electric crackle between their skin and he can feel those nominations rolling in. He loves Yana for it, wants Yana for it. Sheets are changed and tables righted, new lighting set up as quickly as possible, not a moment to lose in case the moment is lost. Another bottle of wine is opened but neither Yana nor Mike are thirsty. Mike will now hit Yana and maybe-fuck Yana, is it really fucking Yana? And Yana will do both back. All to each other. All to a single hand-held camera. All to a waiting, watching world. They are both excited. And because they are good at it, part of it is real.

None of it felt real. I sat by the pool with him and we talked – he talked, I listened – and I liked what I heard. Was surprised to like what I heard. Jimmy had good plans, was looking forward to his new life. Was open and honest in a way he hardly ever was with me, not totally, not without a waiting edge. This was the Jimmy I enjoyed, crawling out from underneath the smart-mouthed bastard I found so infuriating. And so attractive. The attractive was useful though. Happy in his company, I could keep my fear and nerves in check. There was no going back, no changing our minds, but his good mood made it easier for me to be with him. Yana hadn't said I should fuck him. But I thought it might help, would make the point of contact easier, the flesh quicker to pull to me, drag under, leave down. It felt like ages, though it was only an hour at most. All the things Jimmy had left to say took only an hour at most. And then I suggested we go for a swim.

She reaches for him and he is already there. Knows she is coming, has made a place for her, space for her. There is a coming together between them that was not unexpected and yet could not have been pre-empted with awareness either. It is both as they would have thought and entirely surprising. Her skin, his mouth. There is soft touch and harder touch and harsh touch. Pain and delight. The pool is floodlit, light refracting off the dark tiles. The set is still. She is whispering to him, hard to hear, hard for him to hear. When he understands, he is first unnerved and then willing. Ready. He stands now and is bigger than her by far. There is a moment when the disparity looks ludicrous, an equality impossible, and then her tight fist reaches out to take his and she shows her strength. He likes her strength. Likes the show of it. Gives him something to work against, lean against, sink into. He sinks into her. They sink into the bed, beneath the water. Spinning now, colour catches on her skin, light waves across her back, she is holding him so tight, he thinks he might drown in her, might drown. There is real sex and nearly real sex and the faces look the same. And then, so quickly, comes the switch. It is not smiling or laughing, it is held under, he is held under, pulled down. Under her hands, under the water, under the bright studio lights, under the thrashing of last-minute waves. It is suffocating, this much feeling, suffocating and addictive. He comes back for more. She gives it. She comes back for more. He gives it, he is it. He is not.

They part. Exhausted. Finished.

Yana and Mike look at each other, breathing heavy, excited and a little fearful. She breaks it first, she giggles. He laughs, then everyone else does too. Relief. Satisfaction. Completion. Applause.

I came to the edge of the pool, breathing heavy, fearful and a little excited. I laughed quietly, nervously. Tried to breathe myself calm. Relief. Completion. Time to go.

Twenty-four

I have been sitting beside the pool for about ten minutes. I know I should be going, but cannot seem to make my legs move. I have lost the thread of what is supposed to happen now. I look at Jimmy lying face down in the pool and understand I need to see him just once more. There is no time for this and yet I cannot leave. The floodlights are on, the pool is dark blue, refracting fractured light, but there is no one to see. Our natural security here is so good, so safe, we have high fences, thick hedges and no intruders. Our demons come from inside. I get back into the water, it feels cold now, very cold. I am shivering, and I swim beneath him, open my eyes to look up at his. They are open too. I thought dead people were supposed to be surprised. Or peaceful. Jimmy just looks tired. Utterly knackered. It was a hard night, he drank so much, all those drugs, an asthma attack possibly, at the last.

I reach out to bring my fingers near his face. I'm not sure what the story is with fingerprints on skin in the water, I don't think it's wise to test. Too late I realise I haven't watched enough of those TV programmes about forensics, sincere pathologists, hard-working old-school cops, can't read the fat novels, their pages of gore and silent story-telling corpses revolt me. I don't know if they can get fingerprints from skin, but Jimmy is my roommate, my boss's lover. Surely I would have touched him at some time? According to the *National Enquirer*, certain internet chat rooms, I certainly have. Maybe they wash off, these marks of me. In some part of my brain that takes this seriously, I worry that perhaps someone who knows about these things will be able to tell the difference between my fingerprints on his skin before death, and after. So I don't touch him. Though my hand comes close, very close.

I break the surface to breathe – Jimmy doesn't – and study the sway of his back magnified underwater. Beneath again I follow the pattern of his skin. I have always loved the lines of Jimmy's face. He is not really my type, not physically. I know I've said this before, before we fucked, before I created the culmination of Yana's desire, but it is true. Though his behaviour has been both repulsive and attractive to me, his face and body have not. Not until tonight. I like manly men and womanly women. Always have done. *Double Indemnity. It Happened One Night. How to Marry a Millionaire.* I prefer the women, but I like the men too. Women and men. Androgyny does not do it for me, never has, I don't really get it, don't understand the point. It is a melding, hence pointless to me. There to smooth over, not to delineate. In my opinion anyway, each to his own. Jimmy was not my own. But so close. Too close.

They always looked good together, in the popular brother-sister fashion. Seemed strange to me that the tabloids didn't pick up on it more often, how similar they were, he the male of her fe-male. And yet perhaps that was what made them work. He was her complement, complimenting her: 'You are so lovely tonight, you could almost be me.' She looked him up and down, took the point and then laughed it off, but it occurred to me he actually meant it. And then they went out together, shining and loving and bare arms touching, while I stayed at home,

179

Cinderella to their beautiful step-siblings, inglenook servant waiting at the pool's mosaic edge.

Jimmy had planed angles to his face, light glancing off in perfect model poses, and yet his bones were not too sharp. He was softened by big round eyes and smooth, wide lips. Even with his added height, the height that is so foreign here in this city of little men waiting for screen magnificence, he was not imposing. He was neither broad nor narrow. Jimmy was just right. And so she ate him all up. Greedy girl.

We first met Jimmy at an arranged dinner. Felix had already checked him out, of course, Jimmy was just another possibility, a guaranteed and certain chance. Felix needed to know if we liked him, if Yana thought she could make it work, if Jimmy could pull it off. No one asked what I thought, not really, not like I was an equal partner. I thought yes please and this one and I could like him too and he is the one that will do and I'd like to try for him and maybe this one, maybe this one can do it and the impossible can be made true and I can have her totally and she can have him fraudulently and it won't matter and I won't be jealous because I will want him too and my dislike that is drawn to his fierce mouth will understand the situation and it will all be OK. This hard, hard arrangement will all be OK because we want it to be and because it can be and because he is the one. The One. Like any other silly little girl looking for her prince and demanding he make it better.

And the coming and going, the teasing and nastiness, the bitterness that became harder and yet more ordinary as the years passed, were just so many teenage crushes. All on him. On me. Between us. We knew that. I'm sure he knew that. Love is always a choice. I didn't fancy him, but I liked him, some muscle in me that was not usually flexed desired him, and I chose to allow those feelings to develop because it was easier to love them both when they went out leaving me behind, than to hate him for taking her away. Though of course he did take her away. I know that's a strange thing to say. Especially when I am the one who fucks around, not her. But he did take her away. He made it work. If it hadn't worked, if Jimmy hadn't been so good at the part, if we three hadn't been so brilliantly successful together, maybe we would have stopped it sooner, and I would have had Yana all to myself. If he had lied to Felix and then told his dirty tale to some tabloid, sold us both for the price of a house and some land back in Texas, if he and Yana had found they simply couldn't do the kissing in public, that there was no chemistry at all, if Jimmy had turned out to be the bastard he liked to act, if his leaning towards laddishness had been indulged just a sliver more than it was: if − then. Then we would have stopped it. Then we would have had no choice. Then Felix would have had to come up with another way, a better way. Maybe we would have told the truth. Most of it. Maybe we'd have picked someone else instead. Dumped Jimmy and paid him off and worked out another plan, an easier plan, a plan with more truth. But we didn't. Jimmy was our star. And he was well paid and handsomely rewarded and it was good for his career and brought him status and I think he liked it. For a long while. He wouldn't have been so good at being the consort if he hadn't liked it to some degree. Then again, if Jimmy had been bad at it, he wouldn't be dead now. Poor Jimmy. Too good for his own good.

I blow him a kiss and the bubble of it bursts on his mouth. His lips are blue. I'm too cold. I get out of the water and wash and dress and clean the house wherever I have been, taking away the glass I used and the plate. It is easy to simply wash and put them away. I do not worry too much about anything else, am not over-careful. After all, I live here. I have only been on location with Yana for the past week or so. I leave his drugs and alcohol residue where we shared them only ninety minutes earlier, it's a very easy explanation, sad and ordinary. I leave the sheets too. They look like sex. They will need to look like sex. It will make the police more careful with Yana, will give the papers a nice distraction. I towel-dry my hair and pick up my things. There are messages on the answerphone in my office and I am tempted to get them, almost push the button, and then my hand recoils, remembers what it was there for. Lucky. I leave the night alarm turned off. I don't know how much the alarm system remembers. Don't want to chance it. And Jimmy has had so many night-time visitors this past week. Marina can vouch for that.

Of course Jimmy was stronger than me. Far stronger. But I was sober. And better in water. And anyway, I wasn't surprised. He was.

When I walk up the street afterwards my feet fly over the pavement, the sidewalk. I am in another country. This is not the land of my birth. I am long gone from there. I walk along the place where feet go beside the road, beside the cars, beside the danger. It is too early, there are no cars, danger-free zone. But I am not walking. The ground spins out beneath me, behind me. I have blades on my feet, bleach-free chlorine in my hair, blood on my breath. I charge up the hill, the soles of my shoes making no imprint on the road dust below; to anyone else I am merely an early-morning power-walker. Power-walking out the energy he gave me, Jimmy's life sucked into mine. I am not scared or nervous or even worried. I am fast, speeding and silent. Concrete paving stones, set into dry grass verges, like train tracks rolling beneath me. Each one another step away, each one an infinite danger to step on the cracks. I step on every crack. There is no reason to worry about falling through. I am moving too fast to fall through, the momentum of the pool, the night, Yana's decision, my agreement, every single one of those letters. Each incident that has brought me here now sits at my back and speeds me on.

It is like walking through snow. The snow we had when I was a child. The snow my mum says they never have any more, not really, not stopping. She thinks the last proper snowfall was the winter my dad died. I know it delayed my plane. Kept me in the air, circling London until the runway was safe to land. In real snow the streets turn white and it keeps on falling, in front of your face, not just down, but round and spiralling and backwards and forwards and even when there is no wind, the snow moves. It flies up as well, and it makes the stationary move, moves it fast. What was defined becomes unclear, a blur of white melding into itself. The journey home from school hurries on, without the usual signs to mark out the staging posts, technicolour world turned to black-and-white dream, walking home with my bag heavy on my shoulder, houses and shops hidden in the scarf of white, wrapping itself tight around their necks, I get to the door quicker, fast to my mother's arms. And tea. Toast and honey. Warm chocolate milk. Everything in its place.

My walk to the hire car becomes those past journeys home. An unseen run. Not from or to, merely speed and energy. There is a physics equation that explains this. I do not know it.

My hair is still damp when I drive away. I have only been in town for three hours. It isn't long. I am not crying as I drive away. But I think I could be.

When I get back to Yana's trailer I let myself in and climb into the bed in the small end room. It is the bed I left eight hours earlier when they began the night shoot. It is the bed that is now cold. There is no one around. Most people have been let go for the evening, and anyway, Yana's trailer is far distant from most of the others, she cannot stand the noise, requested distance weeks before. There has been no one to see me come or go. Only Jimmy. I fall asleep and I do not dream and when Yana, her long night shoot done, finally dares to ask the make-up girl to fetch me, work is over for the night. I wake because the smiling woman is saying Yana needs me and could I come now, they are all exhausted but wait until I see the rushes, Mike and Yana have done such good work, Yana was unbelievable, there is much to be proud of. I come back from sleep and do not remember where I have been. Not immediately.

Twenty-five

When Jimmy first came to LA, before he'd met Felix, back then when any job might be the big break, he'd played a GSW in *ER*. Brought in on a trolley, left on a trolley, forgotten on a trolley. Still dead. Divorce and desire and vitality swirling above him, over the rib-spreader, under the bloody sheets. After Felix took him on Jimmy progressed from merely playing dead to actually playing dying. The good-looking and ultimately doomed young man in a made-for-TV hospital bed, his decayed body finally Y-cut open by the lust-distracted pathologist, her hidden lover strangely immune to the scent of formaldehyde in her skin. Just before the final ad break, the tough-but-soft scientist correctly uncovered the hint of murder in Jimmy's character's death, came up against the rampant and not unexpected sexism of her business, and then – against the odds, time ticking away – won through in the end. They always do. Cue backslapping and career-ladder machinations. Lost her lover though. They always do. Roll credits. Jimmy's breakthrough part was a surprise gift from the first series of *Six Feet Under*. The light comedy establishing scene, the shock death, the dead-man-talking fantasy shots. It was the high point of his showreel, secured him the audition for his sitcom. The rest is history. Jimmy is history. And well practised at lying on mortuary slabs.

Press Release

It is with great distress that we confirm the sudden death of actor James (Jimmy) McNeish. An investigation into Mr McNeish's death is ongoing. We would ask at this time of sincere grief that press and fans respect his loved ones' sadness and allow them the privacy this difficult time demands. Mr McNeish is survived by his partner Yana Ivanova, and by his son Samuel.

Further details: Felix Berger Associates.

Two young men were first on the scene. Live guys in dark blue, dead blue guy in the deep blue pool. Doug's stomach fell at yet another wet one, his shoes were brand new, cost him half a week's pay. Andy salivated, his fist already closing tight around the fat wad he'd get when he called this story in to his old buddy on *The Times*. He took it all in, the weeping maid – Hispanic, not as old as she'd looked at first glance, kinda cute really – the white-smudged glass top of the patio table, fingerprints and saliva no doubt running a race to the dead guy's brain and gums, the empty beer cans, the open bottle of Jack. Sure the alarm and cameras had been turned off, weren't they always? Who'd want to see themselves caught out on film when the Mrs comes home from her hard week's work? Same old, same old. Just another LA morning made brighter by the starlit address. Doug was already on his radio, calling it in. The forensics guys could fish this wet one out of the pool. And Andy would get himself out of debt. For maybe a week or so. He nodded to Doug, flipped his thumb back to the house. 'I'll check in there.' The maid stepped aside to let him pass, he was on his cellphone before he'd crossed the threshold, who was she going to tell? And anyway, everyone needs a sideline. Everyone trying to get by in this town at least.

JIMMY McNEISH

Jimmy McNeish had a brief, by some standards – though long by many more who never scaled his heights – career in theatre, film and television. His short forays into film acting were welcome and highly praised, especially his work in Nessa O'Neill's *Steel Mountain*, a passionate short film in which Jimmy's tour de force shone through, and clearly contributed to O'Neill's subsequent breakthroughs in European cinema. McNeish's theatre work, while largely confined to his native Texas, first drew attention to his cool good looks and not-so-innocent charm, but it is more likely that he will be remembered for his television roles. From ingenue young man when he first arrived in the city, to his breakthrough work in *Setting the Seen*, Jimmy was always the real thing. Honest – some would say almost naive – in his openness, and completely without guile in his portrayal of the dangerous charmer Eddie Fitzsimmon, Jimmy's faultless comic timing and dedication to the whole shone through every episode. While a consummate comedy performer in his own right, Jimmy was also a true ensemble player, a fact every one of his co-stars will readily testify to – though perhaps it is the mourning of his not-so-famous friends that will bear out this truth even more firmly. Jimmy's closest friends were the sound guys, the writers, the runners. Jimmy could play any role – the one he never chose to play was the star. Jimmy McNeish was one half of a truly magnificent pairing, he was a loving father, and he was a good guy. He was one of us. We will all miss him.

Daniel Markham,
sound recordist.

Scene 8: INT; A SUNNY, OLD-FASHIONED 'COUNTRY' KITCHEN. THERE ARE CHILDREN'S TOYS, SIGNS OF A MESSY LIFE.

We hear Felix's 'goodbye' down the line, see Carla replace the handset. She is slow-moving. Sits down at the table opposite Greg.

Silence. Refrigerator humming. A bird outside. Child calling.

GREG
What?

CARLA
Jimmy's dead.

GREG
Shit. No?

CARLA
Yeah. Asshole drowned himself.

GREG
God. Really?

CARLA
Didn't mean to . . . they think. Drugs I guess.
Probably drunk. Idiot. Fucking idiot.

GREG
Wow. *(pause)* You want a beer?

CARLA
I guess.

(Beat)
GREG
You going to tell Sammy?

CARLA
Yeah. Sure. Later.

GREG
Yeah.

(Pause)

GREG
Did he . . . ?

CARLA
What?

GREG
Did he leave us . . . you know . . . a will or anything?

CARLA
Felix is dealing with it.

GREG
Right.

(Beat)

CARLA
He said he knows Sammy's taken care of.
Jimmy promised he would be.

GREG
Oh. Good.

CARLA
And he figured there'd be something more.
For us . . . for, you know . . . us.

GREG
Sure. OK. *(beat)* Good.

(Pause)

GREG
You OK?

CARLA
Yeah. I'm OK.

I-doll T: I read he was completely waste-d.

Helvetica: me 2 I-doll. & there was a girl there, right?

I-doll T: 3 grls. LOL!!!???

PPx: my sister said they were going to drop him from the series. that's why he did it. they said he'd lost it.

Helvetica: just drugs PPx. 2 many. 2 much, 2 early, 2 L8.

PPx: & they said he had asthma. Maybe it was that.

jnny: asma? Swimming bad for asma?

I-doll T: she must be sad.

PPx: no, drugs bad for asthma. my sister said. She's a doc.

jnny: drugs. bad. baaaaaaad.

Helvetica: who sad?

I-doll T: ?????Yana!!!!!

PPx: nah! it's good for her.

I-doll T: NO!!!!!! (how so?)

PPx: she looks good in black. ☺.☺. ☺. and I heard she was <<with>> Mike Scarling anyway.

I-doll T: right. I read that 2.

jnny: i thought he was gay?

Helvetica: Cool. Nice couple. (✱Scarling. Drooooool!! ☺ soooo not gay!!!)

jnny: << she looks good in black>> (hah!) aah. poor Jimmy ☹.

Yana and Penny sat in the sitting room of the rented house. Filming had been cancelled for the day. The next two days. There were already flowers, bunches of lilies and white roses piling up on the doorstep. Yana was in shock. The network was so fast. She hadn't expected any of this to be so fast. The nice young police detective had come to confirm the bad news (Felix had called an hour or so earlier) and also to ask a few questions. Just a few questions. We have to. Formalities only. I'm so sorry. You understand? Yana understood. The questions were asked and answered. What was there to say? Jimmy was in LA on his own in the house while Yana was up here working, her assistant with her this week. Right. Friends over late at night. Women visitors. The day before yesterday according to the maid. A woman, that night, early on, maybe. I see. I'm sorry, I know this must be very hard for you. No, it's fine, you have to do your job. It's so sad. Can we keep this quiet? Please? The alcohol? The coke? It depends on the coroner's office. Yes, of course. We're so sorry, we'll do our best. Thank you. And then it was time for Detective Gianelli to leave. But the detective couldn't quite make herself go. Not yet. There was still more to see, torn as she was between feeling sorry for Yana and really wanting to have a good look. A good no-holds-barred gawp at the crying woman. This close to Yana Ivanova, without make-up. Amazing, even with the tears. And she was so thin, way thinner than she looked on screen. Angela Gianelli felt her thighs chafing against the constraints of her black work trousers. It was a nice suit, a good suit. Specially picked for occasions like this, she knew she looked good in it. But she was too aware of her body now, the way the edges curved out, spilled into the side of the chair.

Yana was crying again and the English assistant was holding her hand. (It must be weird to be that close all the time to someone so much more gorgeous than you, not that she wasn't good-looking that girl, but all the same, she was hardly Yana Ivanova. Angela knew she'd have hated it, high school was bad enough.) She'd ticked off her question list, it really was time to go. All the basic formalities. There were at least seven people who'd been with Yana Ivanova at the estimated time of Jimmy McNeish's death. There was a time-coded video version of the rushes the detective could verify it on. She didn't need to do that. These women were obviously in shock, Jimmy McNeish had clearly fucked up. This was awful. Like being in a movie, only not the glossy ones Angela Gianelli occasionally pictured herself in. This was one of those sad, real-life dramas, the ones she couldn't stand because the last reel was always all tears. Give her a clean shoot-out any day, a nice juicy, messy murder. Tear-jerkers about love betrayed were so not her thing. And so embarrassing, having to tell Yana about the bed, that they thought there'd been someone else there, earlier that night. It was all too horrible. What an idiot. The manager had told them he thought McNeish maybe used some firm of fancy hookers occasionally. Of course, he didn't know the name of the company, didn't have a number for them. Hell no. What was it with these guys? Why couldn't they just keep it in their pants, Ivanova was meant to be heading back home this weekend, how desperate was he? Christ, if a guy couldn't keep himself just for Yana Ivanova, what hope did a girl like Angela Gianelli have of finding herself a good one? The young woman excused herself, went to the bathroom, had a quick look through the cupboards. Not for work, just out of interest. She was surprised to find Yana Ivanova used the same moisturiser she did. Surprised and pleased. She left feeling sorry for the woman in the beautiful rented house. And skipped her usual afternoon snack.

Twenty-six

On the day of the funeral Yana was more beautiful than I had ever seen her. The fraught passion of the past weeks was gone. This was the perfect Yana that turned out only for very special occasions. Translucent Yana, Yana lit with an inner glow. It's not quite, as they used to say of the golden days movie stars, that Yana can just turn it on – she can usually create the glow for a camera or a packed auditorium, ready to applaud her seat-to-stage rush – but it's harder in real life. It's always harder when small talk and polite chat are the order of the day, and even Yana is not in control of herself to that extent. Sometimes, though, the glow just seems to settle upon her, an aura of loveliness. Often it arrives at a useful moment, granting her access to places or feelings otherwise denied. And very occasionally it's just there. Whatever the indefinable thing that is star quality – the ability to exude grace while not even thinking about it, let alone trying – sometimes she just has it. The day of Jimmy's funeral was one of those times. It was as if she'd put no effort at all into her appearance or her clothes. As if she, Yana Ivanova, was simply there. Pure. Present. Honest. It really worked.

Yana was calm and composed and cool throughout. She was perfectly dressed for the occasion, her behaviour was modest and careful. And she was sad, we both were. It was sad, Jimmy's funeral, incredibly, shockingly sad. Of course his death was a release for us both, no denying that, but we were upset, we were hurting. We'd lived with the man for five years. We loved him. Jimmy had been our friend, our partner in business and, very often, in play. And now he was gone. And though his going was a release for us, it was still a loss. Jimmy was still a loss. We both felt it.

Felix, who was horrified and totally grief-stricken for all of fifty-five minutes when he first heard the news, stage-managed the entire event brilliantly. Pulled himself together and got on with his work, he would save his tears until everything had been made good. He did a fine job, his people did a fine job – created the funeral so that it didn't look stage-managed, so that it looked honest. Which it was. And it wasn't. The tributes did pour in from other celebrities and fans across the world – the order they appeared was down to Felix. Jimmy's little boy Sammy did cling to Yana's hand throughout most of the service – the fact that he'd had a fight with his mother on the plane getting to LA wasn't essential information for the watching public. It just looked really good, broken widow beside small snotty boy. As did the slight hint of dress coat in Sammy's too-long shirt, the one Felix had persuaded him to change into just before the ceremony – LA toys are a fine bribe to a small-town boy. Yana wasn't wearing a veil, but the suggestion of Jackie and John-John was there all the same. She was low-heeled, bare-headed, empty-handed, just Yana until the kid put his hand in hers: then snap! Picture perfect. Carla on the other side of her son, but all eyes on Yana and Sammy. Yana was swathed in a tight-fitted, long-sleeved dress. The black crêpe severe yet moulding and cut to only just above the knee. No jewellery, not even earrings, except for the single garnet she'd been wearing on her ring finger for the past three years. The garnet she had allowed people to assume was from Jimmy. The garnet that was from me. And no make-up, none at all, not even a touch of mascara, ready to run. Yana was face-naked, and all the more perfect for it.

She didn't cry for ages. I did, couldn't stop myself. Carla too. It was all so sad. Kept seeing him cold, wet. Remembering I really had liked him. Often. By the time we got to the mortuary they'd made dead Jimmy look like waxwork Jimmy. Certainly there'd been no shortage of pictures to base their embalmers' art on. I'm sure they did a good job. His hair still looked wet to me. Yana held herself in – gently – all day. She had no tears when we pushed past the crowd outside the small chapel, immediate family and friends only – not the Hollywood wedding version of friends and family, the real thing this time, just thirty-two people. Her eyes were dry all through the ceremony, when only the vicar was in front of her, facing us in the congregation, when only he would have seen her tears, only he would have been able to get on the telephone to his pet journalist (as he later did anyway), but Yana didn't cry for the vicar. Nor when the coffin was lowered into the ground. She didn't cry all afternoon. Until she said goodbye to Sammy, until Carla took back her son's hand and the two official women of Jimmy's life embraced. Then Yana broke down and her shoulders began to shake and her breath came in gasps and she cried, properly cried in Carla's arms, true tears, little boy looking up at the embracing women. And as the sobs cracked through Yana's tight body, the long-lens cameras carefully positioned in trees and bushes throughout the grounds came alive, the cemetery lawn echoed to the chirruping cricket-chatter of a hundred shutters taking flight. The tears were real. Yana was sad, as I was. And sorry. But no regrets. Sometimes we cry in relief, not pain.

In the early evening we all went back to the house for canapés and carefully measured drinks, all seventy-five of Jimmy's nearest and dearest from his work and play. Including Mike and Melissa because they'd come along anyway and none of us knew how to tell her to fuck off – not in that lovely new black dress anyway. The extra twenty or so who turned up at the house had been working during the funeral, filming schedules wait for no dead man. Carla and Sammy were already on their way home. Felix had offered to get them a hotel for the night – or longer if they wanted, nothing would be too much trouble, they could stay in his house if that would be easier – but Carla couldn't stand LA, had never wanted to be there before and certainly didn't want to stay now, as Jimmy's body began its slow settle into the earth. Jimmy's parents long-dead, sibling-free, his wake was peopled only by his non-blood family, those who really wanted to be there. More honest than most then.

In the bedroom Marina had laid out a change of clothes for Yana. Still black but softer now. A silk trouser suit. Something to sit in. Something to collapse in, to get drunk in if she wanted to. (She did want to, but she wouldn't, not yet.) There were clothes laid out on my bed too. Sweet of Marina, very touching when she had so much to do, when she would have loved to have been at the funeral herself, but offered to stay home to get things done instead. Sweet of Marina, and I thanked her. And dressed in remorseless guilt.

As the people began to arrive Yana, Felix and I took our places. He the host, she the widow. And me the same as always. No actual role, no proper place, just there anyway.

There always. No reason for any of the visitors to question my presence, I belonged to Yana, to her house, her household, as much a part of her life as Felix and Marina. I was never handed glasses to refill – or only as an equal hostess myself – but nor was I asked, not once, how I felt. Lucky really, I have no idea how I might have answered that question. Fortunately the twenty-first-century crossover between intimate and staff meant I didn't have to. Just did my job as the paid best friend, unpaid lady's maid – *Upstairs Downstairs* in 25,000 square feet of earthquake-safe bungalow and a status-free sensibility.

Some of the people ate – the canapés were delicious. Melissa was starving apparently. Marina had stayed up all night crying and cooking, Armando came over to help her sort out the tables in the morning. The drinks were willingly poured by Felix himself, no surreptitious looks at second or third refills. Jimmy's funeral, Jimmy's excess, we all knew what it meant. I didn't notice any couples or trios huddling over comfort lines in bathrooms, though that doesn't mean it didn't happen. Just that people were quieter than usual, held back their gabbling mouths, or disguised it as grief. Out of respect for the rumour mill no doubt. People talked quietly, cried softly against hastily hung muslin curtains, wide against the broad windows, light let in, path up to the now-covered pool shut out. Shut out but wanted anyway, needed almost, the Marina-draped curtains twitched back by every guest who thought they might do so without being seen. And some who didn't care as, later on, grief and alcohol began their age-old liquid mingle, emotional mangle.

Eventually time came to get rid of people, clear the rooms before the alcohol took too great a hold and the itching desire to get out there overcame good manners, past the curtains, beside the pool, at the not-yet-shrine.

The never-shrine if Yana had her way. (Way too fond of her beautiful pool to have it claimed by Jimmy's ghost hunters.) I asked for silence and Yana quietly apologised that she didn't feel able to speak, heads nodded sympathy, understanding and – among the few who knew their press contacts would be disappointed – mild irritation. In her place Felix made a nice little speech about Jimmy and his too short life, his glittering career, his would-be wife. Jimmy's mate Dan told stag-night, best-man, bad-taste stories. Best-friend stories. Dead best-friend stories. A make-up woman, another drinking buddy, slurred a few lines of self-centred woe. Jimmy's series producer announced the show would go on – though with its pivotal actor missing and missed and definitely, obviously, clearly acknowledged. (His co-stars' faces split into tiny, not-quite-hidden, smiles of utter relief.) And then it was all over. Time to go home.

We were home. Jimmy wasn't.

We made love that night. Yana and I in the house, our house. Just the two of us. Both crying. For Jimmy and for ourselves and where we were and who we were and the first-time freedom we now possessed. They say it's common to want to make love after a death, on funeral nights, the grief manifests in a fucking desire, procreative passion. Sex is sex, whether it recreates life or not – it still feels like love, make love, be lust, be loved.

Before we fell asleep she told me a story. It was a new one. Yana was telling me something new.

'I met this girl once. It was when I first went to England. And she was exactly like me, only not. You know? We were just seventeen and both ambitious and both beautiful – for girls I mean, for young girls, considering we didn't know how to dress and didn't have any money or anything. We weren't formed yet, not properly. But we both knew we had it. That thing that makes people look at you. It. And we were asked to go down to London together.'

'When you were talent scouted?'

'Yeah.'

'You've told me about her before. Kathy.'

'No I haven't. Not really.'

'OK. Go on.'

'We had these two days to get there, down to London, and we were hitching and stealing train rides where we could – it was different then, security wasn't such a big deal, we felt safe. We were young too. The safety of not knowing how bad the bad things are. And she had these mushrooms, I'd taken a bottle of vodka from the people I'd been staying with, and we just had such a good time. I thought she was going to be my best friend. I told her all my stories and she told me all hers – hers were way more interesting than mine, she'd had much more of an interesting life. I was really impressed with her, excited she was my new friend. I thought we would go down and conquer London together and it would be so much easier because I had her by my side. I wasn't scared then.'

Yana was quiet. I waited, holding her hand in the dark.

'But you ended up going to London by yourself, right?'

'Yeah. She had the looks but not the desire. She wanted it, but she didn't want to have to do the hard things to get it. I felt so betrayed. She became my friend really fast, I mean we only spent two days together, but I guess I sort of fell in love with her, not sexually, just that way you do when you meet a brand-new person and they seem to understand you so well and you think you understand them and you talk about everything, tell each other everything, and they get it, get you.'

'But?'

'But she didn't want it enough. Most people don't. They say they want it – whatever their it is, the job, the car, the lover, the world – only they're not prepared to go through with everything it needs. Or worse, they do, they start, and then give up at the last minute, more scared of success than failure.'

'But you're different.'

Speaking into the dark, explaining herself.

'Yes I am. I'm not scared of doing the hard things and I'm not scared of success. I'm not even scared of failing.'

I'd never thought of it like that, but I knew she was right. 'No. I don't think you are. So what are you scared of?'

'Of not giving it everything. Giving in. Giving up without trying hard enough.'

'I don't think you need to worry about that. It's not like the business is likely to let you give up, not now, when you're doing so well.'

'No. I suppose not.'

More silence. More dark. If Jimmy were here now we might hear him through the cooling night, the hum of the pool as he sat beside it, always wanting reflected light in his dark, a slamming of plates and fridge doors in the kitchen, low voices on a distant TV screen. We heard nothing. Just each other breathing, waiting.

'You did a big thing you know, Pen. An important thing.'

'A hard thing.'

'Yes. A hard thing.'

My stomach was churning. 'I really don't think I can talk about it.'

I felt her nodding in the dark. 'OK. But I want you to understand. I know you did what was needed. You didn't give in. And I'm grateful.'

'I know that.'

'We won't forget Jimmy.'

'I don't imagine we will.'

We were quiet again, creaking house sounds, body sounds, no-Jimmy sounds. Yana turned over to go to sleep. I held my arms around her, tight. She was shivering.

'What happened to that other girl?'

'I don't know. She got off the train at Coventry. She didn't really want to be there, travelling.'

'And you never saw her again?'

'No. But I never forgot her either.'

Twenty-seven

Just the two of us. So easy. Yana was still in mourning, of course, which meant no one even expected her to go out. When she did, when she was brave enough to put on make-up, strong enough to turn up to a party, an awards dinner, a proper work meeting perhaps, to go on with the show and grind her way through the last two weeks of the shooting schedule, she was greeted with soft voices and sincere smiles. And a wide array of grief-curious looks behind her back. Yana had touched death, there was a Jimmy-shaped hole in her life. This gave her – in their eyes – new knowing, she was special. And there's nothing that makes a party more select than one or two guests who are truly properly special. Not the special of work accomplishments or career enhancements – ten a penny in our city. Not even extreme weight loss or radical new marriage bring the proper kudos of really, truly mattering. Accessory-baby is so last decade, death is the new yoga, mourning the new black. In lieu of an actual life-threatening disease taking the hostess's right hand at the table – and God knows AIDS and cancer have done their best, but unfortunately sufferers tend not to look too good on it (and we do like our victims to be pretty) – a grieving widow is easily the next best thing. And way less embarrassing than actual illness. Grieving widowers are pretty good too, but there's really nothing to beat a sad, thin woman, jet beads strung across her prominent bones. I opened more invitations for Yana after Jimmy's death than the two of them ever had before.

I opened no more nasty letters after Jimmy's death though, at least none from that sender, in that style. Yana took it as proof that Jimmy had been sending them. And as long as our mail-box stayed clear of Lonely Hearts ads, there wasn't much reason to contradict her.

Yana completed the filming schedule and everyone said her work was amazing, incredible, so real, so true. They were right. Mike stood opposite her, but she could have been acting with anyone, Yana was doing it all with herself. Playing a broken and bruised character and keeping it small, holding it all in, making herself tiny. The opposite of Hollywood tradition, where actresses clamour for the glamour of pain, and everyone wants it magnified, Yana had to hold it all in, she was scared her real-life truths would shine through. So she kept herself close and played it small. Everyone thought her work was a tour de force. And because she was going through it right then, in that moment, because every person on set believed they were seeing the honesty of her grief, they didn't question the size of her playing. Yana played the victim as if she knew what she was doing, they just let her get on with it. And through her diminution they were able to dream themselves, their own pain, their possibility of understanding her. She held in her pain and gave all the more in her containment. Producers heaved sighs of relief and the movie finished on budget. Only the unit publicist was annoyed – best story of her career and she had to stay away from it on grounds of taste.

And when work was over, after we'd remade the house as our own home base, we did go out sometimes. When it was right to and Felix agreed we should, sometimes even when he didn't. Evenings when Yana couldn't bear another night in and the thought of possible-party was just too good. Yes, she'd have to play sad lady some of the night, forget her grief in passing, maybe nearly-laugh and then drop a tear or two at the right moment, but she was good at that. Is good at that, has been given prizes for that. I was happy to stay in, but I didn't mind the going out either, not really, not now that I had become her accept-able escort. Someone had to hold her hand, be there just in case, who better than her best friend and assistant-accomplice-accompaniment-slave? To the assembled select, I was the other woman who had lived with Jimmy, also loved Jimmy, maybe even once shagged Jimmy. Though only according to the more daring message boards, those with less litigation-anxious administrators. I was the right person to be by Yana's side because I knew her so well. I had known him so well. I could join in her grief.

We were both grieving. In our way. It was sad, all of it, that it had happened and how it had happened and why it had happened. That it had come to this. I tried not to think about it much, that night, the following day. But the image came back to me, unbidden, and often. Jimmy cold in the pool, Jimmy hot on my skin. Jimmy waxy in his coffin, waning in my arms. I was grieving for Jimmy and grieving for the loss of my own innocence. I knew it all now, had stood at the very moment all those dinner party guests were so in awe of, the dividing line. And then pushed him over, held him under. Somehow this brought Yana and I closer together, she understood me more, my dark-night Jimmy fears. And she held me through the shakes and she told me it was the right thing to do and I knew she meant it, believed in me, and we did it together. We moved somewhere else in our lives and we moved there together.

205

We did miss him though. Miss his laugh, miss his jokes —
even those at our expense — miss his smart mouth and his
fine body.

We missed him and we were sorry that he was gone and
we were glad. Pleased and relieved and free. Yana and me.
Just the two of us. It was wonderful, really fucking wonderful. Breakfast alone and no concern that Jimmy would
walk into the kitchen, mock our plates, eclipse my taste
with his, his wants with hers. Midnight swimming in the
pool — that pool, ours again, hers reclaimed — and safely
undisturbed. Pissed off with each other for some uninten-
tional slight and free to shout it, scream it, throw it, be it.
Free to fight without the fear that our fuck-off words
might be heard and recycled at some later date. Free for
fun, for fucking, and fighting. We were a single girl
moving into her first studio apartment, the newlyweds
who finally get clear of their in-laws, an old man released
from the slow death of his now-addled love. All that freedom, all that time to ourselves. And we lapped it up.

Yana won a prize. For the movie. That movie. A big, fuck-
off, you've-made-it prize. Some said it was because Jimmy
had died, some because she was brilliant anyway. Most
maintained her scenes filmed after his death were the
astonishing ones. And a few thought the violence and sex
with Mike were so astonishing that they had to be real, real
fake, false truth. The prize was an English prize and I was
her English rose travelling companion. We went home,
home for me, journeyed first class. I've travelled first class
with her before, never felt I'd earned it so much as then.
First class is weird, the price mark-up is exponential, and
the space is nice, but there is no amount of attentive service that can possibly justify the excess, the highest-class
hooker fees. It's all about location I guess. It so often is.

On this trip I was in my proper place. Beside Yana. Not behind with the bags, or on the other side of Jimmy, or next to Felix with papers and laptop and the paraphernalia of assistance. On this trip I sat next to her on the plane, held her hand at takeoff and landing. Of course I did, she needed me there. On this trip all the extra goodies, freely handed out to those who already have so very much, while those who have not remain back in the poverty coach, seemed fairer than they ever had before. For once Yana failed to complain about the ostentation and the excess in the VIP lounge, didn't bother to disparagingly compare this flight to the poor versions she'd suffered in her less famous youth. Somehow we both felt we'd earned our place this time. The first time I crossed the Atlantic it was to meet up with an ex-lover who'd been living in the States for a year and wanted to play with me for his last three days before he moved on to South America. I travelled from Heathrow on a half-price courier ticket in the middle of the night, allowed no bags other than my carry-on luggage and then waited for four hours at JFK while the US half of the courier company sorted out the paperwork on the documents I was bringing through. The flight was exhausting and boring and I spent every one of my three days in New York arguing with my very ex boyfriend. Flying back then with Yana I felt for the first time that I had definitely worked my way up to the first class cabin, I had earned my seat. Jimmy paying the price, swimming towards me through the jet-lag turbulence until I accepted another glass of champagne, settled back to watch my choice of movies, stretched out full and easy on the bed-seat beside Yana. Jimmy in my thoughts until I put him away.

At Heathrow we were swiftly processed and smoothed through customs into a car and then to town where she and I had connecting rooms in a venerable venereal

Thames-side hotel. Yana Ivanova was recently bereft, what if she woke in the night, called in the night, cried in the night? And what if my bed remained untouched and her pillows were wrinkled on both sides of the bed? Everyone needs helping through the night sometimes, every troubled soul needs a hand, a leg, a warm flank of flesh to keep away the lonely dark. I was Yana's succour. And her slut.

I loved it there. Three weeks back 'home' and yet just visiting. The first time I'd returned since starting work with Yana, starting life with Yana, the first time I'd had the chance. Twenty-two days is just enough to see the family and show off the gloss and the income and be a success and no time at all to get bored, annoyed with the traffic, pissed off with the weather. Or start to wonder about missing it. I never think about missing home, pining for loved ones from before, not if I can help it. Of course I could miss them, but what would be the point? I'm not coming back, I live with Yana, her life is there because her work is there and it follows that mine is too. No point in craving what I cannot have. And so I held the ones I loved and kissed the ones I didn't and offered demi-truths and lots of gossip and just enough star stories to keep me in bubble-wrapped jars of Marmite for the next three years. And we went over to Southend to see my mum. Who loves Yana. She'd visited us a couple of times in LA and quite liked Yana before Jimmy died, adored her after. I watched them, two widows gossiping quietly over a cup of tea in my mother's sunny back kitchen on an early spring morning. I wanted to tell her then, give my mum the whole story, pass on a single truth. Not about me and girls, my mother knows all about me and girls. Told me herself when I was fifteen and simply couldn't get excited over the boy pop star of the moment, was upset that all my friends felt something I didn't. She suggested maybe I check out his bass-playing girlfriend instead.

She's very cool my mum, my dad was good too, but she's not that cool, not hold-it-in cool. I knew that if I told her the truth about Yana and me, she'd have to tell one of her friends, it's the way of motherhood, the child's accomplishments are only properly tangible when shared with someone else. And loving Yana Ivanova had to be one of my more important accomplishments. Unfortunately, gossip that starts 'Well, her mother said . . . ' has a horribly true ring to it. So we spent three nights in my mum's little semi and slept together in the spare room because it was the only other room and if she knew, maybe she knew, she didn't say a word. I've slept with other women under her roof. But Yana Ivanova isn't any other woman and even my mum, who reads glossy trash only at the doctor's, and only if they're running very late, knew that. But she kissed us both goodbye. And she wished us Godspeed. And I felt bad then, for a while. Until I remembered that before the swimming pool Jimmy would have been with Yana in London, and I would have been with Mum, and Yana would have been able to pop in for half an hour at most. And then I was glad again.

When they opened the envelope and read out her name, she turned to hug me, camera on us both, me on screen in my Aunt Patsy's sitting room, Mum whooping at the telly. Yana walked up the steps and held the prize in her hands, that night we took it to bed with us. Slept with it between us on the pillows. To remind us how far we'd come. She thanked Jimmy in her speech and me in her bed. About right.

I was really happy those three weeks in England, like I'd come home in the way I'd always wanted to. A success on my own terms. Even if no one else knew it, I did. I knew how hard I'd worked to get where I was, right beside her. Yana wasn't as relaxed as me, didn't like all the photographers everywhere, not that she ever did, but her angst was different about them, her desire to hide stronger. I didn't know why. The British paparazzi are different to the ones in LA, less deferential. I think they reserve pretend politeness for the royals and screw the rest of us. For all their well-documented intrusion, they're disturbingly royalist at heart and commoners are fair game. I thought it was that, and the possibility of winning, horror of losing. Put her tension down to nerves, tiredness, her desire to hold the statue. She was fine with it in her hand, and at my mum's, just not with a flash bulb in her face. It's a different quality of light in England, all the painters say so.

We had a whole year with just the two of us in quiet mourning and easy quiet. And then another six months to try out the new Jimmy-free Yana. Six months reminding us, not of the years before when he'd been there, but of the past twelve months when – for the first time ever – it was just the two of us. Each fading season made a whole new batch of memories and there were only me and Yana in them. After the first twelve months Yana was able to throw off some of the mourning signs, be slightly freer, braver with herself and her body. In the first months after his death she took two small-but-significant parts in very heavy films, jobs that would enhance her reputation, though they were hell to do. And then, as soon as Felix granted permission, she leaped at the chance of a big lush romantic comedy, an opportunity to show them she could laugh again, an excuse to have a laugh herself. (A way to go for the comedy prize that had so far eluded her.) Well, if Yana Ivanova could make a try-out cinema laugh only eighteen months after Jimmy McNeish's death, then surely she deserved the little man statue? It was a lovely period in our lives. I was with her all the time and no one ever questioned my motives. I did head off for a quick shag every now and then, just to be sure, to keep the stories out there, but never even had to pretend interest in the bloke. How could I? I had my mourning best friend-employer at home who needed all my true energy. I had desire to offer to those outsiders, but not love. Not now, not when I was needed so much.

We had the house to ourselves and our life to ourselves and it was gorgeous. Like a proper couple. Like a real life. With the hidden bits, sure, but everyone has those. Even the straightest, most married couples have those. Another summer, hot and sticky on her skin, in public and out, in the water and out. Only Yana, only me, June and July melting together into August.

And then, just as I started to get used to it, to believe just-we-two was not only possible but might actually be the best option, Felix decided it was time for a change, a new direction. Another leap up the ladder for Yana Ivanova. She needed a new man, could no longer be seen to be totally single. He said the rumour mill was working on her again, Jimmy had been dead coming up for two years, Yana wasn't Queen Victoria, she couldn't stay in mourning for ever, she needed someone by her side. And I wasn't enough, I didn't fill the space beside her, not in the right way. It was time to move on to the next phase of Yana Ivanova's glittering career and her glorious life.

I hated him. He was a bastard, fucker, cunt.
    And he was right.

Twenty-eight

What hurt most was that she didn't argue. Not at all. Not even a quiet wink for me, to let me know it was all right, to make sure I was OK. She nodded, smiled and told Felix it was fine, agreed with him, ignored my anger by her side. She told him we'd start seeing new men whenever he was ready to call them in. Let the auditions begin.

I was furious. We'd been really good, so happy just her and I. The past two years had been a wonderful working-out of the kinks in our relationship, we'd really blossomed as a couple, she knew that, she'd said so often enough herself. And she was prepared to let all that go, take us back into another messy, potentially dangerous, threesome without even a second thought.

'Don't be stupid, Penny. Of course I've thought about it. We both knew this couldn't go on for ever.'

'You've been happy without a man, without anyone else.'

'Of course I have. I love you.'

'Well, tell Felix to fuck off then.'

'Why?'

'Why? Because we don't need anyone else. You and I are enough by ourselves.'

'I don't think so. And neither do you.'

No I didn't. I knew, even though I didn't want to, that Felix was right. And Yana was right to say so. I just wanted her to be less easy about it.

'You want me to shout at him, Pen? Make a fuss and then give in anyway? What's the point?'

'The point is it would make me feel better.'

'You knew what you were getting into. I never lied to you about how it would be, not even right at the beginning. It was always clear.'

'So why not stop lying to everyone else?'

'What?'

She knew what I meant, she just wanted me to say it out loud.

'Come out. We could come out. Other people have.'

'Sure they have, sweetie. And where are they now? Don't be silly.'

She lay down on the sofa, picked up a magazine, dismissed me like I was asking for the moon. Pointless, foolish. Irrelevant.

'But you could, Yana. You're doing so well.'

'Mmm, I am. And this would make all the difference, wouldn't it? Just what I want right now, the slide into once-famous, now-gay obscurity.'

'Some people make it work.'

'Really?'

'They do. There's a fuss at first and then it's all forgotten and everything carries on as normal.'

'That's right, and the last time I looked all the people you're thinking of were men. There have been a few very successful gay men directors and some quite successful gay men producers and even one or two gay men – out gay men – successful actors. Though truth is, of course, we prefer our queers to be English if they absolutely have to exist. And ideally over fifty. But there aren't any gay women in these hills, not girls that talk about it anyway. That way madness lies.'

'And crap biographies.'

'You got it.'

I wasn't prepared to let up though. 'But Yana, you're in a great position right now, they all love you.'

'Yes, and I'd want to fuck that up for why, exactly?'

'For me. So we could be together, properly, always.'

'We can be together always.'

'If we lie.'

'Where the fuck has this come from, Penny? Suddenly you're having an attack of conscience?'

It wasn't that. Not guilt, not that kind of conscience. And it certainly wasn't any political correctness on my part, I just couldn't bear the thought of sharing her again. I hated it. I'd had a hard enough time with Jimmy – and the path of that sharing had led me somewhere I tried really hard not to think about now, somewhere cold, wet, dark. I didn't want to start it again, the thought of the acid jealousy made me sick. But she said that was my problem to deal with, my character that needed to develop. I should be more open.

'Anyway, Felix knows things got hard with Jimmy at the end. He'll find us someone who works for us. He knows us better. Knows our needs.'

'You make him sound like a personal shopper.'

'Isn't he?'

'Fucking hell, Yana, take this seriously, will you?'

Her voice quiet, dangerously low, I should have known better.

'Just leave it to Felix. I don't want to talk about this.'

'Yes and I want you. Only you. I don't want to do that again. I won't do that again.'

'Won't? Is that a threat?'

'Maybe. I don't know. But I hate it, I fucking hate sharing you.'

My voice louder, more shrill, hers soft and slow. Careful. Very careful.

'Go gently, Penny.'

'No. I mean it. I know how much your career matters to you . . . '

'You don't.'

Very quiet, almost unspoken. I didn't know how to shut up.

'I know you couldn't bear to do anything else, I know how hard you've had to work, how far you've come.'

'Really, you don't.'

I was shouting too much, couldn't hear the warning in her quiet.

'Sometimes though, Yana, you have to make a choice.'

Just a look now, her question face, single raised eyebrow, not even a sound.

'I'm your partner. We have a life together, a life in addition to your work. You need to choose what you care about more – your career or your life. You can't always put your life off for work, hide the truth. You just can't. Love has to matter more.'

She sat up then, looked at me. Long and hard. And loving. Held my face in her hands. She was so calm and I was shaking. Desperate for her to hold me and say she agreed, promise that I mattered more, desperate and already lost. I knew better than my words. But I wanted to push it anyway, just in case.

She shook her head. 'You don't know me at all, babe.'

'Of course I do. We've had seven years to learn each other. I know you've been happy since Jimmy went. I know you've loved being just the two of us, you've done some of your best work. I've taken care of you, of us, and it's been good. You've been happy with me, with just you and me. You said so, and I could see anyway, even if you'd never told me, I could see you were happy.'

She smiled, 'Yeah, I have been. I am. Very happy with you, my darling. But you don't know me, really.'

'I do.'

Trying to persuade her, loving to persuade her, I knew what was best for her, knew her best.

'No.'

Yana Ivanova was born in a small town halfway between Moscow and Novosibirsk. Yana's parents were both teachers, her mother an English-language specialist, her father a biochemist. Yana was not planned. Yana was the product not of love or of passion, but a bored late-night fuck. Fine and delicate and huge-eyed, yet also bright and questioning and brave. Yana was not an easy child.

Kathy Duncan was born in Stratford. East London, not upon Avon. Kathy was not planned. Her mother was seventeen, her father just some boy, one boy. Boy enough to run away when she told him about the baby, man enough to stay away when he realised what it meant. Janice tried to look after her little girl, but her heart wasn't really in it. Her heart was in the boy and he was nowhere to be seen. She slipped into sadness and from there to depression and Kathy went to a foster home. For a year or two Janice tried to get her back. But it didn't work, she could never stay happy for long enough to convince the care workers, and the foster parents were good enough. Except they weren't. But Kathy had long since run away when their crimes came to light. Nothing too brutal, illegal, wicked. Just indifference, an interest in the income not the child. They weren't bad people, Kathy's foster parents, they just weren't good people either, they weren't really interested in Kathy. It happens. It happened to Kathy. She ran away. Attention equals love equals life. Not a hard equation, but a hard one to get right, harder to ignore. Kathy ran away and tried her hand at looking after herself. She was beautiful and clever and ambitious and she had no idea how to get from here to there. From this cold life to that place where she knew she would be in the warm light, the loving light.

Then one day, Kathy was shoplifting in a Manchester mall, and met some other girls. Like her, but nothing like. Happy-families girls who thought they had every reason to be disaffected and in truth were merely spoilt. And Kathy watched them and she thought it was funny because one of them looked loads like her. She joined up with these girls for the day, taught them a few tricks. Comfortable girls, not wealthy, but easy in family love, they liked her tricks: mascara up the long sleeve, blusher down her narrow jeans. Kathy was drawn to the lookalike girl, with their matching legs and arms and cheekbones, dark eyes. Her lookalike was foreign, Russian, even more interesting. They hung around the mall all day and she wasn't surprised when the lady from London gave them a card, they'd got some good gear, a really nice lipstick, they looked fine. Finer together, reflecting magnificence. Kathy knew the London lady was a bit more interested in the Russian girl, that accent, the difference. Nothing very different about some poor bitch from London, run away from home and trying to make it in Manchester. But she had good legs, and she was thin, very. And together they certainly turned heads, even just in the shopping mall, that much was obvious. And so they decided to travel down together. Kathy knew how to save money, get rides, steal some model-type clothes from a few of the better shops. Kathy knew loads of things. For instance, she knew the Russian girl was more interesting than her. She knew a foreign name was more exciting to model people. Kathy stole the right magazines, she knew what to read, and when the Russian girl got scared, wanted to back out halfway there, Kathy knew it was a chance. Her chance. Why not? You had to take your chances.

Yana Ivanova died in a back street in suburban Coventry. It was an accident. They'd nicked their train tickets and then hitched a lift and ended up in Coventry for the night. The Russian girl started saying she was frightened of London, maybe she wanted to go home. They needed to be at the scout lady's office the next day, Kathy knew a bloke they could spend the night with. They went to his place and he had some beer, the girl wanted vodka, wanted to show them how to drink vodka. She had fucking good English actually, really good. And so they drank vodka too, the bottle stolen from the worried host parents back in Manchester. And the guy had some smack. Kathy wasn't stupid, she wanted to look good the next day, so she stopped early on, but that girl – it was like she'd never been anywhere before, like she couldn't handle herself. She hadn't, she couldn't. She was worried, frightened about the big city, and foreign. Pete just kept filling her glass. They were smoking, him and the Russian girl. Then she started throwing up and Pete got pissed off and said they both had to get out and Kathy was really upset, she had this bloody Russian chick to look after and nowhere to sleep and it was gone midnight and she wanted to look good the next day, this was such a big chance, but the girl wouldn't stop throwing up and Pete was being such a cunt, telling them to fuck off.

So they went out into the street and Kathy had no fuck-ing idea where they were and the girl looked really rough.

And then she fell. At Kathy's feet. And Kathy was holding both their bags and there was sick everywhere and the girl started sort of choking and Kathy didn't know what to do and she probably could have done something, should have called for help, but she had no fucking idea where she was or what to do and anyway, if she got help, they'd ask all sorts of questions about Pete and the gear and everything. They always ask bloody questions. So she did nothing. And eventually the girl stopped choking. And Kathy thought it was such a fucking shame because they would have done really well together, she'd read the magazines, knew those fashion people liked a gimmick. Matching girls was such a good gimmick. Though being Russian was pretty cool too. Pretty cold now. Kathy took off her shoes, vodka and beer sick staining them. The Russian girl had a nice bag, big and useful, not like the little one Kathy'd had to nick – so hard to nick big things. And the Russian girl had some nice clothes too. Odd that, because Kathy had expected them to be really poor, Russians, but the girl had said her mum spoiled her, treated her like a princess. And it was late then, two o'clock in the morning or something, and the girl and Kathy didn't have much money between them, not for two, but not bad for just one, enough money for just one. And it was time to go.

Kathy Duncan travelled down to London on an overnight coach carrying the Russian girl's things, wearing the Russian girl's shoes. Read her precious diaries. Wore her clothes. Practised her accent on travelling strangers. They didn't know what they were hearing, it sounded about right. Her looks definitely helped, her undoubted acting ability was useful, her perfect if not-quite-definable accents gave her the edge of sexy outsider status, but most of all, Kathy helped herself. Changed clothes in the toilets at

Victoria Coach Station, fixed her make-up. Yana Ivanova went to the meeting with the agency. Kathy Duncan never turned up. No one cared enough to report her missing. No one noticed. Everyone noticed Yana Ivanova.

By September 1990 Yana was living in an overcrowded shared flat off Kensington High Street and slowly but successfully touting her portfolio to the fashion editors of all the London-based magazines. And now, many years since the day Kathy Duncan illicitly boarded a London-bound coach in a cold dark depot in Coventry, her travel documents and precious diaries in a box under her arm, Yana Ivanova is a Queen.

Twenty-nine

There's a fly buzzing on the window-sill. Buzzing in my head. I'm looking at her and trying to understand. But Kathy Duncan is such an innocuous name. The fly keeps throwing itself against the window, it's trying to get out, back to real life – air, water, earth. The thin muslin curtains are long gone. Marina kept them up for a few months and when winter came we wanted light more than we cared to hide the path to the pool. That first summer we were alone was particularly hot, sticky nights, we just needed the water. She did anyway, Yana. Kathy. Her. I don't swim so much any more. It's always cold. The water's always cold.

'What about all the stories, Yana? Your brothers? The Red Riding Hood thing, with that guy?'

My voice is louder than I expected. I'm shouting but I don't mean to be. I clench my fists, push fingernails into skin, breathe.

'From her diaries.'

'Your diaries? The ones in your dressing room?'

'Yes.'

'But the details – surely she didn't write all that detail?'

'Actually it's only detail. Specifics. Almost no feeling. Weird, not like a real teenage diary at all. Maybe because she was writing in English, Latin script. You can read them if you like. The details are in the diaries, the feelings are mine. I had my own Dimitri. Doesn't everyone? Didn't you?'

I remember Nasim Khandir. Fifteen. Depressed. Beautiful. Dangerous.

'Yeah. I suppose so.'

Need more specifics. More truth.

'Is that why you wouldn't talk to Masha?'

'Yes.'

'Or your brothers? Her brothers?'

'The brothers barely knew her. Yana. She told me that – and her diaries make it very clear. They were much older than her. Now they think they know me. They know my money. They're happy enough, they don't need me to speak Russian to them.'

'Do you know any?'

'Russian? A little. A few words I've picked up from the ones who wouldn't shut up, some of the books, her diaries when she couldn't find an English word instead. Not enough to understand. Not enough to talk to them.'

'Do you have brothers of your own?'

'Kathy?'

I nod. Asking family questions about this stranger I love.

'Foster kids. Brothers and sisters at the foster family. I don't know about my real mother. Maybe she had more kids after me.'

'Don't you want to know?'

'No. Not any more, it's too late. Anyway, they probably told her in the end.'

'Who? Told her what?'

'Authorities. Whoever tells bad news. I left my wallet with her body. They would have thought it was Kathy who was dead. They will have told my mother I died. I did really.'

*

Buzzing. The fly will stop eventually. Or not. Behind the fly I can hear the hum of the pool filter, a neighbour's distant car door slam, flight path adjustment and something overhead. Something overhead, she is reaching out to me, her hand out to me, near my forehead. This is shock I suppose. And something I can't grasp just yet. Shock and . . . shock and . . . I open my mouth, it doesn't come. It will. I open my mouth to say one thing, get another fresh-formed sentence instead.

'You killed her?'

Not the words I was expecting. Though maybe Yana was, she didn't have to think about the answer.

'Not intentionally.'

'You let her die?'

'Sort of. Maybe. I don't know. I was scared. I was just a kid. I didn't know what to do to help her. She'd been drinking all night.'

'Weren't you worried they'd try to find her? Yana, I mean? Foreign girl in a strange country?'

'I was her.'

'Oh, yeah.' Adjust the picture, one into two.

More information: 'Anyway, they knew where I was.'

'Where Yana was?'

'I was Yana. The agency called the family in Manchester, they called me, I told them I wasn't going back and I wouldn't speak to my mother, I said they'd have to tell her.'

'They let you get away with it?'

'I was a foreign kid who'd managed to run off from their home. Of course they let me get away with it. If I was this badly behaved brat, at least it made them look less culpable.'

'Your mother – Yana's mother – agreed to it?'

'She didn't have any choice. I sent her a letter, mostly copying stuff from the diaries. I sounded like her. Like me.

Her little girl was desperate to break free. She knew that. Of course she was upset that I was gone, but it wasn't a complete shock that I might run away. Stay away.'

'Well what about Kathy then? Weren't you scared they'd try to find Kathy? The foster family? The authorities?'

Long pause, almost tears in her eyes now. Maybe.

'Who? No one was going to be looking for Kathy. No one had until then. She – I – had been alone for a couple of years. Kathy was over sixteen. The authorities you're talking about had given up two years earlier, not that they cared much even then. Kathy – I – didn't matter to them.'

'Right.'

'I took my chance.'

'Right.'

Sounds again, inside, dishwasher cycle ending, outside, a far car door slamming.

Then a long sigh, her urgency. 'I've done so much to make this life, Penny, make my life. You need to know that. I'm never going back. Backwards. Never.'

Feels like giggling inside, I let it out. 'Stratford?'

'I don't want to talk about it.'

'No, but Stratford! Yana . . . Yana? Kathy?'

'Yana. I'm not Kathy. I don't think I was ever Kathy. Not really.'

'Stratford – it's almost funny. It's so . . . ordinary.'

'I'm not talking about it, that stuff, it's all past. We both have our secrets, the things we don't like to think about. Let's leave it at that.'

'So why tell me now?'

'I figured it was time you knew.'

Holding my hand, pulling me to her, I move, but not easily, I am stiff with confusion.

'You and me. We're it. All we have. You deserve to

know me, in the way no one else will ever know me. Now you know all about me.'

'Is this all?'

'Yes.'

I believe her. She goes on. Explaining, making right, making clear.

'I will find some other man to be with, because Felix thinks it's time and I agree with him. You know you do too, it's how we have to be for this life to work. To have all the good things our life earns, we have to pay that price. But I'm giving you a gift. My truth. Now you know.'

'I could tell people. I could blackmail you to be with me for always. Only me.'

I'm lying. She understands this and shakes her head. 'No you couldn't. There's a swimming pool up that path, remember? I am being totally open with you and absolutely clear. I have never let anything come in the way of what I want to do and I'm not going to start now.'

'And yet you just revealed everything to me.'

'Yes. I love you.'

'I love you too.'

'Good.'

We kiss and I realise what the other feeling is. Shock, yes. And disappointment. The exotic princess is as ordinary as me after all. English. She's just English. A runaway English girl who watched the same *Top of the Pops* that I did, ate Maltesers because they were supposedly light, smoked the cigarettes I too shoplifted, understood enough about the country to wonder what the hell was going on in that hot summer of the Diana farce. Wilting mouldering flowers piled high in sticky cellophane, florists' boom-time, crazy British people mourning their total stranger. She was like me. Yes I was a happy-childhood girl and she was not, yes she had created her life, made her self and her career in a stratospheric rise that I couldn't claim. But her name was Kathy. She was from Stratford. She was like me. I wanted to hear her voice.

'What do you really sound like?'

'I sound like this.'

Soft accented, mostly non-specific American, something else, the Russian thing, twisted underneath.

'No, your English voice.'

'This is my voice, Penny.'

'Your accent then. What's that?'

'This. Me. Like all those other actors who went to drama school in the forties and fifties and trained themselves to be another person, dumped their northern accents at the door to London. All the movie stars who made up new names, new faces, Marilyn Monroe stealing Betty Grable's whisper. I've talked like this for so long now, this is my voice.'

'You're good at accents.'

'Everyone says so.'

The fly had stopped buzzing, given up, collapsed in the glaze-magnified sunshine. Filter timer on the pool turned itself off. We sat in hot afternoon silence. I stared at her. She looked the same and not. Mine and not. I knew it then, never mine. Never mind.

'What are you thinking?'

My head shaking, I didn't know. What else was there besides disappointment? I didn't want to tell her about the disappointment. She was on the back foot right now, confessional sofa, telling her my princess fantasies wouldn't do my cause much good. I wanted to keep the narrow upper hand I held. And I didn't want to disappoint her. Yana believed I loved her for herself. I always had. Mostly.

'I'm wondering why.'

'God, Pen, I don't know. Not really. It was all such a mess back then.'

'You could have just gone as yourself to the agency.'

'I know. And they probably would have taken me on.'

'Kate Moss doesn't exactly have an exotic pedigree.'

'She wasn't famous then. Not quite. And I don't think it was about that anyway, about becoming Yana. Though I wanted to, liked to. I enjoyed it, the deception. It was less about becoming her and much more about not being me.'

'Redefining yourself?'

'Defining myself at all. I was undefined, didn't know what I wanted. I was only a kid, but I knew I didn't want what I had, what I was. This was my chance to leap past all that. All teenagers want it, hell, half the adults we know want it, an opportunity to become someone new. It's what all the diets and break-ups and affairs and cheap makeover shows are all about.'

'And you had the chance?'

'Yes. I did.'

Quiet again, softer, easier, understanding. Getting there.

'It's not that unusual, you know.'

'What?'

'Changing yourself. Not for an actor, not for here.'

'I guess not.'

Movie star pictures, beautiful women parading across our sitting-room floor.

'Norma Jean Baker?'

Yana shook her head. 'Mortenson first.'

'Really?'

'Yeah. And Doris Von Kappelhoff?'

'Knew that.'

'Julia Wells?'

'Julie Andrews.'

'Margarita Consino?'

'Rita Hayworth.'

'Betty Joan Perske?'

'Lauren Bacall.'

'You're good at this.'

'You're not the only girl who ever dreamed of coming to LA, babe. Lucille Le Sueur?'

'Oh not Lucille Ball?'

'No. But she was wonderful.'

'Who then?'

'Joan Crawford.'

'Really? Lucille to Joan?'

'It was a different time.'

'Yes, it was.'

A different time now too. A different feeling between Yana and me. Something explained, almost understood. Both of us lying on the sofa now, me in her arms.

'Anyway, Pen, you've changed too.'

'How?'

'To be with me, to stay with me, even just to stay in the States, you've made adjustments.'

'Yes. I have.'

'And you wanted to.'

'To keep you? Oh yes.'

'But not just me, what your life is, what your life has become. You like our life, we both do, the money, the ease. We make the necessary changes, the accommodations.'

'Everyone does.'

'My changes have just been bigger than most.'

'They sure fucking have.'

Understood. Agreed. Something shifts. Time to move on. We move to another room.

*

Yana's body beneath my hand. Her flesh, the body that has launched a thousand beauty dreams. Advertising schemes and teenage hell. Yana Ivanova's skin is translucent. I know this because it is said in all the right magazines. I know this because beneath my searching fingers I see her pulsing blood, read her stories. We are all the stories of our time-travelling flesh, Yana's skin whispers hidden histories.

Yana's mouth above mine. Her lips on my lips, teeth touch and enamel shock jars, calcium leaches from my bones to join the mingling possibilities. She sucks me into her and I go willingly. Yana's tongue, magnified a thousand times on screen before now, greets mine for the single moment, uncaptured, passed. My manicured fingernail traces her lip-line just as teenage girls copy the same from newsprint possibilities across the land. Yana bites my nails. Her lip-stick marks are real to me, the copycat girls reinvent their own, but they're not quite right. Mama knits the home-made cardigan and it never fits like the shop-bought hope. But trying all the same. Her prize-winning lips to my mouth to my neck to my heart into me. And you talked to Michael Parkinson with that dirty mouth?

Yana's legs twining, twinning, toes and ankle-bones and smooth patella mine to touch and kiss and hold in hand, flesh, mouth. Yana's get-ready-for-summer body, dissected and laid out in a double-page spread of this exercise for that long thigh-line, these crunches for that abdominal dip, this lunge for that hip. I lunge for that hip. I win it.

Yana's hands on my body now. Mouth to breast to cunt to toe to breast to thigh and home again. Hand on my hair, my cheek, testing my waters and dipping her hand in. These hands are good on screen, known on screen, small thumb scar made huge, cuticle-clean, lifeline forced and followed. Yana's hands have soothed dying husbands and new-born babies, balled fists of held-in hate, open offering love-me-now. On screen they are always still, always, unless they have something really important to say. When Yana Ivanova offers a wild poppy in a just-mown field it says the world. Her hands have held the awards the microphones the dresses the stresses the cheques and the hands of the other-famous many, clawed for by the not-famous more. But right now they hold me, hold me tight, hold me in, hold her in me.

Here's a secret: Yana wears glasses when she watches TV. Late-night films in bed, her hand in mine, my other on the remote. She likes it loud, I turn it down. I do not turn her down. She turns to me and in her glasses I see myself night-light lit. Only myself, one Penny per frame, no pictures of Yana or stories of Yana or magnified Yana, in-depth-interviewed Yana, just me. Then she comes so close I see nothing and then there is only Yana, my Yana, the real Yana.

Of course, she is always my Yana and their Yana. She must be famous-Yana and home-Yana. She is both those women and all the others. She is herself magnified by their desires and herself brought back to true size by mine. Even when I try not to see her through their eyes, I still see her through my own. And my eyes are of this world and my wants are of this world and while I know that she shits and farts and bleeds chunky red blood in cramping pain and her morning breath is just as bad as mine, even while I know all this, there is still the residual truth: I am fucking Yana Ivanova. Me. Only me. Only her. A private audience.

And now, as it turns out, I'm not fucking Yana Ivanova at all. But she looks exactly the same. Yana Ivanova is a constructed promise, home-made, hand-delivered.

230

Thirty

Yana accepted, Felix went to work. We were delivered a catalogue of new men. One after the other they paraded before us. Not that any of them knew what was going on, understood their position. Not yet. Each meeting was presented as merely a lunch date to chat about a possible work project, an evening dinner at Felix's favourite restaurant, a breakfast discussion about some vitally important possibility that would come to nothing. It is not unusual to attend breakfasts and lunches, dinners and coffees, to turn up as if they are work meetings. They very often are. It was not unusual for Yana or for any of the men, nor was it odd for me to tag along. In other cities they do deals over drinks and in crowded bars, on the telephone or in the bedroom. Here we like to be seen in the bright light. And trade in flesh none the less.

Felix hand-picked six men. Not one of them knew he had been picked, only one of them would ever be told the truth. Felix assured us that there was no possibility of a mistake. We would definitely like one of them, maybe more than one, in which case his intimate knowledge of the contenders' past would come in useful for the final choice. And once we had decided – once Yana had decided, with my help – the truth would be offered to the Number One Choice. Along with the customary slew of personal-preference bonuses. Felix was certain that whoever we picked would not say no. He believed he had already guessed which one we would pick – he told me so in private – even before we met these men, but he wanted us to choose. Wanted Yana to choose. Needed her to know she was in control here, of her life, her future, her partner. It's what Yana always needs to know.

We were working on an arranged marriage. And in this case the bride was one of the chief arrangers, as was her best woman. It was only the groom who was to be surprised. Felix, the post-feminist, double-cellphone Dolly Levi. His list was short on men, long on past and possibility.

We met John Harte at dinner. His new home, new cook, clearly looking for a new life. Very good seared tuna though. John was the older man of our selection, in his mid-fifties. He was – and still is – a very successful actor, not long out of his first and only marriage, his late-teenage children now live with his ex-wife on the East Coast. On the pro side, John has always had a reputation as a thoroughly nice guy, and a good-looking one at that. Still good-looking. He has a great acting CV. And his ex-wife is a firm friend, his kids seem perfectly sane. As for cons, there was just the one. His perfectly controlled but two-decades-long heroin habit.

Next we went on set to meet Ian Fox, the young Scottish stud-about-town. Very very juicy, rising star, a little too aggressive for modern tastes. Or mine, but then my input wasn't quite as necessary as Yana's. He clearly saw himself in the James Dean/Steve McQueen mould. What he had going for him was that Ian really needed the hike up the ladder that mixing in with Yana would give him – and he knew it. His talent had been sufficient to get him started, but not enough to take him to the next level. He would be very willing and, Felix believed, very well behaved, were he to get the part of Yana's man. But only until he got the lift he needed. Or killed himself.

Marc T. Weringer was the gay one. A producer not an actor, which was a major bonus as far as we were concerned. Obviously he would be completely discreet, having no intention of ever outing himself – or of being outed. He had been with the same partner for the past ten years. And his partner is a leading Republican. Really, no one knows. Or ever will. Apart from Felix, of course. This one meant we would have absolute secrecy assured. On the other hand, Marc Weringer was not an attractive man. Not at all. Properly plain, verging on ugly in a bad light, they wouldn't be quite the golden-reflected couple Jimmy and Yana had been. Except on radio.

Dinner again with Ben Fisher, a newly interesting model-turned-actor. Turned surprisingly good actor actually. But not great, according to Felix – and he should know – Ben was never going to be great. Not that a little exposure to serious fame wouldn't help – there is nothing that carefully rubbing up against influence cannot help. The forward-thinking frottage. He was sweet, a year or two older than Yana. One failed marriage with a girl model-turned-actor-turned-new-Mummy-married-to-rich-guy. He told us they emailed regularly. She'd loved him, he'd loved her, it just didn't work out, she married the guy with more cash. Felix said Ben could do with the career help and we both thought he was quite lovely. Which made his problem all the more surprising – Ben was impotent. Chronically, medically, not-budging, non-psychological, impotence. Not a con for Yana – or me – obviously, but definitely a con for any women he dated. (Safe women, mouths-shut women, Felix-chosen women.) And Ben did date them, every now and then. He just hadn't yet found one who thought his ever-limp manhood was OK by her.

We had a power breakfast with Joseph Neil Pendelton. Absolutely beautiful man, LA local, major pin-up material. Already the past beau of three Academy Award nominees. And one winner. Clever too, lovely family, on the first lap of his career but already looking more than hopeful. Already looking pretty damn special. Joseph was a rising star. Several years younger than Yana, he'd completed two degrees in his early twenties, one in business studies, before deciding he really did want to be an actor after all. It was in the blood obviously – he came from a proper old-fashioned Hollywood family, mother in casting (much older and long dead), ancient father a golden-age director. The big sister from one of his father's three other marriages is a hugely respected television talent, his baby half-brother is getting ready to follow in his footsteps. And the only thing against him was that he was, according to Felix himself, 'Kind of like me, you know? The girl thing?' Joseph Neil Pendelton had a predilection for under-age girls. Twelve, thirteen, fourteen. (Funny the difference those two years makes, isn't it?)

Finally there was Angelo Walden Schlesinger, the African-American-Italian-Jewish hybrid, same age as Yana. Angelo was a respected producer, yet to achieve a major credit. He was best known in properly artistic circles – so not at all in ours. Highly regarded, he wrote important articles and was more than likely to become a very successful essayist when he finally gave up on his movie-making ambitions. Felix, an old friend of his, regularly recommended this should be sooner rather than later. According to Felix, Angelo knew his limitations, realised he needed someone interesting by his side. Hoped that someone would make a difference and take him from where he was stuck to where he wanted to be. More ambition than talent and too properly clever by far for this town. Unfortunately, while Angelo was good, well meaning and generous, he was also very very dull.

We met all six first. One after the other in an eight-day period. Joseph Neil Pendelton was great. We both really liked him, enjoyed his company. Yana looked lovely sitting beside him. But that young girl thing – and we didn't for a moment doubt Felix knew what he was talking about – was just too great a risk to run. Yana and I were risk enough, without taking the chance that someone would one day find out more about him than he wanted known and then look a little closer at his home life, just in case. Yana was never going to be OK with closer scrutiny. We turned down John Harte for the same reason. And Weringer. Underage sex, heroin, and homosexuality. Only one of those was legal, all three would damn us equally. And Angelo was just too dull. Yes he was perfectly pleasant and yes he was great at what he would end up doing rather than what he wanted to do, but in his company, breakfast was interminable. Yana and I almost caught each other out in a nervous giggling fit brought on by tedium. He looked good, but we needed substance as well as stature. Which left Ben Fisher and Ian Fox. And though Ian had the obvious appeal of the rising star, that was also the damning point in our calculations. He was a lot like Jimmy. And neither of us could face that again.

So we chose Ben. He was nice, easy to talk to. He looked best with Yana. Different to Jimmy, opposite to Jimmy – and therefore opposite to Yana as well. And he had more to lose. There is no movie man whose career can stand the whisper of impotence. A Hollywood man can do under-age girls and, if he's really a big enough star, under-age boys. He can do drugs and drink, lots of either. He could fuck his grandmother if he really wanted to – and was playing a part that needed the experience. Just as long as he can fuck, he's fine. Every second relationship in this town is based on hidden sexual or addictive secrets, very few are founded on the masking of abstinence.

We didn't want sex from him, Ben Fisher could give up his quest to satisfy. He was longing to give up trying to satisfy. It had been a hard realisation for him, had taken the past fifteen years, but it was his truth. Just as some women will never have slim thighs, never be able to dry their curly hair sleek and straight, and in the same way that some men will never grow any taller than five foot five, any hairier than bald, Ben's penis was never going to work. Not hard, not sexually, not like that. End of story. Start of new life. He'd finally met the girl who actually wanted him like that. If he wanted cuddles – and everyone wants cuddles – we could no doubt provide. I liked him well enough, what I knew of him. She would learn to like him, it was part of the job, Yana was good at the job. And if he wanted more, Felix could find someone for him. But for now, Ben was burned from trying and wanted a year – or twelve – free from the effort. Ben had more reason to agree. The most reason to agree. Which gave us more reason to agree. He was safest. And after Jimmy, we were ready for safe. I was very ready for safe. Ben said yes.

Of course it wasn't this simple. At every one of the meetings, and then the subsequent re-meetings, I was eaten up with jealousy, too sated with gall to touch a mouthful of the fine foods placed before us. I found fault with them all, wanted to turn down every one. Even after Felix had taken me aside, had a quiet word, and then – when I'd let out a sniping snide comment once too often – threatened a loud word, I still gave in with a bad grace. I wanted to be good, wanted to be open, knew there was no choice. And I couldn't help myself. This was like the last week of the holidays, being forced to shop for a school uniform and new books and unchewed pens. No matter how shiny the new pencil case, it still meant the beginning of a new term. I didn't get over it, but I did shut up. Gave in with a grumbling bad mood teenage daughter attitude and grudgingly accepted pay rises, new car, and a promised week's holiday alone with Yana – every year, without fail. When you have no choice and yet decide to bargain your position anyway, it's best to do so in the angriest possible terms. It makes them agree to almost anything, if only to put a smile back on your glowering face. As far as I was concerned, Ben was the best of a bad bunch. Treating him like the answer to all our dreams was going a little too far. Even more irritatingly, I found him funny. And once caught myself looking forward to seeing him.

Three months after our first meeting, after the private contract had been signed and sealed, and several of Yana and Ben's 'secret liaisons' leaked to the right journalists, we celebrated our new foursome in style. And public. Felix made a few calls beforehand so that the celebrations – twenty-five months, two weeks and six days after Jimmy's death – were noted in all the appropriate papers, paparazzi at the ready. And everyone was very pleased for her. She deserved this after all she'd been through. Poor Yana. Lovely Yana. Hopeful Yana. New Yana. Great shot.

Yana and Ben left the restaurant together that night, heading back to her house, our house, soon-to-be-their house. That was the plan. They were caught kissing as the restaurant outer door opened. That was the plan. Felix and I stayed on to drink, me too much, him just for show. Then he put me in a cab and drove himself home. I made the cab stop at my favourite bar, picked up my favourite waiter, did my old favourite dance, thinking all the while of Ben in the spare room and Yana waiting alone. Not the plan, just my choice. Lucky me, no one to see. When I got in she was already asleep. I think.

Thirty-one

Of course it wasn't that easy. We had to get used to each other, used to being a new three after two years of the ideal two. And Ben needed to accustom himself to us. To my jealousy, Yana's fears. Her paranoias that I now understood in a way I never had before. We needed to get used to him as well. An adult lifetime of personal disappointment had also left its scars, no matter how successful his public life had been. We were careful with each other initially and then less careful and sometimes outright difficult. And like any other relationship we discovered our places of compromise and our boundary points.

Ben didn't swim.

He didn't eat meat either. And he meditated, morning and night. He did drink fortunately, but not to excess, and his idea of excess was a far smaller margin than either of ours. He liked loud music and barely watched television. He didn't particularly like movies, especially not those he was in. He enjoyed the process, not the product. Every morning, when Yana and I were happily still asleep, Ben went for a long walk. He usually came back some time after she and I had had breakfast. This was good, we started the day in our own home, alone. I wasn't as sure of him as I had been of Jimmy, Ben gave away much less of himself, in some respects he was far colder, less of a friend, more of an adjunct to our lives. But he was so much easier. I had no spark with Ben – and neither did Yana, though between them they manufactured the impression of spark fantastically well for the press and their public – and she and I discovered the joy of living with nothing niggling in between. Our home life with Ben, with Ben's influence, became routine, ordered. It was the adult version of our youthful passion with Jimmy. It lacked a certain vehemence, but more than made up for it in ease. Ben was easy, quiet, self-assured, contained. I have no idea what he thought of me, not really, he's never said – we have never had those rows where such things are said – he was my roommate and my lover's public partner. And somehow, even without all the personal knowledge, the intense discussions, the late-night drinking sessions eliding into the confessional, I came to trust him. And when I trusted him, Yana did too. It worked.

Mike and Melissa came back into our lives briefly, when they announced their pregnancy, were famously fecund in every second newspaper, gave birth to a boy, and named him Jimmy. In honour of their good friend Jimmy McNeish. Yana was away filming on the day of the pagan-humanistic naming ceremony but I went along with Ben for ballast. I was surprised to find I needed it.

I have never wanted children. I have wanted to be a mother, briefly, in passing – to feel the helpless abandon of baby love. There have been times when I've looked at Yana and been consumed with a desire for the mingling of her gene pool and my own, I've wondered what our baby might look like. Years ago when I had proper men lovers, not merely for show, I wondered the same – though never with the ferocity I have imagined these futures for Yana and myself. I have seen the pregnant women and wanted for myself their madonna glow, pictured me in receipt of

the interested glances, on the receiving end of the interfering belly-touch that complete strangers offer in approval
and gratitude when yet another member of the species is in
creation. We are still a primal people, we need to see the
recreations, give thanks for the continuum. I have offered
that approval myself, held out the applauding, marauding
hand. The pregnant bump, the tiny baby, they are very
appealing, I am drawn to them, by biology or timing or
both, I am drawn to be them. But I do not want the children who turn into people who make things happen. It is
the cause and effect of procreation that scares me, karma
that pushes the stop button.

I was like this when I finally gave in to the American
landscape and learned to drive. I had avoided driving in
England. It was easy to avoid in England. There, where the
roads and the land are narrow and the people are swaddled
tight into the small island and there are criss-cross train
tracks at every turn, it is easy not to drive. Ecologically
correct and right and good not to drive. Here it is insane,
there is no public transport to speak of, no public land that
does not really belong to the road. And the road cannot be
tamed without a car. The car today is John Wayne's horse,
it makes us who we are, we cannot exist without it. People
do exist without it of course. But they find it hard. And
they do not live in the Hollywood Hills. They live in the
cracks where the gloss cannot get through. I am not those
people. Gratefully. But I thought of them when I sat
behind the wheel for my first lesson. The pedestrians I
could easily mow down, the precise quality of skin it
would take to withstand the shiny metal I now controlled.
Elephant skin maybe, rhino hide. Most walkers, bus-stop
dwellers, do not have rhino hide. I thought of them when
I lay in bed unable to sleep the night before my first driving lesson. The car is a brutal instrument and I was scared

of what it might do. I would be in charge of it, but not. I had heard the tearing of metal on metal, feared the greater possibilities of metal on flesh. There was so much damage I could do in a car, so much more than I could do on foot or in a bus or train. My fault, my hands, my feet. The karma of driving cars terrified me. And then I got over it, and now I drive like everyone else. Thoughtless, mindless, listening to music or the radio. I drive like my mother ironing, concentration on anything other than the task in hand. Only changed to true attention when there is clear and present danger – rain, jams, small children on the side-walk. But it still creeps up on me sometimes, the horrendous possibilities of the tin box. The horrendous possibility of me.

The horrendous possibilities of the new baby. Brand-new person. Someone who will go out and no matter how good, how true, how perfect their nature, will effect change. I don't believe they think about it, those pregnant glowing ones. I don't believe they could think about it, that any one of us might be carrying a Hitler or a Mother Teresa. Serial killer, serial adulterer, heartbreak queen. We make new human beings and we think of the first year or two, five if we are the parents who need to get them on a school list early. But I cannot stop myself from thinking further ahead to where the new people go out and make a difference. Because they will, even the smallest of us makes a difference. Through shyness he snarls at the too-chatty taxi driver who then goes home and hits his kid who grows up to buy a gun and teaches his cousin how to shoot who spends too much on rubber bullets so leaves not enough money for the cleaning woman this week who steals her bus fare and goes to jail for petty theft. And leaves her heartbroken old father to die alone. And the good deeds are no better. Equal and opposite reactions abounding, we are in constant flux. And every time we make a new human being we add to that, without thought for the consequences. My mother had me after all. And now there is no more Jimmy. It's my own fault, I look too far ahead, always have done. It stopped me driving for the first ten years I was legally allowed. It holds me back from my own biology. It did not stop me doing as Yana asked with Jimmy though, I made a leap of love for her. I have always found it is easier to end than to begin. There are, of course, consequences, karmic results, from endings. But they seem somehow more contained than those at the beginning of things.

I sat at the naming ceremony, home-made version, made essentially anodyne by its effort not to offend anyone, and listened to the request for non-specific blessings on this tiny thing. Heard the speaker recalling Jimmy in the naming and remembered the chill of the water. Ben sat beside me generously warm against my cold arms. He thought I was sad to have to remember Jimmy in this way, figured he understood why Yana had chosen to claim work instead of attendance. And then, sitting beside me as we watched Mike and Melissa parade their fertility, Ben might also have felt something else, something beyond his own loss. He is sweet and he is sensitive. Often he knows when to leave a room, when not to speak. More often he knows when not to ask. Maybe he has sublimated sexual desire into psychic reason, or maybe he's just nice. But he knew something else was going on with me that day, hearing Jimmy's name. Ben held my hand and he didn't say a word and when it came time to move on to the party, back at Mike and Melissa's lovely new home, Ben explained that he didn't feel very well and needed me to take him back to the house.

I sat by the pool that afternoon. The water remained clear.

Some months later Felix brought up the possibility of our having a child, Yana and Ben having a child. It was doing Mike no end of good, even Melissa's new career as a cable talk-show host had received a boost from the appearance of her new customised accessory.

Yana, who hadn't come as close to Melissa as I had, thought he was being mean. 'God Felix, you're so nasty sometimes. Surely even Mike Scarling and that woman can have a baby and just enjoy it for what it is?'

Felix yawned, covered his mouth late and slowly. 'Yes they can. They could. I've seen them with it – him – they do love him. Hugely, of course they do, he's a very good little boy. All fine and natural and good. Except that this is the exact conversation I had with Mike just about a year ago. When would be a good time – career-wise, I stress, for both of them – for Melissa to get pregnant? Did I think it was a good move, did I think it would be good for them? It's my job, I see into the future. I can't help it if it makes me a little cynical now and then.'

He went on to explain that Ben could do his part of the deal medically if not actually, and Yana would probably get pregnant with a little assistance. I held my breath and waited for their answer. Waited knowing that this was another one of those times where my future was weighed in the balance of someone else's choice. By now, Yana and Ben were joined in useful friendship. A genetic bond, though, that would cut to the centre of my currently-resting ache. Heart beating fast, face and hands cool, I turned to Yana – and watched her conjure up birth mother, foster parents, Russian family, pretend family, fake life. And I knew she would say no. The ready excuse was her work and her perfect body and the necessary medical intrusion which would be so hard to keep secret. Felix conceded she was probably right. Ben looked only slightly interested – and then slightly less disappointed. Felix thought for a while and then said he'd give out a part story, something about maybe investigating the plight of Russian orphans, the children in the world who have no choice, the so-much-more that this happy couple had to give if they didn't limit themselves to the selfish gene. A nice lie with a long and respected Hollywood pedigree.

We left it at that. Stayed away from Mike and Melissa's little Jimmy unless we had no choice. Worked at being our three. Got on with it. Made actions, dealt with the consequences, kept going.

Thirty-two

I play the bars less often now, it feels as if there's less need. Sometimes, if Felix says so, or if we feel it is right, I go out and claim a man. But Yana and Ben seem very settled, people like the look of them. Both of their careers are doing well. As is Jimmy's. Again. Better than before. Nothing like the glow of untimely death to relight the bathetic comedy of the laughter track – there have been two retrospectives, each one more insightful and excessive than the last. And by the second year after his death there was a nice, persistent rumour, about Jimmy and me, mainly fed by internet chat rooms, those who weren't dealing in conspiracy-theory death dreams – Jimmy McNeish and his FBI/Mafia connections, Jimmy McNeish and his disease-ravaged lies. The rumours about the two of us were easily dismissed as fantasy ideas, but they were useful all the same. People debated the strength of our hidden passion, Jimmy's self-destructive behaviour a result of his inability to decide between Yana and me, her widow weeds transferred to my back. My guilt the reason I stayed on with Yana – guilt and a need to be close to Jimmy's past. It helped actually. Gave me a status I'd not had before, undercut the other rumours, the ones that will never be far from the surface, the ones we work at denying every day of our lives.

Sometimes I look at her and remember she isn't who I

thought she was, she isn't who she sounds like, but not often. I have mostly subsumed that knowledge. It is a truth and it isn't relevant. There are plenty of truths. I live with the ones that work, it works for me. I still love her. I think I love her more now that I know more. What we have been through has brought us closer to each other. What we have done for each other, what she has revealed. Sometimes I look at her and see all our past, wide open and twisted together, crowding in. Other times I look at her and see how much I love her, that she loves me. More often than not I just see Yana. The woman I know as Yana, love as Yana. It's enough.

Yana and Ben are getting married. A proper American marriage in a Las Vegas chapel, all the better for Felix to promote the passionate spontaneity of the happy couple. We have it all planned, the unplanned, impulsive, spur-of-the-moment. She and I have been shopping for her wedding dress, we think red, dark red. We'll be out in Vegas for a series of meetings with the Australian director of her new film, they begin shooting soon in Paris. Ben will visit for the weekend, they'll play the tables for a while, make the decision, call Felix – Felix will grab the next flight out and we think we can just about squeeze in the ceremony before five in the morning. In time for the breakfast news. She's going to look fantastic. I'll need to go with her to Paris, Ben has filming commitments of his own at home. He's been working on his honeymoon talk-show jokes. How totally LA it is for your wife to go on a working honeymoon in Paris with her assistant, while you're forced to stay at home playing Reese Witherspoon's new screen lover. What a hard hard life it really is. Kah-boom!

And of course I still get jealous. How could I not? When the two of them pose for hidden cameras, hold hands in the street, kiss in the car with a long lens somewhere ahead. When he is by her side at the dinners, the awards. But it isn't as bad as before, Ben is much more careful with me, nicer to me than Jimmy ever was. And I don't really feel for him either. We get on, it's easy, but nothing more. That helps. Anyway, I know I have dealt with it once, got over it, acknowledged and taken steps to deal with my pain. I will do so again if I need to. I have tamed my passion. Just as I tamed Jimmy's.

The first time I read Jimmy's diary I was furious. It was in our earliest months together. He was slagging me off for some presumed rudeness – or maybe it was real, probably it was back then, in the first months much of our time was spent fighting for place, determining position. Jimmy took a whole paragraph of his journal to write about how he'd get back at me that night, planned to be on live television with his tongue down Yana's throat. I read the journal when they left for the studio, three hours later I watched him fulfil his threat on national TV. I remember still how much that hurt. After that night I read his journals regularly. It made things easier; showing myself what a bastard he could be reminded me not to fancy him too much. Knowing what was going on in Jimmy's bedroom became a sort of quest for me, I figured if I knew what he thought, I could handle what he did. And for a long time that was the case. I could put up with any amount of his game-playing because, more often than not, I knew it was coming. And while it still hurt, the sting of surprise was removed. But it was after he'd met Melissa, when he started working out how he planned to set me up with her and Mike, what a laugh he thought the whole thing would be, how great to get both Yana and me furious with him at the same time, that I knew I had to act. Even more so when he wrote that Melissa thought it was fucking hilarious too. Not that he'd told her the whole truth, Jimmy was way too clever for that, just that he wanted her on his side in the plan. To her, I was only the assistant, a glorified tooknowing servant, the likes of me regularly needed bringing down a peg or two. It was then I realised that just knowing Jimmy's secrets wasn't enough. I'd have to take action. Knowledge is power, it gives you options. And sometimes you have to act on them.

Writing the letters was easy. Getting Yana so upset was incredibly easy. I knew exactly which buttons to push, the veiled hints to make, I knew how to get her. Of course I did, I loved her, love her. I knew, too, what to write so that in the end, when I showed them to her, she'd decide the letters were from Jimmy – with no prompting from me, other than ensuring she'd find his journal. And I knew how to stoke the letters with Jimmy-clues. I'd leave working out the exact nature of his betrayal up to her. She got it sooner than I thought.

The weird thing is, I didn't know it would all work so well, I'm really not that clever. I was just making it up as I went along, deciding on each step as the last one was taken – none of it was so very careful that I could tell you at which point I realised Yana would have to make the leap to send Jimmy away. I'm not clairvoyant, but I was way more successful than I expected. And though I couldn't know Yana would want to take it so far, though I only started out trying to get rid of Jimmy – just rid of his presence in our lives – Yana was right to ask me to do what I did. We could never have trusted him. And I'd do it all again, the planning, the execution, working out the aftermath, hoping for the right consequences. If I had to. Not that I want to. It's been a hard thing to live with, honestly. Not just Jimmy, but the lying to Yana as well, the setting her up to make her hate him. I don't suppose time will make it all that much easier, I don't believe that time does heal, merely that we get used to our suffering. And I do grieve the loss of my innocence, I know Yana misses hers. But then we all make sacrifices, don't we? Tiny and huge, open and unseen. Every day a choice, every choice a necessity. She and I are bound always, twisted into each other with what we know and what we've done. The glorious compromise of living a life. And always now at the back of my mind the question of how long I will satisfy Yana – and who gets to win if she and I don't make it. All the while working out who to believe, what to believe, every day a new decision.

That's the thing about stories though, isn't it? You have to understand who's doing the telling.

Lightning Source UK Ltd.
Milton Keynes UK
UKOW04f0613120214

226323UK00002B/3/P